His Secret Mistress

By Cathy Maxwell

The Logical Man's Guide to Dangerous Women
HIS SECRET MISTRESS

The Spinster Heiresses
THE DUKE THAT I MARRY
A MATCH MADE IN BED
IF EVER I SHOULD LOVE YOU

Marrying the Duke
A DATE AT THE ALTAR
THE FAIREST OF THEM ALL
THE MATCH OF THE CENTURY

The Brides of Wishmore
THE GROOM SAYS YES
THE BRIDE SAYS MAYBE
THE BRIDE SAYS NO

The Chattan Curse
THE DEVIL'S HEART
THE SCOTTISH WITCH
LYON'S BRIDE

THE SEDUCTION OF SCANDAL
HIS CHRISTMAS PLEASURE
THE MARRIAGE RING
THE EARL CLAIMS HIS WIFE
A SEDUCTION AT CHRISTMAS
IN THE HIGHLANDER'S BED
BEDDING THE HEIRESS
IN THE BED OF A DUKE
THE PRICE OF INDISCRETION
TEMPTATION OF A PROPER GOVERNESS
THE SEDUCTION OF AN ENGLISH LADY
ADVENTURES OF A SCOTTISH HEIRESS
THE LADY IS TEMPTED
THE WEDDING WAGER
THE MARRIAGE CONTRACT
A SCANDALOUS MARRIAGE
MARRIED IN HASTE
BECAUSE OF YOU
WHEN DREAMS COME TRUE
FALLING IN LOVE AGAIN
YOU AND NO OTHER
TREASURED VOWS
ALL THINGS BEAUTIFUL

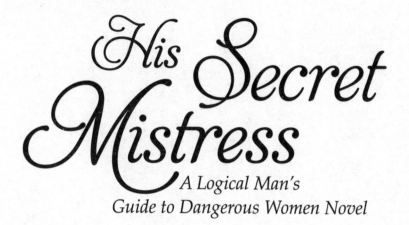

His Secret Mistress

A Logical Man's
Guide to Dangerous Women Novel

CATHY MAXWELL

AVONBOOKS

An Imprint of HarperCollins*Publishers*

First Avon Books mass market printing: March 2020
First Avon Books hardcover printing: February 2020

Print Edition ISBN: 978-0-06-297505-8
Digital Edition ISBN: 978-0-06-289685-8

FIRST EDITION

20 21 22 23 24   LSC   10 9 8 7 6 5 4 3 2 1

This one is for you, Holly Maxwell
With peace, joy, and love . . .

His Secret Mistress

The Logical Men's Society

*T*he Logical Men's Society started as a jest, as many things do.

Over a pint or two in The Garland, where men gathered in Maiden-shop, it was noted that a sane man wouldn't choose to marry. It went against all logic . . . and so the "society" was formed.

Oh, men had to marry. It was expected and life is full of expectations. A man gave up his membership in the Logical Men's Society when that happened and he could only return if he was widowed. But in the years before he tied the parson's knot, the Society offered good fellowship that was highly valued and never forgotten.

And so it went for several generations. The irony of the name of their village, pronounced Maidens-hop, was not lost on any of its members. The Logical Men's Society provided a place of masculine good-will and contentment . . . until the women began to win.

Chapter One

Maidenshop, Cambridgeshire
1814

He'd lost the damn commission.

For a good twelve months, Mr. Brandon Balfour had labored on a proposed design for a bridge crossing the River Thames in London. After repeated requests for elaborate and complicated changes, the Surveyor-General had assured Bran his was the best proposal submitted. He'd all but promised Bran swift approval, and then last night, the council had informed him that they were interested in a new contender. A Scotsman well-known to council members had expressed interest in the project.

And in less time than it took to down a brandy, Bran's hours of work and endless toadying to pompous asses who knew little about what made bridges work had come to naught. That bridge was to have been his signature, his mark on the world, the first important project of his small, struggling engineering firm.

Which meant that right now, the weight of the fowling piece felt damn good in Bran's hand. He was of a mind to shoot something this morning. Rooks were as good a choice as any other. In fact, he'd been so angry after the council meeting, he'd ridden through the night to join the hunt at Belvoir Castle. He'd known he was too bitter and frustrated for sleep. Or to cool his heels in London.

His friend the Earl of Marsden, the owner of Belvoir, walked beside him through tall grass toward a thicket of trees, the rooks' haven. It was shortly before dawn and the air had a hushed, expectant darkness.

Flanking them was Mr. Ned Thurlowe, the local physician and another valued friend. The three of them, tall, well-favored, and confident, were often referred to locally as "the Three Bucks" of the Logical Men's Society. Gentlemen usually envied them and women thought they should be married.

At six-foot-four, Mars was two inches taller than Bran. He was lean of frame with broad shoulders and blue eyes that could be warm and friendly or deadly chilling. His hair was the golden brown of winter wheat.

Thurlowe was the handsomest of their trio. He had wild, untamed looks with dark hair and slashing brows. It was claimed women feigned sickness just to have him place his concerned physician's hand on their brows and more than one had swooned from his touch.

"When I saw you in London last week," Mars said to Bran, his voice low so it would not carry in the predawn air and warn the birds of their approach, "you told me you didn't know when you would be returning to Maidenshop. Didn't you hope your bridge design would receive its final approval?"

A hard stone set in Bran's chest. "We had a meeting last night. I expected to be named the architect but then a new player was thrown into the game. A Scotsman who is a relative of Dervil's."

"Dervil? That bastard." Lord Dervil's estates bordered Belvoir. Years ago, in a dispute over property lines, Dervil had challenged Mars's father to a duel. The old earl had died of the wounds he'd received that day, and the feud between the two families had intensified. Mars claimed he couldn't wait to put a bullet into Dervil's black heart. "Did he block your plans after all the reviews you have been through?"

"He was at the meeting. He suggested an architect with more experience would be a better choice. Apparently his opinion was all that was needed for the Surveyor-General to table the matter."

Ned jumped in. "More experience? You've built bridges, canals, and roads in India. What have you not built? You have letters of recommendation from the Company, don't you?" He referred to the East India Company, which Bran had left three years ago.

"My introductions and references have been presented," Bran answered. "Dervil suggested my work on foreign soil could not meet English standards." Dervil wasn't the first to do so. Establishing himself in England had been a challenge.

"Dervil is a fool then," Ned replied stoutly. "And what is this talk about connections? What does that have to do with engineering?" Ned was a man of science. He was the bastard son of a noted peer, and as such, like Bran, had to rely on his intellect to make his way in the world. They had both been successful, although many wondered why a talented doctor like Thurlowe would prefer to rusticate in Maidenshop instead of try his hand in London.

"Obviously, competence and intelligence isn't enough in the world of politics and power," Bran answered.

"The Duke of Winderton is your nephew and your ward," Thurlowe said. "You returned to guide him after his father died. That is a connection and a damn honorable one."

"A connection to property Dervil covets," Mars pointed out. "And property he would have convinced your sister to sell if you hadn't returned from India and stopped her. So, this is his revenge, eh? I assumed he would show his hand sooner or later. He prides himself on extracting a price, damn his soul."

"Apparently, it is." Bran tightened his hold on the gun. "I spent a *year* meeting their every demand . . ." He let his voice trail off with his frustration.

"Did you say the meeting was last night? And you are here?" Ned asked. "Did you sleep?"

"I was too angry to sleep. Besides, late yesterday, my sister started sending urgent messages for me to return at once. Something about Winderton." Bran was the duke's guardian until he reached one and twenty in a few months. In truth, Winderton had been too coddled by his mother to take over such responsibilities. If Bran had been the author of the will, Winderton would need to wait until he was at least thirty, but the matter was not his to decide. "Do either of you have an idea what she could be in high dudgeon over this time?"

"I saw your young duke drinking with friends at The Garland the other night," Mars reported. "He was blissfully in his cups and appeared happy."

"I passed him yesterday in the village," Thurlowe offered. "He was barreling down the road without a sideward glance on some mission of his own making. You know how he is."

Self-important? Bran wanted to suggest. He didn't. It would be disloyal. Still, how could someone who was only twenty think his opinion mattered to anyone in the world? "Lucy cries wolf every time he doesn't do what she thinks he should. So, I've come to sort that out." *And himself. He needed to sort himself out. If he didn't receive that commission, then what future was there for him?*

His friends nodded, quieting as they reached their destination, a group of three huge plane trees off to themselves. Here was the rooks' roosting place. The birds would wake with the dawn.

Trailing behind the Three Bucks were the oldest members of the Logical Men's Society—Mr. Fullerton and Sir Lionel Johnson. They rode in makeshift sedan chairs carried by Sir Lionel's servants and were more interested in drinking port than shooting birds. Fullerton had been the estate manager for Mars's grandfather back in the day. Sir Lionel had once been the king's ambassador to Italy and he'd been dining out on the honor ever since. Rounding out the hunting party were Mars's gamekeeper, Evans, and numerous servants carrying more guns, powder, and, of course, the port.

A number of lads from the village, warned to silence, brought up the rear. They would race to collect the kill. Mars had offered a penny for every rook stuffed in their bags.

The goal of a rook hunt was to catch the fledglings as they woke. The young birds had the tender meat and there was no sense hunting birds if you couldn't eat them. The low mist drifting across the ground helped to conceal the men's stealthy advance upon the trees.

As the sun began to rise, the nests high in the trees' branches stirred. Against the dawning sky, the birds perched on limbs as if needing to shake themselves awake in the manner of grumpy old men in the morning.

Without a word, the Three Bucks raised their guns. Mr. Fullerton raised his as well, while still sitting in his chair. It was unloaded. Evans was not so silly as to give the drink-addled Fullerton a loaded weapon.

Sir Lionel raised a glass of port. *"Here's to the hunt,"* he shouted.

The clicks and wheezes of the birds went silent as now *they* listened.

It was of no mind. The Bucks had expected Sir Lionel to do something loud and silly. They fired, knowing that they had best not miss their opportunity. Rooks were clever creatures. The old ones would be gone in a flash. But the fledglings, well, they were like Winderton, not so wise.

After each shot, the gun was handed to a groom who offered a freshly reloaded one. The village lads began zigzagging under the trees, stuffing dead birds in their sacks. The hunters' aim was true and a good number were killed.

And then it was done. The birds were gone. They were either flown or bagged.

Mars laughed his satisfaction. He lowered his gun. "Excellent shooting! I'm glad to be rid of those pests." He looked to the boys. "C'mon, lads, all of you, join us at The Garland for breakfast. Andy promises to have a good one for us. We will count the birds there."

That was met with cheers.

"To The Garland," Sir Lionel now shouted, leaning sideways in his chair. "Pick up the pace, lads. We can't keep Andy waiting." His footmen set off at a trot and, of course, Fullerton had to give chase. Both men appeared ready to be bounced out of his chair at any moment. Still the footmen did not stop and led the way to breakfast.

"Evans, you and the others are to come as well," Mars ordered. "If I know Andy, there will be food for a hundred."

"Thank you, my lord." Evans waved a hurrying hand to his men. "Move this along. We must take everything to the house before we can break our fast." He didn't have to speak twice.

Bran's horse, Orion, a huge blood bay gelding, and mounts for Ned and Mars were brought to them by a groom. Orion was not pleased to find himself groomed, fed, and saddled again. Not after a night of riding.

He snorted his disapproval but Bran climbed into the saddle anyway. "You'll rest in a minute," he told the disgruntled animal. The answer was a shake of the head as if to deny the bit that was already there.

The friends rode at a walk to The Garland. The anger that had driven Bran was giving way to a cooler head. He'd needed to be out of the city and in country air.

"What are you going to do with all those birds?" he asked Mars.

"Andy will bake several huge pies," Ned answered. "You know the Cotillion Dance is tonight?"

Bran inwardly groaned. "I'd forgotten." The Cotillion Dance was the biggest event in Maidenshop's active social season. The patroness of the acclaimed Almack's could not rival how the Matrons of Maidenshop organized this dance. Because of the village's close proximity to Cambridge, London, and New Market Road, the countryside was a favorite of the titled, upper gentry and even the rising middle class. Everyone attended the dance.

"Ned worries that the membership to the Logical Men's Society is not what it should be," Mars explained.

"It isn't," Ned groused. "It is truly just the three of us and those blighters." He nodded to where Fullerton and Sir Lionel had disappeared up the road. "The young ones like Winderton are not interested. We need to recruit more gentlemen into the Society or we will disappear completely."

"Especially since you will soon marry," Mars reminded Thurlowe.

The physician looked at him with a blank stare and then said, "Yes, to Miss Taylor." He frowned as if annoyed with himself for forgetting he was promised. Bran didn't blame him. Ned's offer for Miss Clarissa Taylor was not a conventional one.

As a baby, she had been abandoned on the late Reverend Taylor's doorstep. The reverend and his wife had raised her as their own, although the whole village had been caught up in the mystery of the child. They all acted as if she was a part of them.

The Taylors died when Miss Taylor was two and twenty. Squire Nelson and his family took her in, but the Matrons of Maidenshop had decided that was not enough. She needed to be married, and one of the Three Bucks should be the groom. They'd stormed into The Garland, interrupting a night of merriment with their demands.

Mars had refused. He and Miss Taylor could not abide each other.

Bran was not about to marry anyone. At six and thirty, he'd been a bachelor too long to succumb to the parson's noose, especially out of pity. Over the years, Bran had formed quiet, unfettered liaisons with the occasional widow—although for the past year he'd done nothing but focus on that damned bridge commission.

In the end, it was Thurlowe who had broken down and sacrificed himself. He'd claimed to feel sorry for Miss Taylor since she had no family and few prospects. That was two years ago. Ned called on her every Saturday for fifteen minutes and made no move toward marriage.

Anyone who thought the good doctor was ready for marriage, or enthusiastic for it, was a fool. However, the matrons seemed mollified and Miss Taylor appeared at peace with the current situation.

Bran did not understand why the matrons didn't push for an actual wedding, but it wasn't his worry.

Meanwhile, Mars seemed to enjoy chiding their friend on his "someday" upcoming nuptials.

"To interest new members in the Society," Mars went on to explain, "Ned has arranged for a scientific lecture on matters of interest to men for tomorrow to take advantage of those gentlemen who will be staying over after the dance."

"A lecture?" Bran asked with some interest.

"Yes, every gentleman, married or not, is invited," Ned said with enthusiasm. "Mr. Clyde Remy will discuss the late James Hutton's theory concerning uniformitarianism as an explanation for the formation of rocks and mountains. I think that should draw them in."

Uniformitarianism? Bran withheld his opinion, although his gaze met Mars's amused one and he knew they both did not share Thurlowe's confidence. Bran had a deep interest in geology but he didn't know if it was a popular topic to others.

"Andy and I decided rook pie can't hurt our chances of attracting members either," Mars said. "After all, I had rooks to spare. Blasted nuisances."

They rode through Maidenshop now. The dawning sun highlighted the thatched roofs of charming whitewashed cottages and rose gardens filling with fragrant blooms. When Bran had first arrived here three years ago from India, he had thought he'd never seen a lovelier village—or a more English one.

Mrs. Warbler, a widow and one of the busiest of the matrons, owned the largest home in the village. It was built of yellow stone and set at such an angle she could sit in her morning room and see everything going on—and everyone going in and out of The Garland.

In the distance was the lichen-covered stone roof of St. Martyr's, a twelfth-century church the villagers had the good sense to leave alone. Like many churches of that era, it had been built by a nobleman, supposedly a Winderton ancestor, and the property included a long, high-ceilinged stone outbuilding that had once served as a barn. The Cotillion was held there every year.

Down the road a ways was the smithy. Another two miles would take them to New Market Road and the Post House, where a good number of those attending the Cotillion without local relatives or friends would find accommodations for the night. It was a major stop for travelers and could be busy day and night.

The Garland sat at the edge of the village on the banks of a racing stream known as the Three Thieves. There was a story behind that name, but no one knew it to tell it. Upstream, the Three Thieves bordered Marsden land and had good fishing, especially in the spring.

The Garland itself was built like three small cottages hooked together. Mars claimed that inside, it resembled a fox's den with low-ceilinged rooms and walls darkened by age. Save for the time the matrons had stormed it to demand a husband for Miss Taylor, it was definitely a male sanctuary. The Garland was the hub of the Logical Men's Society, and everyone in the county knew it.

The scent of roasting beef and fresh bread greeted the group as they walked through the door. Andy must have been up for hours. He liked to cook on a spit out back and the smoke from it rose above the thatched roofs. Bran was surprised at how hungry he was. He'd been too anxious yesterday to eat much.

The sedan chairs were out front, a footman left to guard them as if they were in London and not the safe haven of Maidenshop. Boys carrying their bags were shoving their way inside, big smiles on their faces. The men dismounted and tied up their horses to the post. Orion grumbled his thoughts. Bran ignored him and went inside. He had to duck to go under the door.

"Come in, come in," Andy called in his soft burr. The old Scotsman stood in the doorway of what he called his taproom where he kept his keg. He was about as wide as he was tall with white whiskers and a shaved pate. "Why, look at all of these birds. I'll make you a pie that will sing itself with these," he promised Ned. "Sit yourselves wherever you like. I'll bring the food out."

A huge table had been set out in the middle of the room. Metal plates were stacked on one end along with knives and forks. Bran made himself useful handing them out. The air rang with the sounds of booted heels and chairs scraping the wood floor as they were pulled out.

Andy had left to bring in the meat on the spit. In the taproom, Ned started pouring tankards of ale and had the lads distributing them. Mars had tucked into the tray of at least seven loaves of cooling bread. One didn't stand on ceremony in The Garland. Once Evans and the Belvoir servants arrived, they began to eat and the room went quiet save for the sounds of hungry men enjoying themselves.

Food helped restore Bran's spirits. And, yes, he realized, being here with his friends was better than moping in London.

Soon, everyone in London connected with engineering and architecture would learn that he hadn't been awarded the commission. At least, not yet. They would wonder why and he and his small firm would be like the rook fledglings this morning—a target for gossip and speculation. His reputation was too new and he didn't know what the damage would be.

Mars began entertaining a group of lads with a story out of his youth when he'd been swimming and Ned had stolen his clothes as a jest. "Just as Mrs. Warbler and her daughters were out for an afternoon stroll."

"Did they see you, my lord?" the youngest boy asked.

"*All* of me," Mars said dramatically and the boys fell off the benches laughing. Even the servants had a giggle.

Bran caught himself smiling, until he noticed the blue-and-white of Winderton livery at the door. Damn, it wasn't even half past eight.

He stood and walked over to greet Randall, Lucy's butler and most trusted servant. "My sister has found me? Or were you just lucky?" Randall had once served with their colonel father in the Guard and was around Lucy's age, which was twelve years older than Bran.

"Just lucky, sir. Will you come with me, sir?"

Bran ran a hand over the rough whiskers of his jaw. "I need to shave."

"She is frantic, sir." A not uncommon situation where his sister was concerned and yet there was a hint of desperation in Randall's tone.

"Very well." Bran waved to his friends. He noted that Fullerton and Sir Lionel were now back at their favorite table in the corner. The potted knight appeared to be sleeping, his head on his chest. Fullerton did not seem to mind since he was animatedly talking to himself.

Outside, Orion stamped his displeasure as Bran mounted. "A few minutes more, my friend." Randall had his own horse and the two rode off. Bran did not ask questions. Randall was extremely discreet when it came to Winderton affairs. Bran had learned how close-lipped back when he'd first arrived from India.

The Winderton ancestral seat, Smythson, was a forty-five-minute ride from The Garland. It could have been faster except Bran refused to push his horse more.

Smythson was a redbrick manse surrounded by gardens that had at one time been designed by no less a personage than Capability Brown. Lucy wasn't much for gardens or management, and her husband's death hadn't made her rise to the situation. When Bran had first arrived as the duke's guardian, the estate had been on the brink of ruin. The lawns had been ill kempt, the stables were a shambles, and his nephew's schooling tuition had not been paid in years. He was amazed they took him back term after term.

Bran had corrected the problems, using his money to do so because at the time Winderton didn't have any. The old duke had been an exceedingly unwise gambler. Bran had learned there was no investment too ridiculous for his brother-in-law to throw money at, no horse too much of a long shot not to wager upon.

Of course, Lucy had not wished for anyone to know the state of her affairs. What Bran had done for the estate and for his nephew was their secret, and, yes, when his nephew acted immature and entitled, Bran wished he was at liberty to tell him a few hard facts.

His sister had always stopped him . . . but someday, he needed to sit the duke down and explain.

As it was, Bran had successfully turned the estate around. It was profitable again and meeting its obligations. The gardens were well-groomed and the stables organized. The money generated by the estate was going into a fund that was earning Winderton 3 percent, Bran's gift to his ward. However, Winderton was fast approaching his majority; the time would come for him to take over, ready or not for the responsibility.

A groom waited to take Orion and the other horse. After dismounting, Randall led Bran inside and up the front stairs to the Dowager Duchess of Winderton's private quarters.

Lucy was still in her black dressing gown and lace cap and standing in the center of the room when Bran presented himself. She was a handsome woman for her age with gray streaks beginning in her dark hair. Her figure was plumper than when she was married. She blamed her eating as well as everything else on the need for comfort in her loneliness. Bran thought the extra stone or so of weight suited her. Both brother and sister had the Balfour "silver" eyes.

She launched into him. "I sent my message demanding your immediate presence late yesterday morning. You should have been here last night."

"I was required to attend a meeting about the bridge—"

"The bridge. *The bridge,*" she mocked. "I'm so tired of this bridge, especially when I need you here. Christopher needs you here."

"I saw Christopher in London a few weeks ago. He was fine."

"He is *not* fine now." She began furious pacing, her arms gesturing wildly. "You must talk sense into him because he is not listening to me. And *don't* tell me you hurried to Smythson because I know you went shooting with your fellows this morning. The Logical Men's Society! An excuse for men to behave like boys, if you ask me." Lucy was an important member of the Matrons of Maidenshop. "That you would choose them over your sister—" She made an exasperated sound before chiding, "And don't deny you wouldn't, because you did so today."

Bran couldn't take her charging around him a second longer. He caught her, a hand on each arm, and guided her to the wing chair in front of the cold hearth. Sitting her, he knelt on one knee and said calmly, "The hunt was before dawn. I assumed you were asleep."

"I haven't been able to sleep since Christopher said what he did. It was horrid, Brandon. *Horrid.*" Huge tears welled in her eyes and rolled down her cheeks, reddening her nose. Lucy had never been a pretty crier.

Bran pulled his handkerchief from a pocket and offered it to her. "Lucy, I am here now." He kept his voice low and controlled. "What has His Grace done to set you in such a tizzy?"

Lucy lowered the handkerchief and visibly struggled to regain control of herself. "He says . . . he is going to marry an *actress.*"

For a second, Bran didn't think he'd heard her correctly.

At his silence, she elaborated, "He has met an *actress* and he vows that she is the woman he has been searching for. The one he must have. He claims his heart is set afire for her."

Bran rose, not trusting himself to speak immediately. He pulled a straight-backed chair over to his sister's and sat. "An actress," he repeated.

Lucy nodded her head enthusiastically, causing the black ribbons in her cap to bounce.

"You have been sending messengers and tracking me down while I was trying to prepare for the most important meeting of my life because Christopher is taken with an actress?"

"Not just 'taken.' He wants to make her *his duchess.*"

She sounded so sincere.

And suddenly all Bran could do was laugh. A good, hearty, well-isn't-this-life laugh. Her offended stare brought him to his senses. "Lucy, he is almost one and twenty. Of course he wants an actress. We all do at one time or the other."

She shook her head. "Not a mere *flirtation.* He informed me he plans on *marrying* this woman."

"He won't."

"He said he will."

"Lucy, he's twenty. He says a good number of things he won't carry out."

"You should have seen him, Brandon. It was as if he'd grown into a man as he was telling me all of this."

Bran gave an indifferent shrug. "He still has plenty of manly growing to do. An actress might help him with that."

Her brows snapped together. "I don't want her near my son."

"Says every mother since the beginning of time."

"Stop patronizing me." Lucy twisted the kerchief tight in her hands. "I know my son. He is smitten and he'll do something foolish if we don't chase this woman away. Worse, she is *older* than he is."

His nephew was sounding wiser and wiser as this conversation progressed. Bran feigned a frown to hide his grin. "Fine, I will talk to him."

"He won't listen." She spoke to Bran as if he was a child. "This woman has bewitched him."

"When did he meet her? In London, the duke said nothing to me about any woman."

"Yesterday."

The word stopped him.

"Yesterday?" Bran shook his head. Mars and Thurlowe were not going to believe this story. "Lucy, he met her yesterday and he was bewitched on the spot? And you believe him? You have better common sense than that."

"You should hear him. He's not himself." Indignant color rose in her cheeks.

"And how did he meet this actress yesterday?" Bran tried to hide his skepticism. He was not successful.

"He came upon a troupe of actors on the road. Their wagon had broken down and he offered to help. He saw her and fell in love. He said it was that quick." She snapped her fingers for emphasis. "He told me there isn't anything he won't do for her."

Until he beds her, Bran thought, but wisely refrained from voicing this observation. In truth, he was a bit relieved his nephew was not so wrapped around his mother's finger. In fact, in London, Bran had suggested His Grace come for the Season. There were responsibilities to the title that the duke must understand and he wasn't going to learn them doing his mother's bidding in Maidenshop.

Bran patted his sister's hand. "All right. I will talk to him."

"He won't listen. I've talked and talked. We must buy her off. Pay her to leave. That is the only way that we can keep him from her. Truly, Brandon, he acts possessed. He was *humming* before he left the house."

Bran wasn't about to waste good money on an actress. "You are taking this too seriously. It is the normal course of things for young men to do. A rite of passage even."

"Are you trying to make me feel better? You aren't."

"Very well," Bran said patiently. "I was once in love with an actress. Heart and soul and you can see I survived the adventure." Barely . . . but he didn't need to say that to Lucy. If it hadn't been for his actress, he wouldn't have taken a position with the East India Company. He had literally exiled himself to be away from her.

He also realized that he himself had been a bit naïve like Winderton. His actress *had* made a man of him. Certainly, she had set him on the course that had made him a very wealthy man. This one might do the same for his ward and nephew. "He will be all right, Your Grace. He will."

She bit her lower lip as if to stop it from trembling. "I thought Christopher was safe from that sort of woman here."

"And that is why you don't want to let him go?"

"His father died. He needs guidance."

"Thomas died almost four years ago," Bran corrected quietly. "It is no longer an excuse to keep him tied to you. Young men must learn their own lessons and they often do it through trial and error. If you don't let him go, then he'll do things like making an actress his duchess."

"Those types of women are crass."

"They serve a purpose."

Lucy put her hands over her ears and closed her eyes, acting like a child herself. "I don't want to hear it. I wish Thomas was alive. I wish nothing had changed."

"Nothing stays the same forever, Lucy." And yet how many times over the past three years as he'd struggled to establish himself as an architect and engineer had he wished he was back in India where no one questioned his talent, his intelligence, or his connections.

She reached out to place a hand on his arm. "Please, pay her off. Do I have the money?"

"Enough. If you spend it here, then someplace else will suffer."

"Do it."

"Very well."

His sister released her breath with a sigh. "Thank you."

"Where is this actress located and does she have a name, or shall I just question every actress in the troupe?"

"Kate Addison. Christopher set them up on Smythson property. He offered our land for their use. Can you believe it? They are camped close to the Cambridge Road."

His sister continued with directions and worries, but Bran had stopped listening. *Kate Addison?* Memories he'd thought safely tucked away and hemmed in by regrets flooded his mind.

Just like that, everything came roaring back.

How many Kate Addisons could there be in the world? Especially amongst actresses?

Perhaps he misheard?

Perhaps this was the culmination of all his frustrations over the past twenty-four hours? A universe preparing him to hear a name he'd prayed to be erased from his life—?

"*Brandon*, are you listening to me?"

"I . . . am," he lied. And then, because he had to know, he said, "How much older is she than Winderton?"

"Oh, lord, I don't know. I haven't asked many questions. All he had to do is say she was older and, well, what man wants a woman older than himself, I ask you? Last night, he suggested he would take her to Cotillion. Brandon, I don't know what I will do if he walks into the dance tonight and fobs off this ill-mannered person on our friends."

"Not to worry, Lucy, I will stop it." There was no patronizing indulgence in his voice now. If this actress was *the* Kate Addison, she would not gain a foothold into his family. That woman had upended his life—and he'd be damned if he let her do the same to Winderton.

All thoughts of shaving or an easy slumber in his bed vanished. "The Cambridge Road?"

"Yes. In fact, Christopher might be there. He left the house and has not returned—"

She spoke to the air. Bran was already out the door.

Chapter Two

"*I believe* it would be better if the fox jumped out from behind a barrel or some such barrier instead of how you have him trolling around," the Duke of Winderton said. He was a young Adonis. Dark brown hair, square-jawed, tall, gray-eyed, with a bit of weight around his middle . . . and an absolute confidence his opinion mattered in this world.

Except it didn't, not in this world where Kate Addison was proudly in charge.

This was her troupe. In a sunny clearing surrounded by sheltering trees, she and her actors had marked the "stage" out on the ground for their rehearsal. Later, they would take the planks they carted around and turn them into a proper platform for performing. They'd put on this play she'd written based upon *Aesop's Fables* countless times and had never *once* needed an outside opinion, ducal or otherwise.

She was, however, pleased with their location. If the troupe's wagon had to break down, the clearing was a good place. It was on a main road with a path cut through the trees that provided a natural attendance gate. This was also an obviously well-heeled area of the country.

The troupe's tents had been set up and their trunks with the tricks of their trade stacked neatly inside the larger, where the men would sleep on low cots. The women lived in a smaller tent set off to the side. Most troupes thought nothing of everyone sleeping in the same quarters, but Kate, who'd had years of experience sharing her private life with fellow actors, insisted on privacy for each of the sexes.

Next to the main tent, a paddock had also been hastily built for their horse Melon, a nag of dubious heritage who worked long and hard for them. Kate always ensured that Melon received the best of care.

Her acting company was not overlarge. Four men, two women, and Kate. Each had a story for why they had joined her. Nestor had been mocked for being Irish and given only the smallest parts in other troupes. He trusted that Kate would treat him better, and she did.

Mary, who served as her wardrobe mistress and who was one of the finest actresses Kate had ever met, had been denied roles unless she'd responded to the lecherous desires of the men in her last troupe. She'd also been paid a pittance of what she'd earned. They had treated her like their whore. But if she had been a whore, she would have made more money.

Then there was young Robbie whom Kate had saved from being beaten almost to death by a heavy-handed poorhouse warden.

Jess had been a milkmaid with a winsome face and the golden blonde looks men admired. She had been turned out by her master when it was discovered she was with child. She'd lost the baby. Mary had discovered her working on the Manchester streets and brought her to Kate.

John was the quietest of the group. He'd latched on to her troupe when she was just forming it and was as steady as they came.

Finally, there was Silas, a former soldier and her most trusted confidant. Silas had been a member of Kate's former company and had readily agreed to leave with her when she informed him she was striking out on her own. That was five years ago, and now here they were, heading to London. Well, heading to London if they could afford to have the wagon fixed.

And if she didn't throttle a duke.

The actors not playing in the scene lounged around with more than a passing interest in what was happening. She, who was known for her tart tongue, could see the smirks and sly glances they exchanged. They knew she wasn't really speaking her mind, at least, not like she would with them, because insulting important locals was never a good policy.

Furthermore, the duke had been generous. He'd used his own men to haul their wagon off to the wainwright for repairs. She'd purchased fodder for dear Melon at a very good price from his stables. And it was on his land that they had set up their camp for their performances and he was not charging rent. No, what he wanted was something more costly—her tolerance.

Did she know that he fancied himself her savior? That he was enamored of her?

Oh, yes. Unfortunately.

He wasn't the first she'd had to delicately handle, although it was a terrible bother. Kate was too busy to be acquiescing to male pride this way. It was one of the chief annoyances of her life. There were times she just wanted to say, "Yes, yes, I know you want to kiss me *but you can't,*" and have them leave her be. They never picked up on her polite hints. Especially the young ones.

And dukes whom you owed a debt to were trickier to dodge than most. She needed to be nice to Winderton, at least until the wagon was fixed and she could continue on her way to the city. She'd already rented Drury Lane for her troupe's London debut. The date was fixed seven weeks hence for their performances and she was determined to make it, even if she had to carry all their goods herself.

Fifteen years ago, just when her acting career was beginning to take hold, she'd left London in disgrace and ruin because of a terrible betrayal. She'd never given up acting. The desire to perform was deep in her soul. However, she'd steered well clear of London.

But life had a habit of turning dross into gold. Last year, her brother had inherited a ducal title. He'd married an heiress and attending the wedding in London, Kate had realized that time had gone on. Those who had hurt her were no longer there. She could return, if she dared—and she did.

Since that wedding, she'd envisioned bringing her troupe to London. She'd planned for it, saved for it. She had a second chance at a dream that had burned bright inside her ever since she was a child. And nothing would stop her—not a lovestruck duke, or a broken axle and wheel, or that a week earlier, her lead actor Arlo Durbin had run off in the night with the local vicar's youngest daughter and the troupe's cash box.

Arlo's betrayal had infuriated Kate. Then again, what man could be trusted?

Her purpose was to do what she always did—to dust off her skirts and move forward.

She could ask her family for help. Her brother was very wealthy now and he had always been generous, even when he'd been poor. She wouldn't, though. Kate had pride. She also wanted to succeed on her terms. She was older, wiser, and tougher than the lass who had been silly enough to believe in love. The past years had sharpened her instincts. Few men played her for a fool, which made Arlo's thievery and defection all the more biting.

Fortunately, Kate was an optimist, especially when she had her eye on a prize. Maidenshop was the perfect sized village for their performances. They could make a tidy sum in a week or two. Then they would move on to London and victory.

That is, if she didn't lose her temper and strangle the local duke.

"Here, see?" Winderton moved over to his imaginary barrier and feigned being a fox peeking out around it. He was a princely dressed fox in well-tailored clothes and he smiled at Kate as if she must agree with his position.

She did not. Behind him, Nestor, the actor actually playing the role of Mr. Fox, mocked his earnestness with a roll of his eyes.

Since the duke had latched on to Kate the day before, the actors had teased her unmercifully about Winderton wanting under her skirts—such was the way actors talked *and* something Nestor himself had tried, until Kate had set him firmly in his place.

No one climbed under her skirts. A woman's power came in being in control. Sexual congress upset that balance. She'd learned that lesson the hard way.

She forced a bright smile. "An interesting idea, Your Grace . . . though Mr. Fox can't jump out behind a barrel because he is supposed to be on the other side of the stage. The 'trolling around' was him taking himself to where he needed to be."

Winderton placed a hand on his chin as he considered her comment. Then he said, "Well, Mr. Fox can move around on the barrel side of the stage. I definitely believe he must be over here."

She kept her voice oh-so-sweet, a warning to anyone who knew her well that her patience was growing thin. This was *her* troupe. She'd built it from nothing. The only opinion that mattered was hers. "You make an excellent point, Your Grace. However, from the angle you prefer, the audience wouldn't believe Mr. Fox can't see what the crows are doing." She nodded to Thomas and Robbie. They didn't wear costumes but flapped pretend wings to demonstrate their characters.

"But if he was behind a barrel—"

"The crows would still see him in that location."

"Ah—" the duke allowed.

"Thank you," Kate answered. "Nestor, your line—"

"Which is another matter," Winderton interjected. "I don't wish to usurp your authority—"

Then why are you doing it? Kate wanted to shout. She clenched her teeth behind her smile.

"Wouldn't it be better for the fox to be more forthright?" The duke puffed out his chest and hit it in dramatic demonstration. "Instead of telling us what the crows are doing, he should just shout, *'Begone now.'* There is more action to it. A small change, but better, no?"

A small change?

To *her* play?

Behind her, Silas pretended to sneeze, releasing the sound with the words, "Be careful."

Yes, be careful.

Before she carved the duke up with her tongue and served him for nuncheon.

Her hands hidden in the folds of her skirts had clenched into fists. She forced herself to stretch out her fingers. Winderton didn't know he was being ridiculous. He actually thought he was helpful. That he had a *right* to be helpful—

Be careful, careful, careful.

She nodded to Silas that his message had been received. They'd been run out of the last village they'd visited; the vicar had not been pleased with Arlo stealing his daughter. They couldn't afford to have that happen again.

And yet, she could not give in.

"Interesting suggestion, Your Grace," she purred, using that tone men liked, the sound almost submissive. "I hesitate to share that if I make that change to the line, well then, when Nestor says his line about how crows are never to be trusted, your very appropriate, and *interesting* change, will not make sense. We need to look at this as a whole, don't you agree?"

His ducal eyebrows came together, warning Kate he was not going to give up easily. "Nestor? The Irishman, right? What is his exact line?"

It took all her will for Kate to *pleasantly* say to Nestor, "Please speak it for His Grace, Mr. Fox."

The Irishman jumped into action. He did more than she asked. Apparently he believed he could command the situation better than herself. God save her from male arrogance, a prayer she had to repeat daily. The part had belonged to Arlo and Nestor seemed eager to prove he was the better actor.

"I'm over here, Your Grace, pretending that I can't be seen, but the crows know I'm there so I tell the audience, 'A crow may think he's a sharp-eyed one, but he lacks the instinct of the fox.' *Instinct*, of course, is the important word."

"I see," said Winderton.

"I'm so glad," Kate answered. "Now let us continue the rehearsal. Nestor, take your place again—"

"I still don't like the line," the duke interjected.

This time, Kate was direct. "This is not the time to change dialogue, Your Grace." She didn't finish with a smile. She couldn't. She had reached the end of what little tact she possessed. One more push and she'd push back. Hard.

He must have caught a hint of her mood. "It was merely a suggestion."

She lifted a brow.

His lips curved into an easy smile, his teeth white and straight. He'd probably conquered many a heart with that smile, and his title, and now he was using it on her.

Kate was too old for nonsense. She had work to do. Turning to the Crows, she started to tell them exactly where she wanted them, except Winderton—right in front of everyone—leaned in close to whisper in her ear, "Come to the Cotillion Dance with me tonight. You said you would think about it, and I have given you more than ample time."

Over the past twenty-four hours of their very short acquaintance, he'd mentioned the dance a dozen times.

She would not go. She was no fool. Her showing up on Winderton's arm would cause a small scandal. And since, thanks to Arlo, she'd just left one, she'd rather not indulge in another.

Silas had disagreed, as had others in the troupe. "Granted you'll have tongues wagging. But then everyone for miles around will rush to the performance to have a closer look at you. And there you will be—our Juno." Juno was the role she played in the fables. "Besides," Silas continued, "you deserve a spot of fun. You can't keep your guard up forever."

Who said she couldn't?

Silas was male. He would never be able to comprehend how much of their souls men expected from women.

"The parish dance?" she repeated as if she'd not heard the duke mention it before. A guffaw sounded from the usually quiet John and she could have boxed the man's ears.

Winderton acted oblivious to anyone but her. He moved closer. "Miss Addison, you can't refuse me. Not after all I've done for you."

That was the wrong thing to say.

But she'd not take him down a peg publicly. Instead, she took his hand, laced her fingers in his, and drew him away. He came willingly . . . like a lamb to the slaughter.

Some seventy feet from the tent was a large sheltering oak tree, which stood out from all the others. Its branches were so long and weighty they almost touched the ground. It was a good place to hide from eager ears and eyes.

The duke followed her docilely enough, ducking his head to go under the branches. He straightened when they reached the tree trunk. "Don't turn me down about the dance. I won't accept it."

She raised his hand she held and confessed, "I must." She gave him a light, reassuring squeeze and then attempted to release her hold.

He wouldn't let her. "Why?"

"You know why."

"Because of what others think?" He laughed. "I make my own rules."

How simple life was for the entitled.

"You barely know me, Your Grace—"

"What I know I like—very much. I've just spent the morning with you. I'm not here because I am not interested—"

"I am well aware that you are interested, Your Grace—"

"Then say 'yes.'" He stepped toward her, his booted toe touching the tip of her shoe. "Say, 'I would be honored to attend the dance on your arm, Your Grace.' See? It is easy to give me the answer I wish."

It had been ages since Kate had allowed *any* man this close. The young duke smelled of cloves and the open air. He was taller than Kate, which was unusual. She looked most men in the eye. She'd had to duck under those branches as well.

"Your Grace, I am not good at this."

"What? Refusing invitations? Then don't. Or being told that you are lovely?" He attempted to pull her closer.

"I'm as vain as the next woman and I am also realistic," she answered, trying again to retrieve her hand without yanking.

"I am pragmatic as well and I merely state the truth. It isn't vanity to recognize that you are a beauty."

Kate was annoyed. "You are being ridiculous. I am as old as a crone when compared to you."

"Age is not an impediment to attraction."

Oh, he believed he was silver-tongued. "It *is* when I am old enough to be your mother."

"We both know that is not true. I am almost one and twenty."

"Dear Lord, you are younger than I thought—"

"Then don't think. *Feel*. Embrace what could be between us." In turn, he tried to embrace her. Kate ducked under his arm, the movement forcing him to release her hand. *Thank, God.*

"Miss Addison, listen to me," he said, reaching for her again.

"*No.* I don't want to hear it." She stepped back to ward him off.

"And what do you believe I'm going to say?"

"It doesn't matter, because you truly are an innocent. You are sincere, so I must save you from yourself."

"I don't *want* to be saved. I have been waiting for you all my life."

"Yes, all your *twenty* years."

"Age is only a number," he countered. "Besides, I'm wise beyond my years. At least wise enough to recognize that you are not like any other woman I have known and therefore worth pursuing."

She could scream.

"Your Grace, I built this troupe from my own hard work."

"And I admire what you have done."

"You don't *know* what I've done." She spoke with the annoyance of a big sister. "You can't possibly understand how hard I battled to reach this point. To overcome the people who would not take me seriously, who attempted to undermine me every step of the way."

Annoyance crossed his face, and there it was—proof that, no matter how earnest, he was like any other man of her acquaintance. Well, except for Silas. She trusted Silas.

"I don't think you understand me," Winderton said quietly with great drama. "I'm *in love* with you."

Kate could have laughed. She'd heard that before as well. Men wanted what they could not have. She drew a deep breath and squared her shoulders. "I thank you for the compliment, Your Grace. Unfortunately, I am not searching for love."

"I thought love was what we all want."

"Especially women?"

He stiffened. "Don't treat me as if I am naïve. Nor am I jaded like so many of my contemporaries. When I first saw you yesterday, my heart *burst*. There is no other word for it. I *burst* with love for you."

But Kate *was* so jaded that she didn't believe him. What she suspected was that he'd had a "burst" of lust, something very different from love. Lust could make men do irresponsible and astounding things . . . including lashing out at those they purported to "love." Still he was young, and she knew he'd mistaken lust for love. He didn't yet know the difference.

He took a step closer; she stepped back and hit the trunk of the tree. She had little room to move. He looked down at her, his expression intent. "I can't believe you don't feel what I do. You must. Or else you are lying to yourself. Trust me, Miss Addison—*Kate*." He said her given name as if testing it and finding he liked it. "Trust what is between us, Kate." He leaned toward her, his lips puckering—

She gracefully stepped aside and avoided those lips. "Your Grace, I cannot."

"Because you won't believe."

There was that. And men never liked hearing she didn't share their feelings.

The one thing that worked was a crisp telling of the truth. "My place is on the stage. I was born to it. My mother was an actress and her mother before her. I will not let anything or anyone stop me from going to London. It may surprise you to learn that I was once lauded as the most talented actress in the city. And then my opportunities were stolen from me. I was disgraced, humiliated." *Betrayed.*

Bile rose in her at the memories. She'd been such a goose back then. She was wiser now.

"I go to London to reclaim my place on the stage, and no one will ever chase me off again. I'll look the devil in the eye, if I must, and he'd best be afraid." Her words gave her strength.

Winderton listened with unwavering gray eyes. Eyes that seemed to tickle a memory in her. "Do you believe me afraid of strong women? I'll be right beside you to meet the devil."

His offer startled her. He would take up her cause? For a second, she believed him—it had something to do with his haunting eyes—until he added, "Come to the dance with me."

And then she knew the truth. He hadn't heard a word she'd said. Men were infuriating—

"No, don't deny me outright," he cautioned, as if he believed he could read her mind. "Think on my request. It is a simple one. I will wait for your answer."

"But you won't accept a no?"

"That is right." He punctuated his words with a roguish grin that brought out a charming dimple and began walking out of their forest hideaway. Kate followed.

"You are a dreamer, Your Grace."

"That I am. I dream of you." They were out from under the tree's limbs. "Send word when you are ready to say yes."

"That won't happen."

"It might." He walked the distance to the tents and picked up his hat off the trunk where he'd set it earlier. He placed it on his head at a rakish angle, and then untied his horse from a tree branch. He mounted. With a wink at her and a cocksure wave to her actors, he was on his way.

Silas sauntered over to her. "He acted happy when he left."

"You know me better than that. Come, we have much work to do." She clapped her hands toward the others. "Places. Let us rehearse 'Mr. Fox and the Crows' twice more. Then we will do Silas's prologue followed by 'Country Mouse and City Mouse.' Later, while we build the stage, Robbie and Jess, you will take some handbills around and spread the word of tomorrow's performances."

"Going to the dance on the duke's arm would spread the news fast enough that we are here," Nestor commented.

Kate didn't bother looking at him. Her coldness didn't deter the Irishman. He added slyly, "Who knows? He seems taken. Isn't a duke who all you women dream about?"

He was being provocative. She ignored him and focused on the business at hand. "Nestor, we'll start with your line. Begin—"

The sound of galloping hooves interrupted her concentration.

God help her if Winderton had returned.

She deliberately ignored the rider. That didn't stop her actors from craning their necks to see who was coming.

Kate thought to chastise them—and then an awareness, almost as if the air around her became suddenly charged, made her look in the rider's direction as well.

It wasn't Winderton.

Instead, a powerful chestnut galloped right into their small encampment heading straight for where she stood at the edge of the marked-off ground.

The rider reined in. He was a tall, broad-shouldered man with a hat pulled low over his eyes. He looked right at her, and, again, her every sense responded to him.

Few Corinthians could have dressed as well as he did. His boots, in spite of the dust, were London made and of the finest materials. Buff breeches encased long, muscular legs and no local tailor had the skill to create the cut of his bottle green jacket.

Nor did this man while away his time in clubs. He was strong, vital . . . his unshaven jaw was lean and his scowl fierce.

It took all Kate's courage to stand her ground. He eyed her as if she was beneath his contempt. That only made her hold her head higher, her back straighter.

He spoke. "Miss Addison?"

Abruptly, immediately, she recognized him.

Her heart pounded. She fought against a wild dizziness. Now, Arlo's stealing her money, running off with the vicar's daughter, the wagon breaking, all of it was nothing when compared to this fated meeting.

"Do you remember me?" he asked.

How could she ever forget that voice? Low, deep, a hint of masculine raspiness. Many an actor would have sold his soul to possess it.

Except now it lacked any hint of warmth or a once-earnest shyness. Instead, it demanded she acknowledge him. As if she had been waiting for years for him to decide to *honor* her with his presence and should now bow in submission?

Long ago, when she had been trusting and in love, Kate Addison had given herself to Brandon Balfour. In turn, he'd sold her out, abandoning her as if she was nothing more than chattel to be handed from one man to the next.

Her sister Alice had warned her that those who had hurt her would reappear in her life again. It was the way of the world, Alice had assured her. And Kate had best be prepared because when those people returned, she would get to mete out justice . . .

Brandon Balfour sat on his mighty steed and wanted her to *recognize* him, to *remember* him.

She would not give him that satisfaction.

Her smile polite and serene, she answered, "I'm sorry, good sir, have we met before?"

Chapter Three

*K*ate Addison *didn't recognize him?*

Bran's self-assurance eroded slightly. He had expected to be her reckoning, her past catching up with her. He had assumed she would remember him on sight and fall to her knees in remorse and fear over how callously she had once treated him.

He was eager for her to realize what she'd let slip through her grasping fingers—because he was no longer the lowly, unknown architect who counted his every penny. No, he was a man of the world.

Yes, he was still trying to establish himself in London but his years in India, and shrewd management, had made him richer than any of the peers and nabobs who had once tried to seduce her, the acclaimed "Aphrodite" of the London stage, with money and gifts.

Of course, a reckoning was a flat thing when the other party didn't even recognize you.

Granted, almost fifteen years had passed since they'd last seen each other, but still . . . she had loomed large in his imagination, no matter how much he'd tried to deny her.

It also didn't help the awkwardness of the moment that she was still beautiful. No wonder his nephew had fallen at her feet. In her demure day gown, a dress so well fashioned even Lucy would not have faulted it, and her thick, raven-black hair artfully styled, Kate could have easily passed for a member of the nobility.

She must be what? Five and thirty? Her hair was as shining as if she was twenty. No age lines creased her features except at the corner of her eyes, and that was as it should be. She'd always enjoyed a good laugh. The sound of it had charmed everyone around her.

Then there was the hue of her eyes . . . they were the deep, shadowy blue of storm clouds and yet, he remembered, sometimes they could turn as brilliant as crystals. He'd never seen their color anywhere else. He had looked—

Blinding insight struck him. Claims of happy bachelorhood aside, if you had asked him fifteen years ago what he had expected by six and thirty he'd say he would have a wife, children, and all that wedlock offered. For the last decade and a half, there had been times when he'd come close to marrying, and yet he'd always pulled up short *because of Kate.*

He'd met lovely women, suitable women, but none had ever stirred his soul the way she once had. It was as if she had ruined him for others—

God, he was pathetic, because she didn't even recognize him. Therefore, he was not about to act as if he remembered her.

They were not alone for their meeting. They stood in front of a ratty-looking faded blue tent that he assumed served as the living quarters for her actors. Several of them, men and women of various ages, watched their meeting with great interest.

"*Miss* Addison, I take it?" He hadn't meant to put quite so much inflection on her address. Any other spinster of her age would have blushed out of humility.

Not Kate. She coolly met his eye. "You know I am. You asked for me and you spoke directly to me."

"I was being polite."

She cocked her head as if she didn't believe him. "And you are?"

"Mr. Brandon Balfour, the Duke of Winderton's guardian."

Even with his name, and his relationship of power over the

duke she gave no sign of recalling him. Briskly, she asked, "How may I help you, Mr. Balfour?"

That voice. Throaty and yet with a hint of spun honey and precise diction. He'd adored the sound of it. There wasn't the slightest hint of feminine submissiveness, something he was surprised he admired—and there he was again, falling under her spell.

Forget Winderton. She was a threat to *his* peace of mind, to his *sanity.* Any thoughts of being diplomatic left Bran's mind. He wanted her gone from Maidenshop and he didn't give a devil's damn of what anyone thought of him. "I'm here to tell you to leave the area. You have one day to pack your things and be gone. If you aren't, the magistrate will be paying you a visit." He knew Mars would not be pleased with his threat, but a friend was a friend. Mars would use the weight of his office if asked.

That broke her composure. "On what grounds are you ordering me to leave?"

"Ah, Miss Addison, you are more clever than that. You know why I want you gone."

"Because of the duke's kindness toward us?"

Bran didn't hide his contempt. "Is kindness what we are calling it now?"

She drew herself up, facing him as if she was a cobra ready to strike. "Very well," she corrected herself. "Are you threatening a group of actors plying their craft because the duke is infatuated with me? He is a grown man. Almost one and twenty. He can make his own decisions."

"But not without my permission, *if* he wants his inheritance." Bran liked letting her know the power he wielded. "Twenty-four hours," he reiterated and started to turn his horse. He'd had his say.

Kate's voice stopped him. "See here, you can't just order me to leave. Warlords no longer exist. We gave up the feudal system centuries ago."

"Not in Maidenshop," he tossed back at her. Orion, still fussy because he believed he deserved a good long rest, pranced as if he was a spirited animal fit for a king and not the most hardheaded creature in the district. Bran gave Kate a mirthless smile. "Don't test me, Miss Addison. I will win."

She moved toward him. "And what if I told you I'm not interested in Winderton? That he is safe from a harpy like me? Will that make you see that your high-handed orders are ridiculous?"

"Actually, it makes me more fearful for his soul than before. I would not wish for Winderton or any other *decent* man to fall prey to your wiles." Her spell was that powerful. Just the sight of her brought back aching memories of the night they'd shared. He'd worshipped every inch of her skin. Its taste had reminded him of sweet strawberries and her scent was that of a field of wildflowers—

The temptation to dismount, to walk up to her to see if her kiss was as he remembered was strong. He had to remind himself that, while he had been her first, he'd not been her last. She hadn't even waited twenty-four hours to be faithless to him.

And a woman like her would adore stirring up the rivalries of men. Bran would not let that happen.

"Good day, Miss Addison." He put heels to horse and rode away.

His nephew would be furious with him once he caught wind of this story, and he would hear of it. Bran would be wise to confess all to his nephew himself. There had been too many witnesses.

However, duke or no, his nephew was Bran's responsibility for another few months and he was willing to use every means in his power to protect him from a Delilah like Kate Addison.

"ARE WE leaving, Kate?"

It was Silas who asked, but she knew the entire troupe wanted to know.

She'd watched Balfour gallop away, hoping that his horse bucked and he broke his neck. That didn't happen. And now she had a decision to make.

She faced them. Most appeared worried. They knew her purse was almost empty, that she had few resources left. The trip to London was costing more than she had anticipated. There was also the small matter of their wages.

The last thing she had needed was Brandon Balfour and his threats.

Still, she'd not given him quarter. She'd held her own and she was proud of it. She'd need that courage to face down her past in London.

Her gaze went to where Balfour had disappeared down the road. He'd changed from those days long ago. He'd grown into a man, yes. His strong jaw and gray eyes that had the ability to see right into a person's soul were still there, but little else of the things that had once drawn her to him. He'd become one of *them*, those powerful men whose narrow thinking had driven her off the London stage—and he had been part of their machinations, she reminded herself. He'd always been one of *them*. She'd been too infatuated with him to realize it.

Now here he was—looking down his nose and threatening her, branding her a tart. He knew nothing about her . . . except that she had once trusted him. And she wanted nothing more dearly than to make him squirm in the most uncomfortable way possible for betraying her. She, who disregarded most men, deeply needed to bring this one to his knees.

"Well, Kate?" Silas prodded.

"We are not packing. We've announced two weeks of performances."

"Then we take him on?"

She smiled with an assurance she wanted to feel. "I will not be threatened. Besides, we still need two wheels and an axle for the wagon to move."

A ripple of laughter went through the men and women of her company. "I promised you London," she said, "and London you will have. I always keep my promises." That last was for *him*, betrayer of young souls, self-appointed warlord, supposed gentleman.

"That man isn't going to be pleased we are still here," the usually quiet John observed. "And local authorities can be nasty."

He was right, of course. Balfour worried for his nephew; who knew what he might do?

Well, she now had a score to settle, and she was about to give Balfour something to truly stew over.

"Robbie." He jumped to obey. He was slight of height with curling blond hair. "Find the Duke of Winderton and tell him that I have changed my mind. I *accept* his invitation to the dance this evening."

Silas stayed Robbie with a hand on his arm. "Are you certain, Kate? That man Balfour will be furious. You are poking a hornet's nest."

"Oh, I'm doing more than poking. I'm taking a paddle to it." She nodded to the wardrobe mistress. "Mary, do we still have that saucy costume?"

"The one with the bold blue stripes?"

"And the cherry bodice. I've a mind to wear it this evening."

A low whistle and a hum of excitement met this announcement from everyone but Silas. "Kate," he warned.

She rounded on him. "Earlier, you pointed out that my going, especially on the duke's arm, would be a good advertisement for our performances."

"In something a bit more circumspect."

"Oh, no, Silas. The last thing I want is to be circumspect." She turned to Mary. "As I remember, the bodice is—" She made an imaginary cut line low over her breasts.

"It is."

"Let's make it a touch more brazen. We need to school the honorable Mr. Balfour on the danger of threatening Kate Addison."

"But you need to go easy on the lad," Silas cautioned, referring to the duke. "He's smitten, Kate."

"If anything, my performance this evening will put him off me."

"I wouldn't be certain of that," Nestor responded.

Chapter Four

Once he reached the main road, Bran reined Orion in. His gloved hands shook with anger, while every masculine part of him reacted as if he'd been waiting for Kate to reappear in his life, as if he had somehow known their paths would cross again, and was ready for the chase—something he would not let happen. He was done with her. He'd cut her out of his life once. Pride alone dictated he would not give her any quarter.

Still, he hadn't expected to come across her practically in his back garden. His local residence at the Smythson Dower House was little more than a mile away. Fate had placed her right next door.

She also seemed determined to countermand him. Yes, he'd had the last word, except he *knew* she would rebel. Her chin had been too high and her eyes had blazed with suppressed defiance.

Oh, yes, Kate was not one to docilely obey.

The question begged, what was his next step?

He knew Lucy would be waiting for a report. He also should search out Christopher and explain his actions. Better his nephew hear about the confrontation with Kate from his lips than from hers. Winderton would not be pleased. He'd long ago grown tired of having to listen to Bran's dictates.

Or, Bran could go to The Garland for a tankard and a moment to steady himself.

Without another second's hesitation, he steered his horse toward The Garland.

Maidenshop was full of activity. Mrs. Yarborough, the dressmaker, was open early and with good cause. Pony carts, a coach, and several mounts were tied up outside. Presumably the owners were collecting gowns for the Cotillion.

St. Martyr's rector was instructing a group of men in the cleaning of the grounds. He nodded to Bran as he rode by. A small army of women with their arms loaded with fresh cut flowers from their gardens bustled around the church's old stone barn decorating the hall.

As Bran approached The Garland, Mrs. Warbler and several of her friends stood outside her door across the road. They all stopped their conversation and gave him a squinty-eyed look.

Conscious he was being watched, Bran dismounted and tied his very tired horse to a post. "Just a bit longer," he promised Orion. The answer was a snort. Bran ignored him and went inside.

The remains of the breakfast feast had been cleared away. The widowers, Mr. Fullerton and Sir Lionel, still sat at their table in the corner. They looked over the rims of their tankards as Bran walked in. "Balfour," Sir Lionel croaked out in greeting as if he hadn't seen him only hours ago. Both men were already at the bottom of a barrel.

Removing his hat, Bran nodded to them before turning to Old Andy who appeared to snooze in a chair by the taproom door. At the sound of the door closing, the man roused himself to see who had entered. "I thought you would be plucking birds," Bran said.

"I have the boys in the back doing exactly that now," Andy said. "Then they will wash behind their ears and make a few pennies tending horses at the dance this evening. They are all good lads. Stout or ale?"

"Ale." Bran could do with something stronger. He flung himself in a chair on the opposite end of the room from Fullerton and Sir Lionel.

"Are you attending the dance tonight?" Andy asked bringing him his tankard.

"Can I avoid it?"

"Not now that you are in Maidenshop," Andy assured him. "Was Mrs. Warbler out on her step? She was there earlier."

"She was."

"Then she and her group of biddies will hunt you down if you aren't at that dance. They won't rest until all of us are under a woman's thumb, including me." He set the brimming tankard on the table beside Bran's chair.

"Which we are equally determined to avoid," Mars chimed in. He came out from the taproom. He was without his coat and his sleeves were rolled up. "Save for Sir Lionel who flirts with Mrs. Warbler outrageously."

"I do not," the esteemed gentleman answered, proving that his hearing was remarkably good, even in his cups. "I'm waiting for the damn woman to go inside her house so that I can sneak out of here."

"What happened to your chair bearers?" Mars asked good-naturedly.

"He sent them home," Fullerton said. "Don't know how we will make it without them."

"I'll have a cart sent for," Sir Lionel answered. "I say, my lord, this seminar tomorrow—is it going to be boring or can we expect some entertainment?"

Mars removed a rook feather from his rolled sleeve. "Depends on your point of view. I imagine Thurlowe will find it fascinating, our friend Balfour may be interested, and the rest of us will be learning more than we wish about rocks while enjoying what promises to be a fine day with a keg or two."

"Ah, then it will be entertaining," Sir Lionel declared.

The earl took the chair opposite Bran's. "I thought I heard you out here."

"What have you been doing?"

"Plucking birds. It turns out I am a capital feather plucker."

"That is only part of what people say about you," Bran assured him with a laugh, and downed the rest of his ale. A bit of the tension inside him started to ease.

Mars nodded when Andy silently asked if he wanted a drink. "Apparently Balfour is ready for another as well." There was a deceptively light tone to his words. Bran ignored it, but nodded his head that, yes, he wanted another.

"So was your dear sister's concern urgent?" Mars stretched his long legs in front of him.

Beyond urgent. Bran kept the thought to himself.

"And apparently you haven't slept yet. Up all night, weren't you—riding?"

Bran did not trust the quizzing. Or the way Mars studied him. He kept his silence, relieved that Andy didn't waste time coming out with two tankards. The old man set the drinks in front of them, and Bran had a powerful urge to suck down the second tankard as quickly as the first.

Mars's presence stopped him. Bran sat, his elbows on the arms of his chair, his shoulders hunkered as he watched the earl take a drink. Mars wiped the corner of his mouth with the edge of his thumb. He looked from the untouched tankard to Bran and his brooding. "Come out back." He didn't wait for Bran but rose and walked through the taproom door.

Bran itched to drain his tankard. It was uncharacteristic of him, yes, but right now he felt ready to crawl out of his skin. Instead he followed Mars, taking his untouched ale with him.

The taproom was a small antechamber leading to the kitchen. Tankards hung on the wall and several kegs, at least enough to keep the men of Maidenshop happy, were stacked neatly in a corner.

In the kitchen, a few boys were cleaning up after the plucking. The naked and cleaned birds had been stacked on a great tray on the center aisle table. Andy nodded to them as Mars and Bran came through.

"Will you start cooking now, Andy?" Mars asked.

"In a few hours. I'll steam them before baking them in the pie," Andy said. "Keeps the meat tender."

Bran nodded dumbly. He was not a cook and right now, he didn't have an appetite for anything save the ale he carried.

In truth, he envied Mars's easiness with people from all walks of society. The boys would never wave and bow to him the way they did to the earl, even when the man wasn't paying them pennies to help with a hunt. Thurlowe was much like Mars. As the local doctor, he was extremely popular and welcomed into every home in the parish.

Only Bran seemed ill at ease when it came to social situations, and that had always been true—except with Kate. For her, he'd called on all his courage and overcome his natural reserve.

"Whatever you do will be appreciated," Mars answered Andy. "Expect a crowd. I'll talk it up tonight. We'll have a good turn-out on the morrow if those who have traveled for the dance don't leave early."

"I hope so. Mr. Thurlowe is anxious over the matter," Andy answered.

"All the more reason to do what we can to make his seminar a success. We want Ned happy." Mars nodded for Bran to follow him through the back door.

Several chairs and a table were outside the back door. Two chairs were close to the stream where the sound of water would prevent any conversation from being overheard. Mars led them there. He sat and indicated Bran should take a chair.

Bran didn't sit. He was too unsettled.

"Go on, spill it," Mars ordered. "Something is bothering you. Is it the bridge commission? Your sister?"

Bran was not one for talking about himself.

"Either tell me or down that ale you've been carrying as if you would like to throw it at me." Mars took a pull from his own drink for punctuation.

"Christopher has his eyes on *an actress*." The words flowed out of Bran, surprising him with their ferocity. God, he sounded like Lucy.

And Mars's response had been his. "As we all should." The earl tilted his chair back.

"Not this one. I've ordered her gone. I want her away from Winderton."

"I never thought you one to discourage a man from sowing his oats. What is he? Almost twenty-one? What are actresses for?"

Bran had a strong urge to throttle his friend, and realized it was jealousy. He did not like hearing Kate spoken of in that manner, even though she'd proven it to be true. "Not with her." He spoke slow and deliberately.

Mars brought all four legs of his chair down. "Balfour?" His brows came together. "Is it possible that you know this woman? You . . . and an actress?"

"You act as if such an association is perplexing."

Mars shrugged. "I mean no offense. It is just that, well, you are rather conservative."

"Not dashing enough for you, eh?"

"Don't take a bite out of me. I'm on your side. Still, I must be honest, there isn't a single woman between here and the coast who wouldn't like your ring on her finger. And most of them think you are as poor as a church mouse and live off of Winderton, versus the other way around. Don't worry. Neither Thurlowe nor I have told anyone," Mars said in answer to Bran's frown. "Although, I think you are foolish for not telling Winderton the truth."

"And let him know what a fool his father was?" Bran shook his head. "I wasn't ready for that conversation, especially with Lucy swimming in her mourning black."

"You can't put it off forever."

"I can for another month or two. When the time is right, I'll sit him down and explain. He actually isn't that bad off. I've done well in rebuilding the Winderton coffers."

"Except you still own the deed to Smythson. His family were fools not to have it entailed."

Bran agreed. "Everything I have will go to him upon my death," he answered.

"Unless you marry and have a child."

Bran snorted his opinion of that suggestion. "I see no reason to marry . . . unlike you who will need to do so sooner or later to breed an heir."

"I pray it is more later than sooner."

"Do you think about it? Marriage, that is?"

Mars shrugged. "No, in fact I don't know how most men do it. How can I settle on just one woman when there are so many waiting to be sampled?"

The earl routinely kept a mistress in London although he cycled through them frequently. He did have fickle tastes. And Bran had noticed that his friend seemed of late to prefer the country life. His trips to Town were becoming less frequent—a complaint his latest paramour made to anyone willing to listen. Usually when a mistress complained she was being neglected, it was a signal she was looking for a new protector. Seeing Mars stretched out in his chair, apparently enjoying the sounds of the running stream, Bran doubted if he cared if his current lady bird flew away.

Mars looked over at him. "So how did Winderton meet the actress? He hasn't left Maidenshop that I know of."

"She is in a traveling troupe. Their wagon broke down right at the edge of the estate."

"Ah, fate."

Yes, *fate*. Bran took a pull on his ale. It no longer tasted good to him. "I knew her once. We met years ago. Before I went off to India."

"Was she yours?" Mars asked, a hint of surprise in his voice.

His? A memory came to him, of that one very special afternoon and the aftermath, his noticing the bloodstains. His pride in recognizing that she had chosen him. His silent vow to protect her with his life, with all he had to offer . . .

He weighed how much to say. "No."

Mars leaned forward. "But you wished her to be?"

"I was young. A fool." And daffy in love. Enough so that when she went off with Hemling she crushed his heart. He'd been stunned that she could turn to another as quickly as she did—

He'd never understood it . . . save for the other man was a marquis. She'd thrown Bran over for a title. For rank and privilege, although look at her now.

"And now she is setting her hooks into Winderton?" Mars asked.

"That is the reason I ordered her to leave. I said if she didn't, I would have the magistrate on her." He shot a guilty glance at Mars who groaned.

"God, I hate the job. How did I end up with it?"

"We appointed you, remember? You were in London and they asked Ned and me what we thought."

"Well, what are friends for?" Mars's brows came together in concern. "Does she know of your connection to the duke? Perhaps even before she came?"

"And this was all planned? I don't think so." The question surprised Bran. "Kate didn't react one way or the other when I mentioned my relationship to the duke. In truth . . ." This was humbling to admit. "She didn't recognize me."

In the trees along the bank, a pair of sparrows were hopping from limb to limb. It was peaceful here—and completely at odds with the turmoil inside him. "Christopher told his mother he plans on marrying Kate. He wants to make her a duchess."

"I wager the dowager needed the smelling salts on that one."

"More like the brandy bottle. She wants the actress gone. Meanwhile, Winderton will be furious that I interfered. He is headstrong enough to challenge me." There was a beat of silence and then Bran added, "That would not be good. My sister would probably load the gun for him. On one hand, she demands her son do exactly what she wishes and yet, her every mother's instinct will go on the attack if someone upsets him. When he learns what I've said to Kate, he will definitely be on fire—and who knows which side Lucy will choose?"

His comment surprised a sharp bark of laughter from Mars. "Not only have you made me happy that most of my family is dead, but you are an excellent reminder that no good deed ever goes unpunished."

That was true. The more Bran had done for Lucy and her son, the more wheedling and demanding she had become. Of course, he had only himself to blame for keeping Winderton in the dark about his late father's shortcomings.

Mars leaned forward, cupping his empty tankard in his hands. "So, do you want advice? Based upon what I am observing?"

"If you will." Bran was at a point that he'd listen to the devil himself.

"Bed the actress before Winderton does—if he hasn't already, that is."

Bran almost fell out of his chair. *At one time, bedding Kate had been all he could think about,* and he definitely wouldn't mind having her again. His loins leaped at the thought, making his leather breeches uncomfortably tight.

"My nephew would consider it a betrayal."

"He'd see exactly what sort of woman she truly is. Certainly not Duchess of Winderton material."

"He'd be furious."

"Perhaps."

There was a beat of silence. The temptation was strong. Could Bran take her into his bed? And if he did, what price would he pay? Kate was a viper. "I wouldn't touch her."

Mars looked away as if he was biting his tongue, and then his lips twisted into a rueful smile. "Well, if you were forceful enough in your demands today, this Kate will be gone and you won't have to do anything."

"I was forceful enough."

The devil appeared in Mars's grin. "It just struck me. This woman must be—what? Over thirty?"

"At least thirty-five, however, she doesn't appear it. I can't criticize Winderton's taste. She is a beauty."

"Will she be when she is forty or fifty? Women don't age well. They can turn overnight like a pear gone to mush. Talk to Winderton man-to-man. If he wants an older woman, tell him he would be better off going, say five to eight years older at the most."

Bran shook his head. "He should put off even *the idea* of marriage for five to eight years. Ned and I have both been after him to join the Logical Men's Society. He needs some depth. There are times I don't understand him. He seems to float through life."

In a helpful tone, Mars said, "If you wish, I would be more than happy to take him aside and suggest he play with his actress, but not marry her. Or, I could take *her* aside?"

"I'll handle the matter," Bran answered, suddenly realizing what it would mean to let Mars close to Kate. The earl would find her delectable and then Bran would have an even larger problem.

His friend laughed knowingly.

And it actually didn't bother Bran that he was transparent to Mars. In fact, he marveled at how close he felt to both the earl and Ned Thurlowe. He'd not had trusted friends before. "Thank you," Bran said. "I am in a better mood than when I arrived."

"I'll see you this evening?"

"This evening?"

"The Three Bucks at the Cotillion Dance?"

"If you will be there, I'll make an appearance."

"If we don't, we'll be hounded by the biddies." Mars referred to the Matrons of Maidenshop.

"I'll need some sleep." Both he and Orion had earned it. He handed his tankard to Mars and started walking toward the corner of The Garland instead of going through the building to claim his horse.

Mars fell into step beside him, dangling the empty tankards in one hand. "By the way, do you think Ned will ever marry Clarissa Taylor?"

"He said he would."

"Wish to put a wager on it?"

"What side would you be taking?"

"That he will . . . eventually."

Bran shook his head. "Then there is no sense in a wager since we both agree. Thurlowe gave his word."

"I can't imagine a duller choice for a wife than Clarissa. She is lovely enough . . ." Mars let his voice drift before saying slyly, "However, the woman I want to meet is the one who has you tied up in knots—"

Bran rounded on him. "I'm not in knots. I cut her out of my life and I don't look back. I just don't wish for my nephew to do something remarkably stupid."

He didn't like the disbelief in his rakish friend's eye. Mars wisely, for once, stilled his tongue.

Riding back to Smythson, Bran found Winderton in the stables. The duke was preparing to ride out as Bran came in.

He greeted his uncle with, "Mother said you had come from Town. For the Cotillion, I take it." He was so young. So confident, and, yes, so arrogant.

Bran remembered him as a ruddy-cheeked cherub when he was a child and, in his uncle's mind at least, Christopher hadn't changed much. He had an open, trusting attitude about life. That Smythson had been practically falling down around his ears through most of his childhood had never seemed to register on him. In fact, neither Christopher nor Lucy acted aware of the lengths Bran had needed to take to secure their futures. The servants knew. They hadn't been receiving reliable wages until Bran's tenure.

"Yes, I did come for the dance," Bran answered because it was easier to lie. "Do you mind if I ride with you a moment?"

"Weren't you just coming in?"

Bran looked around the stable and said, "I'd like a word in private."

Christopher lifted a brow in question, then nodded. A few minutes later, they were making their way down the drive. Orion put up a bit of a protest over being hauled out of the barn. He was ready for his paddock.

"Just a few minutes more, old boy," Bran promised. To Christopher, he said, "Your mother is worried."

The duke didn't prevaricate. "About Miss Addison."

"Yes."

"I knew you didn't come for the dance. She sent for you, didn't she? She threatened to do so."

"She tells me you wish to marry this actress. I told Her Grace that you would never make such an alarming misalliance. Why, you've known her less than two days."

There. He'd put the objection out in the air between them.

And Winderton dismissed it. "Love is something more than just alliances. Besides, my generation takes a more generous view of the classes. The old standards no longer apply."

"Tell that to the gatekeepers. There are always standards whether we like them or not."

His ward gave a small, self-indulgent chuckle. "Yes, there are standards, except I am a duke. All doors are open to me. Always."

"But would those doors be open to your wife? Society can be closed-minded."

"Then those people would not matter to me."

How simple it all seemed to him. And such was the position of someone who had received too much, too soon, and had little knowledge about the balance of power.

Bran was tired and his patience thin. He decided to be direct. "Your Grace, you know your responsibilities. You understand the terms of guardianship because I spelled them out to you very clearly."

He had Winderton's attention now. The ducal lower lip turned mulish.

Bran continued. "Be warned, you are close to receiving your inheritance and the fullness of your birthright—*if* you have my approval." There had been at least that caveat in the father's will.

"I will not be turning anything over to you if I fear you would do something that would be considered stupid."

That knocked Winderton out of his smug complacency. "Is being *in love* stupid? Is wishing to choose a helpmate and settling in to take care of *my lands* and *my people* stupid?"

Ah, yes, Kate had made a conquest.

"You have much to learn about the world," Bran replied. "She might not want you! Anyway, you don't want to be tied down too soon."

"Says the man who enjoys being a bachelor. I'm not like you, Uncle. I want Kate and I will have her."

They were more alike than Winderton thought, but Bran kept his own counsel on that matter. This was tricky business. Christopher was determined to see Kate as an angel. There was also something in his nephew's voice toward him that Bran had never heard before—mistrust.

They were almost to the front gate. Bran brought Orion to a halt, realizing it might be wise to leave well enough alone. He'd planted the seed. Now let it flourish. "Your choices don't have to be mine, Chris. I've never set that yoke upon your shoulders. Beware of making promises, especially to women. They are wilier than men." Especially when a title and promise of a fortune were involved.

"I don't believe Miss Addison has an evil bone in her body. And the world is changing, Uncle. We modern men like women with lively minds."

"So you say. My observation is that the world is full of marriages that should have been avoided."

Bran looked in the direction of the house where he knew Lucy waited for a report. He'd said enough. Pushing the matter would only make it worse . . . especially if Kate told him that Bran had ordered her to leave, and she would. Extracting Christopher from her called for a delicate balance.

Making a show of shaking his head as if he was coming to his senses, Bran said, "Then again, you might be right. Still, remember that your mother and I care for you very much. Your well-being is important to us."

Gracelessly, the duke answered, "Provided I do as you say."

Bran wanted to bark back. It took willpower to hold his tongue.

At his uncle's silence, Winderton finally said, "You needn't worry. I know what I'm doing. I know what I *want* to do." On those words, he rode off with a wave.

Bran knew the interview with Lucy would not go half as well.

Chapter Five

As Bran had predicted, Lucy had not been pleased with his report that he'd given the actress until the morrow to leave. She'd wanted Kate chased out of the village with pitchforks and tar immediately.

Since that wasn't going to happen, she'd exacted a penance—he should be her escort to the dance. "His Grace has warned me he will be attending with friends," she'd said. "I will not go alone."

Bran decided to be agreeable and do as his sister wished. So he took her to the dance.

The duke had joined with them for an early dinner before taking himself off to meet his friends at The Garland. There was usually a good group of young men who drank Old Andy's ale before rolling over to St. Martyr's barn where the dance was held.

Bran wished he could have excused himself and gone with his nephew—however he doubted if Christopher would have welcomed his company. Over dinner, his ward had been deliberately quiet around him. Bran decided to let him be.

Besides, after several hours' sleep, Bran had regained his perspective. A duke needed his pride. He could tolerate Christopher's sulking.

The decorations committee had outdone themselves. The old barn was lit up as if it was Vauxhall. Paper lanterns were strung from one end of the interior to the other, giving the barn's white-washed walls a festive air. The bouquets of spring flowers Bran had spied the ladies carrying in earlier were on tables and around the punch bowl.

A trio of musicians sat on one end of the long room playing their hearts out for the enthusiastic dancers in front of them. Elsewhere were tables and chairs for those who didn't wish to stand. Friends and relatives from other villages and counties attended so the whole event had the air of a well-regarded "crush," that description of any gathering where people had to bump into each other to move.

Everyone hailed Bran as if he was some sort of long-lost prodigal. Questions were asked about why he'd stayed in London for so long. He was bemused by the way people in Maidenshop believed that their little village was the privileged center of the universe in the same way Londoners were quite certain they were the gifted ones.

However, it was good to be in the midst of everyone.

Mars was on the dance floor with one of Squire Nelson's pretty daughters. He came dancing over with his partner and brought her to a halt. While Miss Nelson curtsied, Mars bowed and said to Lucy, "Good evening, Your Grace. I hope I have the honor of escorting you on the dance floor this evening."

Lucy actually blushed. Still, she answered haughtily, "You are outrageous, Marsden. Can't you see I am still in mourning?"

Bran frowned his apologies to his friend over his sister's rudeness, however the earl laughed off her querulousness. "We should all be so honored to have a wife who mourned us for years after our death. My mother was happy to see my father go."

"I'd mourn for you," Miss Nelson said pertly.

Again, Mars laughed. He always took everything easily. It was one of the reasons Bran envied him. The earl rarely overthought a thing. "If you knew me better, you might not."

"Will His Grace be here this evening?" Miss Nelson was so bold to ask.

To Bran's surprise, Lucy, who usually disparaged the local girls, smiled indulgently. "Yes, he should be here shortly."

A becoming pink rose in Miss Nelson's cheeks as if in anticipation of seeing Winderton, and Mars said, "I fear I shall be supplanted."

"As you should be, my lord," a new voice chimed in. Mrs. Warbler joined their group. She was known for the bad wig she wore. It was a vivid shade of red and piled high on her head. Bran half expected her to sport a patch. She had at her elbow a ruddy-faced lad of perhaps twenty years or so. Bran did not recognize him. The lad had a pronounced Adam's apple and could have used at least a stone more in weight.

"Miss Nelson," Mrs. Warbler said, "you promised Mr. Fitzsimmons a dance, did you not?"

For a second, guilt crossed Miss Nelson's face as if she had been avoiding Mr. Fitzsimmons, however she recovered nicely. With a pretty smile, she said, "I've been looking for you. Shall we go for this next set?"

The awkward young man offered his arm and made a tongue-tied expression of agreement.

Miss Nelson shot a regretful look at Mars from under her dark lashes before taking the proffered arm. The couple moved to find their places for the next dance set.

"I wager he doesn't say two words to her the whole dance," Mrs. Warbler said to Lucy.

"Of course he won't," Lucy replied. "Isn't he related to Vida Fitzsimmons?" Vida was a spinster of indeterminate age and was always included in the pack of matrons.

"Her cousin from Newcastle."

"Then it is best he doesn't speak," Lucy answered, opening her fan and lazily waving it past her lips as if to hide her tart comment.

Mars gave a mock wince. "I fear what you say about me when my back is turned."

"That you should be married," Mrs. Warbler snapped. "Come, Lucy, we are all gathered in our corner. Excuse us, gentlemen." The matrons didn't wait for acknowledgement but made their way over to where others of their party had gathered in a grouping of chairs and tables. Their watchful eyes scanned the present company. There would be many tart comments this evening.

"Punch?" Mars asked.

"Have you tried it yet?"

"Weak. However, I hear Squire Nelson is one of many with a flask who is planning to give it some bite. Meanwhile, the Reverend Summerall keeps promising to water it down."

"Nothing changes around here, does it?" Bran observed. This same conversation could have taken place before he'd left for India years ago. And while London seemed to change weekly, every time Bran returned home, he was struck by how predictable Maidenshop was.

"Very little," his friend answered. "That is what makes it perfect. We know exactly what to expect."

As they started for the crowded punch table, they saw Ned standing attendance next to Clarissa Taylor and made their way over to him. If ever a couple appeared uncomfortable, this one did. They stood side by side like strangers waiting for a stage to arrive.

In truth, Clarissa was a lovely, biddable woman. Her hair was the color of the richest honey and her eyes were cat shaped and green, the sort of eyes that lingered in a man's mind. If she'd had any fortune at all, she would have been snapped up. Unfortunately, her dubious parentage, her lack of dowry, and her studious nature kept her on the shelf.

Bran didn't think Thurlowe was making a bad match, just an uninteresting one. Then again, he'd just realized he'd spent a good chunk of his life moping over Kate. Who was the greater fool?

Ned and Miss Taylor stood with her guardians, Squire Nelson and his wife. There was another couple with them who were introduced as Mrs. Nelson's sister and brother-in-law from Surry.

Ned acted relieved to see Mars and Bran. Miss Taylor greeted Bran warmly, yet gave the most civil acknowledgement to Mars, who answered in kind. It was well-known she considered him a wastrel and that he thought her a bore.

Meanwhile, the squire's wife, who delighted in Mars and his rakish ways, would have adored for him to pay court to one of her four daughters. She inquired saucily if they had their eye on any of the ladies. "Such as the one you just danced with, my lord?" She meant her daughter.

Mars mumbled something about how well Miss Nelson presented herself and that pleased her mother. "She'd make an excellent countess," she was so bold to say.

"Martha," the squire warned with a frown of embarrassment.

"She would," his wife protested undeterred. "And what of you, Mr. Balfour? I know your sister would be pleased to see you married."

True. Lucy dropped many hints. "Unfortunately, I'm not ready to give up my membership in the Logical Men's Society."

Mrs. Nelson rapped on his arm with her fan. "You bachelors." She sighed. "I rue the day they ever decided to start that silly club. It truly is spoiling the lot of you."

"That isn't true," Mars said. "There are more married men than there are single ones in Maidenshop. Your husband was once a member."

"Until he saw the light. Man was made to be married," Mrs. Nelson declared. "I for one am pleased that your numbers are dwindling. I can't wait for the three of you to join the married ranks. Then there will be no one left in that club except for those two old fools, and they can have each other." Her sister beamed her agreement. The squire and the other gentleman acted as if they wished to ignore this conversation.

Thurlowe could not let such a comment go. After all, this was the campaign near and dear to him. "The Logical Men's Society is more than just a group of bachelors. We have seminars like the one we will have tomorrow with Mr. Clyde Remy. He will discuss the late James Hutton's theory concerning uniformitarianism and all gentlemen, married or single who are interested in natural philosophy, are invited."

"Uniformitarianism?" the squire repeated.

"Rock formations," Bran offered helpfully.

Mars added, "There will be rook pie and all the ale you can drink. Free."

"Rook pie, eh? Andy baking it?" the squire asked. He had a pronounced belly that indicated his enjoyment of good food.

"Of course he is, sir," Thurlowe answered.

"I should like to be there," the squire said, ignoring his wife's frown. "There will be others?"

"All gentlemen—again, married or single—are invited," Mars answered.

"Ah, good." The squire nodded to his brother-in-law. "Now we have something to do on the morrow while the ladies continue with their chitter chatter about what happened here." His wife sighed her opinion. "Oh, don't be that way, Martha. I'm here tonight, aren't I?"

She didn't answer.

"Miss Taylor, I believe we should dance," Ned said and she agreed with great relief.

"Excuse us," she murmured, placing her hand on Thurlowe's arm.

Mars and Bran moved on as well. They had not gone far toward their destination of the punch bowl when Mars muttered, "Thurlowe appears miserable."

"Trapped perhaps. Not completely miserable. Miss Taylor does not appear any happier."

The earl made a mock shudder and then noticing a larger group of gentlemen injected both he and Bran into their number. "Tomorrow, at The Garland, we are starting a new tradition."

"What is that?" asked Simon Crisp, a man of middling years who farmed property not far from Belvoir.

"We are calling it a seminar and offering free ale and rook pie."

"Capital idea," said Crisp.

"I like the price," another gent agreed.

"Spread the word," Mars pushed.

"We will," Crisp answered. "And the punch has more bite now. We've done a bit of doctoring," he said with a wink. "You should try it, my lord."

"We will, won't we, Balfour?"

Before Bran could answer, there was a sudden shift in the mood of the room.

Crisp and his companions looked past Bran to the door and fell silent. The musicians wound down the jaunty reel that they had just started. All eyes were turning to the entryway, and Bran knew the unexplained prickling sensation at the back of his neck was a warning.

Slowly, he faced the door.

There was his nephew attired as if he was about to be presented in court. He wore white knee breeches and dancing shoes. His jacket was claret and his hair was styled as if he was the Sun God himself. This was not how he'd been dressed at dinner.

In a room where a good number of the men wore their boots, the duke stood out. No wonder so many matchmaking mothers had their daughters at the dance. Here was the Catch of Maidenshop. Mars could just move over.

However, Winderton wasn't the reason the room had gone *very* quiet.

Kate Addison hugged Winderton's arm, but this was not the Kate Bran had left this morning. *That* Kate, in her modest day dress and properly styled hair, could have passed for a Lady of Quality.

This Kate was the conjuring of every erotic image any man had ever held.

Beneath a wide-brimmed hat with no fewer than three bouncing purple ostrich plumes, riotous curls framed her face and tumbled down past her shoulders as if she'd just risen from her bed. Her breasts were mounded up and over the smallest bodice Bran had ever seen. They appeared as if they were being offered on a platter to the slack-jawed gents in the room.

And the skirt—

Bran had never given much thought to skirts before. He did now. In a room full of the tastefully soft colors of innocence or the deep, jeweled tones of properly married women, Kate's skirt of wide blue-and-white stripes almost obscenely outlined the feminine curve of her hip, the indent of her waist, the length of her legs.

Her hand was wrapped around Winderton's arm with unseemly closeness while her other hand held a shepherd's crook festooned with colorful ribbons, a warning if ever there was one that she was here to gather souls.

She was bold. She was beautiful. And there wasn't a man in the room who wasn't having fantasies, Bran included . . . because he could recall too well the perfection of her figure.

However, Winderton's smug expression brought Bran to his senses. He'd ordered Kate to leave. It would have been the easiest path for her to choose.

Instead, she chose to defy his command and twist his ward around her little finger.

A challenge was being issued. A challenge he would meet.

"God in heaven, what has just arrived?" Crisp asked in round, awed tones.

"Balfour's worst nightmare," Mars suggested. He shot a wry glance toward Bran. "What are you going to do? And do you need help?"

His smile grim, Bran ignored the latter question, but answered the first, "Why, I shall welcome her, of course." He moved forward.

Chapter Six

$\mathcal{K}$ate had made a magnificent entrance at the Cotillion Dance. There wasn't an eye in the room that wasn't on her. And now Brandon Balfour knew she wasn't going to let him run her off.

She was inordinately proud of her costume. It had turned out brilliantly. She rarely wore her hair down and even she was surprised at how long it had grown. Mary had done an admirable job of curling it.

The pièce de résistance to her ensemble were her green buckle shoes. In defiance to current fashion, they had a small heel to make her even taller than she was. They curled up at the toes. She remembered she had found them on some tinker's cart and had thought them fun and possibly useful for any part that called for a witch . . . or a siren.

Granted, when the duke had arrived to escort her, he had appeared a bit taken aback at her costume, and yet he'd not made a complaint. He was too inexperienced to put a woman, especially one accustomed to her own decisions like Kate, in her place.

He'd stumbled over his compliment and had struggled mightily not to stare at her bosom, which was there for all to see. Mary had cut the bodice very low.

To his credit, he hadn't leered. He *had* swallowed hard several times, partly from the expanse of skin and partly because this was a village dance. Kate had taken pity on him and informed him of his uncle's threats.

From that moment on, Winderton became her ally. He'd even insisted on returning home so that he could change his own clothes to something fancier. "Let us both give Maidenshop a vision they will never forget," he'd declared and Kate had agreed.

Consequently, they were one of the last couples to arrive. Their appearance could not have been more perfect.

Kate had to give the duke credit, it took courage to defy his uncle . . . courage to offer her his arm. A lesser man would have suggested they not go out. A ruder one would have other ideas.

And it made her quite like the young duke, in spite of his directing her actors.

A hush had fallen around the room. The ladies hid their shocked expressions behind their fans. The men hid nothing at all.

If Kate had any doubts about her ensemble, they vanished as soon as she saw Mr. Balfour heading in her direction with a very determined step. "Prepare for battle, Your Grace."

The duke nodded, squaring his young shoulders.

The room seemed to hold its collective breath, watching, anticipating, expecting a scene that Kate was ready to deliver.

She leaned even closer to Winderton.

Her movement wasn't lost on Mr. Balfour. His step toward them paused slightly, almost in midair—and then he abruptly moved to join a couple beside them, speaking to the pair as if it had been his intent all along.

Which was a lie, she wanted to tell him. She knew he had meant to say something to her and the duke.

She had not dressed this way to be ignored.

And just like that, the music started. The dancers eagerly moved back to their places. Mr. Balfour found a partner and stood up for the set. The rest of the room save for several men who were already too deep in their cups to notice, followed her eagerly as Winderton led her to stand in a less conspicuous place.

The grand moment was over . . . before it had even begun. Kate felt decidedly flat, a bit annoyed at how much she had been anticipating locking horns with Mr. Balfour.

Her gaze went to the dance floor. This was definitely a country society, with no uniformity of dress or deportment. Some men wore pantaloons and their dancing shoes. For others, their two concessions to this being a special occasion appeared to be a clean shirt and a wash behind their ears.

In truth, Mr. Balfour stood out from all of them in his marine-blue coat and white breeches. She watched him move through the dance steps and she knew she wasn't the only female to do so. He had definitely changed from the awkward young man who had once captured her heart . . .

The duke tugged on her arm. "Come, I wish to introduce you to my mother. I've spoken about you and I know she is looking forward to meeting you."

"Perhaps this isn't the right time?" She was starting to realize that Silas might have been right. She may have not thought this through. She'd made her statement but she wasn't comfortable exposing this much of her chest for the rest of the evening. Her goal had been to teach Mr. Balfour that he could not and would not dictate to her. She'd envisioned a grand scene, the dialogue somewhat murky in her mind, in which he ended up being completely humbled.

Instead, she found herself in the middle of a charming country dance that appeared to celebrate all levels of its society. There were matrons gathered in one strategic corner of the room where they could watch over all the proceedings. Young men, some yeoman, some gentlemen, others tradesmen, crowded the punch table. They were under the watchful eyes of the local, blushing beauties dressed in their finest. The music was spirited and happy, the conversation loud, and the laughter a welcome respite to someone like Kate who too often felt like Atlas with the world upon his shoulders.

"Kate, there is no good time to meet Mother. We have already shocked her. Now I must introduce you to her so she knows I am proud to be with you."

What could she do? She'd chosen this role and she'd best play it to the hilt.

Boldly, almost defiantly, Winderton led her through the crowded room. People stepped aside, gaping openly at Kate. There was no humor in the looks women sent her, their eyes narrowed in disapproval. They clearly saw her for the interloper she was, on the arm of the most eligible bachelor in the county . . . and one clearly many years her junior.

As for the men, there were a few randy, low-pitched guttural hums as she passed them. She was tempted to knock manners into them with her crook. Instead, noticing the color that crept up the duke's neck, she distracted him with a compliment about how it was obvious everyone admired him. She had no desire to have a duel fought over her, especially when she was regretting her choice of dress.

But no one would know that. Kate knew how to brazen things out. She decided she had a role to play and she would play it well, adding an extra swish to her hips as she walked. She ignored the fluttering of fans and the buzz of furious whispers.

With game determination, the duke waded the two of them into a formidable gathering of older women who had watched them approach with looks akin to horror. There was no mistaking which one was the dowager duchess. She had the Balfour gray eyes, though she was not as tall as Kate had expected and her hair was as dark as her brother's.

She appeared much older than Balfour, although the cut of the black gown was too matronly. Winderton had told Kate his father had died several years ago. That his mother was still in mourning spoke volumes about her character. This was not a woman who embraced change.

"Mother," Winderton said almost with shy eagerness. "I wish

you to meet Miss Addison. This is my mother, the Dowager Duchess of Winderton."

Kate made her curtsey. She couldn't go too low with it. Not with her breasts in danger of tumbling out. "Your Grace."

No gloved hand was extended to her. The dowager barely murmured, "Miss Addison," as if the name would choke her.

Kate thought of her parents, of the times that the local gentry, people very much like those at this dance, had shunned them because of their opinion of her mother. They'd ignored her father's excellent family connections. He had been the youngest son of a duke, albeit a duke who had disowned him when he'd married the actress Rose Billoy. Their contempt had included the daughters of that marriage.

Still, Rose would not have approved of the way Kate was behaving this evening. Rose may have been an actress but she had been a woman of good taste and genteel demeanor. Kate had always thought of herself in the same fashion—and yet, here she was, dressed as the most common of tarts.

Still, it didn't make sense to Kate, who truly adored her profession and prided herself on her accomplishments, that other women would frown upon her. Didn't all women left without family or benefit of a husband have to survive? What was wrong with a woman supporting herself with Shakespeare and Sheridan? Why was being a governess or a dressmaker better than being an actress? How could they brand her as disreputable when she wrote plays about morality tales like *Aesop's Fables*?

Instead, the matrons sat in their corner appearing scandalized. Their eyebrows hit their hairlines. They held their breath as if she tainted the air.

And poor Winderton was caught between his pride, his lust, and his mother. Kate debated between telling him she pitied him or to buck up.

Her thoughts were interrupted by Mr. Balfour's deep, resonant voice. "May I beg an introduction, Winderton?"

In a blink, any regret Kate was feeling vanished, even as her heart beat faster. The moment was at hand. He had finally decided to engage.

"If you will excuse me, Your Grace?" she said to the dowager, not waiting for permission before confronting her nemesis with a small, very cold smile.

Winderton appeared relieved for the interruption. It was almost as if he had thought his mother, upon meeting Kate, would give her blessing to this match and had just realized the error in his thinking. Men could be amazingly naïve.

"Miss Addison, this is my uncle, Mr. Brandon Balfour. Uncle, may I present Miss Kate Addison, a very talented woman in her own right. She writes the plays her troupe performs. Of course, I believe the two of you met earlier."

That was apparently a jab at his uncle.

Mr. Balfour handled it with false warmth. "Yes, but not with a *formal* introduction, Your Grace. One must always pay attention to the niceties of good manners."

The matrons were listening fervently to their every word.

"Then you have now been formally introduced," the duke declared. "Miss Addison, my uncle is one of the premier architects in London."

Kate had not known that.

Mr. Balfour had the good grace to bow his head at the compliment. "My nephew is very kind to me. I am working to earn that title."

Winderton gave an indulgent laugh. "You will. He hopes to build a bridge across the Thames."

"I understand another bridge is exactly what London needs," Kate said pleasantly, as if she hadn't been ready to punch Mr. Balfour in his arrogant nose mere hours ago.

"One can hope," Mr. Balfour acknowledged, as if he hadn't threatened to run her out of the village. "Ah, look, Your Grace, they are setting up for the next set. Certainly you and Miss Addison wish to join the *young* people?"

Yes, he put a slight emphasis on the word *young*.

"Miss Addison, will you honor me with this dance?" the duke asked.

Dancing was the last thing Kate wanted. Now, she would like to return to her troupe, remove the shoes that had started pinching her feet, and retire to her bed. Alone.

"Of course," she answered.

"I imagine you have never been to a country dance like this?" Mr. Balfour suggested.

What? Did he believe she'd been born in a gutter?

With pride, she announced, "My sisters and I were considered the belles of Huntingdon, not too far from here. I always enjoyed dancing." She flashed Mr. Balfour a brilliant smile as she put her hand on the duke's arm. This time, she didn't lean too close to the duke. She'd made her point . . . and perhaps it would be best if she started negotiating a bit of distance between herself and Winderton. She was using him, yes, but she didn't wish to lead him on.

As the duke started to escort her away, Mr. Balfour called out, "Miss Addison, would you like for me to hold your crook? It might be awkward on the dance floor."

He was right. It was turning into an annoyance. "Why, thank you, Mr. Balfour," she answered with the same veneer of politeness. He took the crook from her.

"Thank you, Uncle," Winderton threw over his shoulder.

The area for dancing took up half the room. Foursomes were being set up. Several gentlemen nodded to the duke to join their groups. Winderton chose one made up of people close to his age.

Kate didn't dare look at Mr. Balfour because she was certain he noticed how out of place she looked, especially with the silly hat and its billowing plumes. She felt like an exotic bird ready to take flight. The smile she'd kept plastered on her face began to feel more like a grimace.

The duke introduced her to the couples around them. She could tell he was popular and would have been even without his title. Like his uncle, he had an air of confidence, and in some ways Winderton reminded her of the young man Balfour had been—except the duke had wealth and position while Balfour had not.

"It is nice to meet you," a young woman said perfunctorily while avoiding eye contact. In contrast, the white-clad debutante by her side stared with undisguised disgust. Their behavior was actually rather comical, until the debutante asked her companions in a pseudo-whisper, "Do you think it will be hard to dance in such a hat?" She punctuated her question with a snicker.

"It shouldn't be," Kate answered serenely, interjecting herself into the conversation. "After all, I dance with my feet and not my head."

The ladies smirked their opinions of her words to each other, but the gentlemen laughed as if Kate had made the wittiest remark. They also seemed to be squeezing in around her . . . and the duke appeared at a loss over what to do. In fact, they almost disregarded his presence. Not one of them met her eye because they were busy ogling her chest—

"May we join this foursome?" Mr. Balfour asked. He edged in, which meant others in their group had to take a step back. Mr. Balfour was accompanied by a lovely woman with large green eyes and a smooth complexion. "You don't mind," he pressed pointedly to the closest man leering at Kate. The man was almost a foot shorter than herself, which made his attention very uncomfortable.

"Of course not, Balfour." The lecher knew this was not a request he could ignore. He moved with one of the snickering ladies to join another foursome with a respect he had not shown for the duke.

Winderton didn't hide his relief at seeing his uncle.

Kate tried to. "Ah, Mr. Balfour. I thought you were guarding my shepherd's crook?"

"It is well protected," he said before making the necessary introductions. "Miss Addison, this is Miss Taylor, a good friend."

Miss Taylor was of medium height with tawny hair. "Miss Addison, I adore your outfit. It is so refreshing to see patterns."

She spoke with genuine feeling, even if it might only be kindness. However, Kate's first instinct was to dislike her. Intensely. There wasn't any reason for it, save that Miss Taylor stood beside Mr. Balfour.

It annoyed Kate that she had noticed—

"*Oh,*" Miss Taylor said as if startled. "Your *shoes.* They are green. How *magnificent.*"

In an about-turn, Miss Taylor became Kate's favorite person. At her exclamation, other women, overhearing, looked—including the smirkers. Kate lifted her skirts slightly. "They are different, aren't they?" And now worth the pinching of her toes.

"Charming." Miss Taylor's gaze held undisguised admiration. "They finish off your ensemble. They are so much fun."

"I thought as much." Kate would have told her about the tinker's cart, except a gentleman leaned into their group.

"All this fuss over shoes?" he said. He was tall, blond, and had an air of easy nobility.

"As if you gentlemen don't carry on about boots, my lord?" Miss Taylor shot back archly. There was no humor in her voice, just mild disdain. She did not like the gentleman. Kate wondered why.

His response was a cold smile.

The duke stepped in. "Miss Addison, may I present to you the Earl of Marsden. My lord, this is Miss Addison whose theater performances starting on the morrow will be all anyone in the county will be able to discuss."

"Well, then I must make it a point to attend," the earl answered as his gaze went to Mr. Balfour. A look seemed to pass between them, some private jest.

Kate decided Miss Taylor was right to dislike Lord Marsden.

She also knew Silas would be pleased, as was she, at the mention of the performances. Everyone around them had heard the duke's prediction. They might have a good crowd on the morrow.

And then the duke offered another piece of information. "Marsden acts as the local magistrate. You would be wise to stay on his good side."

"I will endeavor to do so, Your Grace," she murmured, remembering Mr. Balfour's threat to let loose the magistrate on her.

Thankfully, the musicians struck a chord. There was a beat of silence and then they broke out in a lively reel. The dancers roared their approval.

Kate needed a second to catch the pattern. It had been some time since she'd danced. But once she started, her feet seemed to know where to go.

All pretenses amongst the dancers evaporated. There was the joy of movement, of music, of good fun. Feet stomped. Skirts swished. Even the stuffiest of personages twirled and skipped. The reel was one that was played faster and faster. Kate quickly found herself almost out of breath and laughing.

The duke and Miss Taylor were great partners. When Kate missed a step, they just shushed it away and encouraged her to go on.

Mr. Balfour was even passably pleasant.

Of course, the hat was a silly thing on her head. A single pin with a paste jewel on the tip held her hat in place. The plumes bounced and waved and the brim flapped up and down at Kate's exertion.

The green shoes were another challenge. She vowed she'd never wear them again, even on stage, if they would just carry her through this evening.

The whole room, even the observers, began clapping. Shouts went up, encouraging the musicians and dancers. It was as if the two groups were pitted against each other—and when it was over with a big crashing chord from the instruments, the musicians threw themselves back in their chairs as if done up. Triumphant, the dancers laughed and bowed practically into each other's arms.

Flush from the exertion, Kate turned toward the duke but found herself, instead, facing Balfour. A hank of hair had fallen over his brow. He appeared boyish—and a slate of memories roiled through her. In that instant, she recalled his kiss, his touch . . . his promises.

And those memories of how gullible she had once been to have believed him almost took her to her knees.

She whipped around, embarrassed to have considered him with any favor. Miss Taylor held a hand to her chest while Winderton steadied her by holding her other hand. Kate couldn't help but notice that *here* was a good match.

Removing the pin, Kate took off her hat. It felt good to remove the blasted thing.

A gentleman yelled, "To the punch bowl!"

His order was quickly seconded. Kate, Winderton, Miss Taylor, and even Mr. Balfour seemed to be swept off the dance floor. New couples quickly formed to take their place. By their rosy cheeks and giddiness, she guessed they had already visited the punch bowl.

"Let us see to refreshment for the ladies," Mr. Balfour suggested.

"Good idea," the duke answered. "Miss Addison, may I leave you a moment with Miss Taylor?"

"Of course."

The two men walked away, joining a stream of men on their way to procure refreshments for their ladies. Kate had no doubt that Mr. Balfour would use this opportunity to give his nephew an earful.

She was also conscious that there were cliques of women around them. Kate focused on Miss Taylor.

One of the most handsome men she had ever seen approached them. He had an air that was both studious and slightly anxious.

Miss Taylor smiled her welcome and introduced him to Kate as Mr. Ned Thurlowe, the local physician, and her intended.

There went Kate's plans for a match between Miss Taylor and the duke. When they were young, and she had still lived at home, her older sister Alice had always claimed Kate was a terrible matchmaker.

Mr. Thurlowe was all that was polite but then excused himself from the dance. "I've received word that the Widow Hastings has taken a bad turn. She is having difficulty breathing. Her son has sent for me."

"Of course you must go," Miss Taylor said.

"I am sorry to leave you. It seems as if this happens every time we are together."

"It will not be a problem."

He smiled his appreciation and left. Kate felt his parting was decidedly unlover-like. The two of them had not held hands, not even touched. "It is a pity he must leave on such an important evening," Kate offered.

"He is in demand," Miss Taylor said. "He is dedicated to the healing arts."

"That is admirable."

A moment passed and then, almost as if she could not help herself, Miss Taylor murmured, "Of course, he won't miss the seminar he has planned on the morrow, no matter who takes ill."

"Seminar?"

"He belongs to a local society," Miss Taylor answered. "They call themselves the Logical Men's Society."

"Sounds heady."

"It's not. The village women would adore to see it closed down. The society is for men who are unmarried. It has gone on for years. I'm told there was a time when many didn't marry just because they enjoyed being part of the society. That isn't the case today. Their numbers have dwindled. Mr. Thurlowe is the chairman of the group and he wants to add to the membership."

"When the two of you marry, their numbers will go down by one."

"Yes," Miss Taylor said, drawing the word out. "It is a conundrum for him. I know he means to marry me . . ." Her voice trailed off.

"How long has he been courting you?"

"Almost two years."

"And you haven't grown impatient?" Kate wondered.

A pensive look crossed Miss Taylor's lovely face. "I was a found-ling, left on the parsonage doorstep. I have few options available to me. Mr. Thurlowe was extremely kind to offer for me."

"There are other options beyond marriage for women."

Miss Taylor gave a start. "I didn't mean to insult you—"

"You haven't," Kate replied calmly. "It is just that you are promised to a man who is making you wait? For nearly two years? While he participates in a club that encourages *bachelorhood*?"

"That sums it up." Miss Taylor lowered her voice to confide, "In truth, I'm not that anxious to marry."

"I can understand why." Kate shook her head. "Is there any-thing men won't join? Can you imagine us having a spinster club? Why, no woman would want to be a member."

"If we held our own special lecture on rocks, we could shut the men out."

"Shut them out?"

"Yes, on the morrow, Mr. Thurlowe has arranged a lecture by a Mr. Remy. He is a natural philosopher who will discuss a theory on how rocks were formed. I should find that very interesting."

"Will not Mr. Thurlowe include you?"

"He says he wishes he could," she answered as if quoting him. "He fears my presence might offend those in attendance."

Kate had heard these arguments all her career. There were actors and the managers of other troupes who left her out of dis-cussions or closed off opportunities to her troupe because they claimed to fear offending anyone by having a woman give orders. Or her opinion. Or sit at the same table.

She looked around the room. Most of the men, if they weren't on the dance floor were gathered around the punch table, laughing with each other, gossiping, bragging . . . all the traits men criticized women for but practiced in abundance themselves. Several kept looking over at her, their thoughts plain on their faces.

"Mr. Thurlowe says the Logical Men's Society was formed to support men and their minds," Miss Taylor added.

Kate could not stop herself. "I think he's speaking rot."

Miss Taylor blinked as if stunned at Kate's audacity. "I don't know," she said uncertainly.

"Do you know many men?" Kate responded, matter-of-fact. "There is very little on their minds." *Save for the dress she was wearing.* "Your presence would be an improvement."

Her words sparked a laugh out of her new friend who quickly quieted as if ashamed of herself. "Mr. Thurlowe is truly quite kind. If not for his offer, I'd have to support myself as a companion or a governess. I cannot stay with the squire and his wife indefinitely."

"Or you could be like me," Kate pointed out. "There are other things women can do to fend for themselves. We just have to be bold."

Miss Taylor's gaze took in Kate's dress. "I don't think I am as daring as you."

"You might have more courage than you believe you have. When one doesn't have a choice, one becomes whom she was meant to be."

"Perhaps."

"I'll tell you right now that you have shown great fortitude standing next to me. We have been the focus of all the wagging tongues."

Miss Taylor laughed agreement. "They are all trying to over-hear us. Especially the group of women to my left. I grew up with gossip. There has always been speculation over my birth, the names of my parents. You will have to work much harder to create more gossip than I have."

Now it was Kate who laughed.

"Oh dear," Miss Taylor said under her breath, changing the subject. "I wondered why the men haven't returned. The dowager has intercepted her son with Miss Judith Hollingsworth. Her father is a chancellor at Trinity. Her aunt lives here and they must have brought her to the dance."

"To meet the duke."

"Of course." Miss Taylor cast her a glance.

"Good. He is a very nice young man."

"Who likes *you* very much."

"In this dress, they all like me," Kate sagely noticed. "And I don't blame his mother for doing her level best to interfere with his pursuit of me."

"Miss Addison? Are you saying you *aren't* interested in His Grace—?"

Before Kate could answer, two gentlemen of the same age as the duke barged right in between she and Miss Taylor. One was the short dancer who'd stared rudely at Kate's bosom. The other had a long slender neck and an even longer head.

"Good evening, Miss Taylor." They didn't even look at her. *They had their backs to her.*

"Mr. Michaels, Mr. Shielding."

"May we be introduced to this fascinating creature?" The short Mr. Michaels smiled. His teeth were brown. Kate tried to hide her shock and took a step back. The time had come to leave.

She'd made her point to Mr. Balfour. Contrary to her early hopes, she would have to warn Silas that sales for the performance tomorrow might be sparse. Given the stares she'd received this evening with her stunt, she doubted if any woman in the parish would allow any member of her family to attend her plays.

Such was life.

Miss Taylor spoke as if having doubts about introductions. "Miss Addison, this is Mr. Michaels and Mr. Shielding. They are both solicitors."

"Ah, the lawyers," Kate said, amused by Miss Taylor's reluctance and the gents' eagerness. Then again, of all the species of men, lawyers could be the most worthless.

"I want this next dance," Mr. Shielding said without preamble or manners. He was obviously intoxicated.

Before Kate could politely refuse, Mr. Michaels hit his friend's arm with his fist. "We agreed that I dance with her first."

Mr. Shielding ignored him. "May I?" he pressed, bowing clumsily.

The next punch was to the side of Mr. Shielding's head. The force behind the blow was impressive because of the height disparity. Mr. Shielding fell back, tumbling against the tight-knit group of women who had no doubt been jabbering about Kate. They were caught by surprise. Mr. Shielding landed on the floor and tried to rise by pulling on skirts. There was the sound of ripping material. Women screeched their alarm. Several started to fall and punch cups, fans, and an impossibly red wig went flying.

In a blink, Mr. Shielding and Mr. Michaels were caught up in their own drama. Regaining his feet, Mr. Shielding, with a shout of, "You are an unruly bastard, Douglas!" dived into Mr. Michaels.

They plunged into the next group of people. Behind them, a frantic woman started screaming, *"My wig. Where is my wig?"*

Those who attempted to separate the fighting friends ended up in the middle of it as they retaliated for fists being thrown at them. Men left the punch table, their hands forming fists. The music stopped as more women began screaming.

Outright chaos broke out. It was as if the room had separated into warring tribes.

Kate was jostled this way and that. She became separated from Miss Taylor. She tried to back away from two men who were shoving at each other.

A strong hand grabbed her shoulder and swung her around. *"You,"* the woman who had lost her wig snapped. "You are the cause of all this."

"I wasn't—" Kate said, but her words were cut short.

"Whore."

Few had ever dared to say such a word to her face. "You are mistaken, madam," she shot back. Her palm itched to slap the older woman's face for her impertinence, except Kate had better manners.

Unfortunately, that word was a rallying cry for the women. Kate found herself surrounded. The lady whose dress had been torn by Mr. Shielding's clumsiness reached for Kate's bodice and would have grabbed it save for Kate forcefully pushing her away. With a cry, the grand dame fell back against a man ready to throw a fist. It almost connected with her chin. He stopped himself in time and was rewarded by the woman fainting into his arms like a deadweight.

Kate had to leave.

This was madness.

Tables and chairs were being overturned. There was shouting, grunts, crying, and, yes, she would be blamed.

Kate searched for an escape. She would not be able to reach the entrance. Battles were being fought everywhere.

However, she did notice a side door close at hand. Quickly, she dodged combatants and pushed it open. It led into a small dark room that had been used as storage at one time or another. The light from the other room revealed a half door only three feet high. This explained why no one else had tried this escape. They probably all knew it would not be simple.

Her heart pounding in her ears, Kate attempted her escape. She could not go back out there into the melee.

Fortunately, the door wasn't locked. With a good hard shove of her shoulder, she pressed it open, feeling the cool night air with its hint of freedom.

Dirt had built up against the door on the outside making it hard to open. Using all her strength, and heedless of what her efforts were doing to the dress, Kate put mind and body to the door. With another mighty push, she moved it open wide enough for her to wedge her shoulders through and then ungracefully climb out of it.

She had to crawl a few feet. All was dark here. She shakily rose up. The green shoes were really pinching her toes now, but she did not care. She was more worried about what was popping out of her bodice. Businesslike, she pushed herself back into some semblance of order, and she was safe.

"Thank you, God," she whispered fervently.

A voice answered, and it was not God's.

"Well played, Miss Addison. Well played," Mr. Balfour said. He leaned against a tree not more than five feet away, her shepherd's crook in his hand.

Chapter Seven

At the sound of his voice, Kate Addison jumped like a school-boy caught in a prank, and Bran smiled, pleased.

It was dark on this side of the building. However, Kate stood outlined against the barn's white walls. There had been no mistaking her disarray. What little moonlight was here highlighted the naked curve of her breast.

Images of Kate entwined in his sheets shot to his mind. God, he had dreamed of her breasts—

Bran stepped back into the shadows as something on him grew prominently, putting *him* in disarray. Who knew what Kate would do if she knew she still held power over him?

Sounds of what had become a brawl came from the front of the building where it had apparently spilled out into the front yard. Horses in the care of servants or the local lads called out alarms. The Reverend Summerall's voice could be heard over the din shouting, "Order! Good order!"

However, here, it was quiet. They were hidden by the building, moonlit darkness, and a line of trees and shrubs.

Kate straightened, her stance defiant. She looked around as if realizing they were alone. "How did you know to find me here?"

"I saw you escape through that doorway. It is an old storage room with only that small door. I wondered if you would try it or be foolish enough to risk making your way through the crowd."

She frowned in the direction of the noise at the front of the building. "I did not intend for this to happen. It isn't my fault." She spoke as if to herself.

He had to answer. "I don't see why we can't blame you. As I remember it, fights usually broke out around you."

She glared at him then. He could feel the heat of her anger through the cool night air. "That was many, many years ago. And I did not start *any* of those fights either. You gentlemen tore at each other all by yourselves. I also did not start this nonsense."

"Next you will be telling me old Mrs. Warbler began everything."

"Does she wear a wig?"

Bran had to smile, he couldn't help himself. "The worst in the country."

"Well . . . I won't tell you what you don't want to hear." Kate shook off her skirts as if either ensuring she was all at rights or warding him off. Perhaps both. She began walking as if to leave him. He wasn't ready for her to go.

It was a heady thing having her alone.

"Don't you want your shepherd's crook? I was tasked to watch it."

She stopped, frowned, released her breath. "Yes, I do need it." She held out her hand. "I'll take it now."

"Your manners, Miss Addison," he chided. "Where is your gratitude?"

"You are an ass, Mr. Balfour."

"There is a children's story about a lovely princess who would say and do such ugly things toads would hop out of her mouth every time she went to speak."

That caught her attention—and for a second, they both stood as if transported in time. Back then, he'd earned her attention by telling her stories. After her theater performances, he would linger by the building's back door with all the other men besotted with her. Once, she'd paused in front of him. It was his chance to catch her notice. Instead of praising her beauty like everyone else, he'd surprised himself by blurting out a story. It was one of

Aesop's Fables about Venus and a cat. Bran collected stories. He found them charming.

His method of catching her attention had worked. From that evening on, she'd always stopped to hear a story from him.

But that was then.

"What are you saying about me, Mr. Balfour?" Knives had duller edges than her tone.

And his memories were dust, the sort of things evil witches used to trick men. "You knew coming to this dance with my nephew would stir the pot. You dressed provocatively, and, I will say, completely out of character, to do what? Set people's teeth on edge? Give my poor dear sister a fit of apoplexy?" He paused and then added softly, "Humiliate my nephew? My family? Myself?"

Her hands curled into fists. He braced himself, ready for her ferocity. Kate spoke her mind.

Then, instead of giving him a lashing with her tongue, she drew a deep, shuddering breath. Her fingers straightened. "Go on with it, Brandon. Spill out all your venom toward me." Her voice was quiet and hard. "Warn me off. Tell me I am not suitable. But don't waste my time with your pettiness. Or pretend that you have done nothing to harm me."

"Harm you?" Dear God, he had worshipped her.

Her eyes slitted like a dragon ready to breathe fire. The corners of her mouth tightened, as if she held back a desire to wish him to Hades, and yet, there was something else he sensed in her attitude, something unsettling—disappointment.

She took a deep breath and released it slowly. "You may keep the shepherd's crook. I pray you carry it in good health." Her words sounded like a curse. She set off around the barn, the white stripes in her dress catching the moonlight and outlining her body.

And Bran found himself following. Where did she think she was going? "I wouldn't advise you to go around front. Not until the fighting is over. Your appearance would probably prolong it."

She gave a small start as if she hadn't expected him to be so close. "Can't you leave me alone?"

"I merely make a suggestion."

She kept walking.

He trailed behind. "So, where *are* you going?" he had to ask when she didn't turn the corner of the building but kept walking forward.

"To bed, Mr. Balfour. Alone."

"I imagine that doesn't happen often." The words came from a place deep inside him. An ugly place. An angry one.

Her back stiffened. He braced himself, ready for battle.

She walked on.

Bran knew he should let her go. After this night's business, Winderton would see the wisdom of avoiding actresses. Or, at least, Kate.

Why, he would probably never touch one again . . . and neither should Bran.

Yet, doggedly he followed, her shepherd's crook in his hand.

They had to climb a swell of earth to reach the road. She stopped before climbing it. He waited, wondering what was wrong.

Kate bent over and, to his surprise, removed her frivolous green shoes, the ones he and every other man had gawked at when she'd shown them. She started up the hill in her stockings.

She'd rip them.

She didn't seem to care.

This time, Bran let her be. "Well, good travels on the morrow, Miss Addison," he said after a moment.

She answered with a dismissive wave of her hand. She didn't even bother to look at him. Instead, she glanced over at the barn hall. Bran followed her line of sight.

Either Reverend Summerall had been successful in ending the fight or fresh air had led to cooler heads. Everyone was going inside. There was still the sound of tears and a few boisterous voices called out with good humor as if the whole incident had all been in good fun.

"I'm ruined," she said almost to herself.

Bran felt a momentary pang of empathy.

He quashed it. He'd not orchestrated this evening. She had. "I'm certain you will be a success in the next village you visit."

Her chin lifted, her shoulders squared, and in that moment she metamorphosed from a disgraced outcast into a goddess of war. "London. I'm going to London as soon as I fix the wagon. And we can't leave until it is fixed." She looked down at him, her shoes in one hand, the swell she stood on giving her the height advantage. "See, Mr. Balfour, you didn't need to scheme against me. I have no desire to stay in a place like Maidenshop with its smug conceit. The world—the real world—is too big for small minds. But as of now, I have no choice. There is no way out."

In many ways, Bran agreed with her, except her charge raised protective hackles. "First, you wore that dress to tease those small minds. And do you truly believe London is more unbiased than Maidenshop?" He almost laughed. "Societies are all the same. What happened tonight could have happened in London, India, Ceylon or any place a group of people gather."

"Oh, I am very aware that people enjoy sitting in judgment of what they can't have. Many have tried to teach me that lesson— and they have failed. I refuse to bow to any of them."

They weren't more than three feet from each other and yet the distance could have been from here to the heavens. Her wild, loose curls created shadows around her face. She appeared un- tamed, strong, determined—

"I hate you for what you did to me that night."

Her words went right through him.

Stunned, he repeated, "Hate me?" *He'd done nothing to her this evening. It was he who should hate her*—and then he realized she'd said "that night."

Not tonight. *That* night.

He went still.

"I *trusted* you," she continued, the intensity of her emotions almost forcing him to take a step back. "I will never forgive you for what you did."

"What *I* did?" He was confused. He had been the wronged party. She'd jilted him.

As if seeing his confusion, she threw out a clue. "The Marquis of Hemling."

"Your former lover?" The words tasted bitter.

"*Don't* ever call him that. He was not my lover. He is a hideous man." She moved to the very edge of the road.

"That is not what I heard—"

"He *forced* me."

Her hard-bitten words startled him. He couldn't have understood her correctly.

His confusion charged her anger. Ruthlessly, she said, "He tried to take everything from me for something as ridiculous as a wager. Did you know there were bets made on what man would claim me? Did you know that, Brandon?"

He had. Wagers had been placed in the betting books of every club. The reason men were flocking to her. The one who won her would pocket a tidy sum. It was not an uncommon wager on actresses. Men enjoyed a hunt.

"The question I have, Mr. Balfour, is how much did he pay you to betray me?"

"He? Pay me?" Bran's stomach hollowed. What the devil was she accusing him of?

"Don't pretend you weren't part of his plan."

"I didn't know anything about a plan."

"*You* wrote a note to me asking to see me. He was about to kidnap me because I thought I was seeing you. My guard was down—"

"There you are," Christopher's voice called, interrupting them. He must have spied her on the road from the front step of the barn hall, which would not be hard to do with Miss Addison's outrageous stripes. "I'm coming." He bounded up the road toward her, a young rabbit with long legs and energy. "I was worried that you were caught up . . ." His step slowed as he saw she was not alone. He came to a halt, looking from Kate to Bran, and not happy to see them together. "Uncle."

Bran nodded, his mind racing over Kate's accusation. He'd not written a note. Not to Kate that night, or any night—

"You should return to the hall," the duke said, speaking directly to Bran, a new hardness in his voice. "The reverend has given everyone a lecture. Mrs. Warbler is still hysterical. People are starting to leave. Mother is looking for you."

Then, as if his order would be obeyed, he focused on Kate, his voice gentler. He moved toward her, his arms out. "I was beside myself when I couldn't find you. I feared the worst."

Mercurial creature that she was, Kate changed in a blink from avenging goddess to misunderstood actress. "It was frightening." She actually sounded meek. "I didn't know what to do. I escaped out of a side passage and then I discovered your uncle wandering around. He helped me to the road."

Some of the tension left Christopher, but not the distrust. Young men without the seasoning of life could be proprietorial. They thought they controlled the women who attracted them. The duke had staked a claim and the side glance he shot at Bran said he would fight to defend it.

"May we go?" Kate asked. She reached out and tapped his arm for his attention. "This has been an upsetting evening."

"I'm sorry. This has never happened before. Please, I'll see you home." The duke, all gallant and solicitous, offered his arm. She took it and just that simply, he was conquered. He even held her steady as Kate suffered to put on her green shoes.

Meanwhile, Bran could only watch. And he felt silly holding a shepherd's crook. He thrust it forward. "Here. You don't want to leave this behind."

"Why, thank you," Kate said. She sounded serene, calm—as if he had imagined the revelations of the last fifteen minutes.

Winderton was the one who took the crook.

And then the couple walked away without another glance in Bran's direction. Christopher used the crook as his walking stick while Kate leaned against his other arm.

"Perhaps the punch had been made too strong," he was telling her. "I will most certainly speak to the village council about the matter. I fear there were a number of gentlemen who thought it wise to add their own choices to the punch." He sounded stodgy.

Kate said something in answer, but Bran had to turn away, his blood beginning to boil.

He'd been dismissed. By his *ward*. *A cub of a man*. He wanted to finish the conversation he'd started with Kate. He wanted to know about the damn note.

He wanted—

God, he wanted his sanity back.

Bran took off walking, although not toward the barn. He wasn't going to follow his nephew and Kate. Instead, he'd go around. He also knew his earlier words of advice to Winderton had fallen on deaf ears. His nephew was easy prey for a woman like Kate. She had more world experience. She also had a motive—vengeance. She hated Bran.

He also wondered if he had been that gullible at Christopher's age? Had she controlled him? As he remembered, they'd both been very young together.

Inside the barn, amazingly the dance appeared to be taking up where it had left off. Yes, as his nephew had said, a few people had left but the majority were still there. The musicians were once again playing. Couples danced. There was a scrape here and a black eye there but nothing that deterred the enjoyment of the rest of the evening. Indeed, those with wounds sported them proudly. And, of course, the punch table was busy once more.

The Reverend Summerall came up to Bran and spoke in his abrupt manner. He was of middle age with gray showing in his brown hair and a strong, hawkish nose. "This is better, eh? Informed them all they were not going to ruin this year's Cotillion."

"I am impressed they listened to you."

"Didn't want to. I had to convince them. I told them we English knew proper manners—although I put in a blow or two myself. It is all a bit of sport." He chuckled his satisfaction.

Matters were different amongst the matrons, who wouldn't have agreed with the minister. The ruin of an evening they had planned and organized for months was far from sport to them.

Mrs. Warbler and Mrs. Trent-Longford were surrounded by commiserating friends. Their feet were propped up on chairs. Mrs. Trent-Longford appeared to be weeping silently into a friend's shoulder while Mrs. Warbler, her wig back in place, held a hand to her forehead. She lay back in the chair as if she would expire at any moment, Mrs. Nelson holding her hand. Lucy sat between the two women and fanned them.

At the sight of Bran, Lucy excused herself and rushed to him. This was not going to be good.

"Where is my son?"

"Escorting Miss Addison home."

Her eyes filled with alarm. "And *you* let him go?"

"Lucy, how could I stop him?"

Her face crumpled and Bran feared more noisy tears. "He will be fine." He kept his voice low.

"Did you not see what happened this evening? The dance has been ruined."

"There was some excitement, although I honestly don't believe Miss Addison instigated it. And everyone seems at ease now."

"Only because they think of themselves. Dear Mrs. Warbler has been thrown into a fit of vapors that I have no hope of her recovering from."

"Was she injured?" he asked, concerned.

"That horrid actress tore her wig off her head in front of everyone. She is humiliated."

"Perhaps we should send for Mr. Thurlowe."

"Brandon, you mock me."

"I don't mock you," he said with something less than infinite patience. "I'm trying to help you keep the matter in perspective."

"A trollop has wedged herself into my son's life and you tell me to have perspective? I'll never accept her. *Ever.* And I warn you something terrible will happen if you don't stop it."

"I'm doing what I can." Which wasn't much. "He is a man, Lucy, not some child that I can order about."

"He'll ruin himself with her."

"Then he won't be the first," Bran snapped.

Lucy's hand flew to her mouth in horror. "She's done this before? She has ruined other men?"

"*No.*" Bran prayed for patience. "And men aren't ruined. They just end up looking stupid. Christopher will not be the first, and certainly not the last, if that comes to pass. Now, Lucy, don't cry, not here." *God, help him.* "I will set this to rights. Trust me."

"I trusted you this evening." Heads were turning in their direction. A weeping duchess always drew attention.

Before he could say more, they were interrupted by Miss Taylor.

"Excuse me, Your Grace, Mr. Balfour, do you know what happened to Miss Addison? She disappeared when the excitement started and I hope she is fine, although I don't see her anywhere."

Lucy's tears dried instantly. "You needn't worry, Miss Taylor. Her kind is like a cat. They always land on their dirty paws." With those words, she went sailing off to the matrons who quickly gathered around her with far more commiseration than her brother had.

"I'm sorry," Miss Taylor apologized, flustered. "I was only asking because Miss Addison seems to be missing. I didn't mean to upset Her Grace."

"My sister lives to be upset, Miss Taylor. Think nothing of it. Miss Addison is fine. The duke has escorted her back to her quarters."

"That is a relief. She wasn't the one to step on Mrs. Trent-Longford's gown. The culprit was a very tipsy Mr. Michaels. And then Mrs. Warbler was so out of control, especially after she lost her wig, that I did fear for Miss Addison."

"That is kind of you."

He noticed Mrs. Nelson coming toward them. "Miss Taylor, I believe Mrs. Nelson is searching for you."

The lines of her mouth flattened. "I suppose she is." She turned back to him. "Please, if you see Miss Addison, tell her that I am sorry for how the gentlemen behaved. They were rude and I am quietly furious at all of you." On those words, she left to see what Mrs. Nelson wished.

Mars came up behind him as if he'd been waiting for Miss Taylor to move on. "This has been the Cotillion Dance of the century. Did you see Sir Lionel throw his drink in Reverend Summerall's face when he tried to break up that fracas? Apparently, Fullerton and he had placed a wager on when the fight would end and Summerall was upsetting Lionel's bid."

"I can't say I did," Bran confessed, not wishing to say where he'd been during the brawl. "Then again, shouldn't you have been the one to restore order?"

"I warned you that I would not be a good magistrate. My thought was to let them all work the energy out of themselves." He lowered his voice. "And to think Thurlowe's goal is for all the young idiots in the village to join the Logical Men's Society."

"He is more interested in his seminar plans and shaping intelligent minds."

Mars shuddered his opinion on that subject just as several men approached the earl to share their thoughts on the fight.

Listening, Bran marveled at how quickly stories changed. According to these gentlemen, a few of the lads had taken advantage of the "quarrel between the ladies" to land a number of licks of their own— and they had relished the opportunity. Whereas poor Mrs. Warbler, Mrs. Trent-Longford, and the distraught Lucy, surrounded by her friends, appeared as if they would never recover from tonight's misadventures.

And Kate?

She'd survive.

The thought brought him back to their conversation, to her accusation. He'd never betrayed her, in any fashion.

At least, not that he remembered, and he remembered almost everything about her.

Bran caught himself watching the door, waiting for his nephew to reappear. The actors' encampment was only a mile away. Christopher should not have been gone this long. A light supper was ready to be served, then the dance would reach its end for the year. Tradition dictated that the Duke of Winderton would bid all a fair and happy summer . . . and he was not there.

An hour passed. Winderton did not return.

Lucy kept trying to meet his eye. Bran ignored her until Mars suggested that if Winderton wasn't available then the dowager should bid everyone adieu. The thought threw Lucy into a fit of vapors.

So, Bran did the honors, apologizing to the present company that the family would not be observing all the formalities this year but that he hoped everyone had enjoyed the evening.

Mr. Michaels, who leaned his shoulder against a support column as if he'd fall if he stood straight, called out, "Best Cotillion ever." He was seconded by Mr. Shielding, who sported a very bold black eye.

With that, Bran gathered Lucy and shepherded her home.

"He didn't return," she said in round, anguished tones.

Bran's response was brooding silence. He didn't want to think of Kate in his nephew's bed. Then again, he didn't own her. What she did was not his business . . . except his nephew *was* his responsibility.

"He wouldn't have her in the house, will he?" Lucy worried.

"Not if he has any sense."

His words came out harsh. Lucy gave a startled look and fell silent.

At the house, Bran escorted her in. She ran up the stairs, her black skirts flying as she raced to her son's rooms. Bran stood in the doorway, listening. He heard Lucy's voice, then a man's answer.

Lucy came to the top of the stairs. She moved as if she was walking toward the gallows. "His Grace is not at home."

Not my business, Bran warned himself. *Not my business.*

"Sleep well, Your Grace." He started to leave.

Her voice stopped him. "Aren't you going to do anything?"

"He is making a man's decision, Lucy. There isn't much I can do." On that note, he gave a short bow and left.

He began walking to the Dower House. With every step, he reminded himself that what Kate and his nephew were doing was of no importance to him—except it was.

Vivid memories of Kate in his arms brought him to a halt when he was within sight of his home, and he knew he was as obsessed as Lucy was—but not for the same reasons.

Kate's accusations still echoed in his head. He knew there would be no sleep for him until he had answers.

He had to talk to Kate. As he'd begun to process her charges against Hemling, questions brewed in his mind, questions he needed answered or he would go mad. He began walking in the direction of her camp.

KATE STRUGGLED to quiet her busy mind.

All was quiet around her save for Mary's genteel snores next to her mixing with Silas's bullish sounding ones coming from the men's tent. Jess, the milkmaid, had chosen to sleep with Nestor in the men's tent. Kate wasn't particularly happy about the liaison, except she'd learned after years of living with different troupes there was little she could do about it. Her one rule was that there would be no fights.

Tomorrow, she would have to confess to her actors that, because of her own arrogance, she had made a miserable muddle of things. She hadn't had the energy or courage to tell them this evening. Winderton had escorted her home where everyone was sitting around a fire waiting for her.

He'd been all a gentleman should be, respectful and flattering. He'd told her before they reached the camp that he wanted to kiss her, but he wouldn't. "I want to give you all the respect you are due, especially after this evening."

Kate was relieved. The situation could have been tricky. "Apparently the duke has honorable intentions," Silas had muttered after the nobleman had left. It was obvious her actors, like members of a clan, had been waiting up to watch out for her. From Silas, it was expected. He had guarded her from the very beginning.

However, the concern of the others was actually quite touching— and tomorrow, she would have to tell them that they would be lucky if three people showed up for their performance. She might never be able to pay the wainwright for the wagon repair. Or their wages.

But this wasn't what was keeping her awake.

No, her thoughts strayed to Brandon Balfour, and to the humiliation and shame that she'd thought she'd put behind her fifteen years ago. How dare he plead innocence?

How dare he act as if he hadn't abandoned her—

"Kate."

Brandon's voice was no more than a whisper, and yet she heard him with sharp clarity.

She sat up. She should stay where she was. *He* was the reason she couldn't sleep. The reason that her life had fallen into pieces.

"Kate? I must speak to you."

Was she imagining his voice?

Pulling her heavy hair over one shoulder, she put her feet over the edge of her cot and stood. Her nightdress was a heavy cotton. She picked up a shawl and threw it over her shoulders before stepping out of the tent.

The forest around them was quiet. She listened, and then she saw him.

His dark silhouette stepped away from the night-shadowed trees. She was surprised she'd heard him from that far away.

"Come here, Kate. Come here." His call was barely a whisper and, just like in the tent, she understood him.

This man was the curse of her life.

Kate didn't move. She stood rooted to the earth as memories she'd tried to hold at bay flooded her. She remembered his stories, his laughter, the feel of his lips on her skin. She'd *trusted* him, *compromised* herself for him and he'd almost destroyed her—no, she realized suddenly, she'd *let* him destroy her. She'd let his betrayal color her thinking of herself in every aspect of her life.

Because of him, she'd believed she'd disappointed her parents. *Because of him,* she'd allowed herself to be practically held in slavery. *Because of him,* she'd walked away from London. Because of him, she'd branded herself—but no longer.

The time had come to face this demon and put *him* firmly in her past.

Chapter Eight

Bran watched her shadowy form emerge from the tent.

He stepped back into the tree line, waiting, knowing now that she would come.

She wore a heavy gown with a shawl and her wildly curling hair was down around her shoulders. She reminded him of Artemis, goddess of the moon, stepping out into the night.

Except she wasn't a goddess of grace and beauty. She'd used him. She'd tossed him aside for wealth and privilege. His love had meant nothing to her.

He could not forget why he was here. "Is my nephew in your bed?"

Even in the waning moonlight, he could see his question startled her. She stopped. Studied him a moment, the set of her mouth grim. She bent down.

He waited, wanting an answer to his question.

Kate straightened and before he knew what she was about, she threw a rock at him with surprising strength. The stone hit him in the shoulder and it hurt.

"What the devil—" Bran started, stepping back.

She bent down, picking up something else—acorns!

He wasn't about to let her throw those at him. They could be vicious little missiles. He started forward, but she was faster. She threw all she had in her hand. Several hit him right in the face.

They smarted. He turned his head, grimacing, which gave her time to pick up a stick. Kate attacked, her arm raised as if she would lash him with it.

Bran leapt toward her, reaching her before she could him. He captured her raised arm.

"Where is Winderton—"

His voice broke off with a wheeze as her knee came up and delivered an almost mortal blow to his manhood.

He doubled over, releasing his hold. He couldn't breathe. He couldn't think. He was done in. He backed away.

Kate could have left then. She could have flailed him with her stick. She didn't. She stood over him, glowering.

Bran looked up at the stars and wanted to howl. His voice came out guttural, "Why the devil did you do that?"

"Oh, Mr. Balfour, I've wanted to do that for a long time."

She didn't sound penitent at all.

"Are you happy?" he barked. He reached out, finding a tree to lean against, praying for the pain to subside.

Kate had the audacity to smile, the expression wicked in the moonlight. "As a matter of fact, yes, it was satisfying. And, no, your nephew is not in my bed. So, there, you have your answer. Good night."

She would have turned on her heel but Bran was not ready to let her go.

"Wait," he called, his hushed voice sounding loud in the night.

"For what? You to insult me again?" She snorted her opinion—and yet she did not leave.

Bran tried to straighten. The pain still radiated. "We have unfinished business between us. We should discuss it like civilized people."

"Oh, no, we can't. I've come a good way from the young woman who was gullible enough to be snatched from the street."

That caught his attention. "Snatched from the street?"

Instead of answering, she again started for her encampment.

"Kate," he called, trying to keep his voice quiet. *"Kate."* If he wasn't quick, he would lose her.

Determination drove him forward. His gait was lopsided. However, the pain was subsiding. He caught her as she stepped out of the line of trees, hooking his hand around her elbow. "Kate, talk to me."

She attempted to yank away. "Why should I give you a moment more of my time?"

He wrapped an arm around her waist and pulled her to him. Her dangerous knee lifted again, except he was ready for her. He blocked her movement with his thigh. "Talk to me, Kate."

"Let me go." Her voice sounded feral.

"I will, once you answer my questions."

She shook her head as if to deny him. He tightened his hold. It was a good thing she had almost gelded him or he would not have been able to be this close to her and *not* have reacted. She was naked beneath the nightdress. Granted, he'd seen canvas tents that were thinner than the gown she wore, but she was naked.

Immediately, he recalled those hours when he'd been naked in bed with her, of her toes wiggling as they touched and teased his. The intimacy of the image stirred life back into him.

"One question," he pressed.

"Let me go."

He released his hold.

She stumbled back, however, she surprised him when she did not race to the tents. Instead, she repositioned her shawl around her shoulders, drawing it closer to her, her arms crossed. She did not trust him and certainly did not like him. Her eyes were cold and silver in the night. "What is your *one* question?"

Bran felt as if he'd been given a moment of grace. He kept his distance from her, not wanting to do anything that might make her run again. "You said I sent you a letter and it led to you being 'snatched from the street.' That is what you just said. Do I have that right?"

"Is that your question?"

She was harsh. "No," he hurried to answer, not trusting her patience. "I want to know about the letter."

In truth, he *had* written to her—love notes in poor attempts to woo her. He'd slaved over those few letters. Had even attempted poetry. But he had never sent any of them.

Now, older, more experienced, and far too jaded for anyone's good, he was startled by what a lovesick fool he'd been.

"What did the letter say?" he asked, his voice quiet in the night. "And what made you think it was from me? Because, Kate, *I* never wrote you."

Her chin lifted as if she had expected that response. He held his hands out as if to assure her he meant no tricks. "When did I send a letter?"

"I received a letter from you right before my performance after we—"

Her voice broke. Her arms crossed tighter. She took a breath and amended her original thought. "After you . . . had me."

The anger had returned to her voice. An accusation that he did not understand.

After he'd had her? As if he'd pirated his way with her and she'd not been the willing, mercurial bed partner who had haunted his dreams all these years?

Oh, he wanted answers about her choice of words, because as he remembered that night, they had been joyful bed partners. The moment they had finally allowed themselves to touch, a power beyond all reason had taken over. They had fallen into each other's arms as if they had not been able to contain themselves—and she had been just as willing as he had.

"Kate, I did not write a letter."

"I received one."

He took a cautious step toward her. "Why would I need to write a letter? We had agreed that I should meet you backstage after the performance. I was there. They told me you had left. You had hurried off, but we'd agreed to meet at the theater and I waited."

He'd been dogged. The back-door manager had told him she'd been eager to leave. He had even speculated that Kate had an assignation, one obviously not with Bran.

He'd hated the man's sly, knowing looks as he'd cooled his heels. Kate was the "Aphrodite of the London stage." What would she want with an insignificant nobody when she could have claimed a prince? "Tell me about the letter."

"You asked me to meet you on St. Clement's steps. That is where I hurried off to."

"I did not write such a letter."

"You signed it."

"I couldn't have. The letter was not from me. My word of honor." She seemed to search his face for truth, her stance rigid in the moonlight, and then, an ugly sound, one of sudden horror, escaped her. It was uncontrolled, bitter, heartbreaking. She began to collapse.

Bran moved forward to catch her. She shook her head, warning him away. Sinking to the ground, she hid her face in the crook of her arm and began weeping. Her hair fell forward as if to shield her shame.

He knelt, wanting to take her up in his arms and afraid he would upset her further if he did so. Her soft sobs tore at his heart. "Kate, what is it?"

With heaving breaths, she gathered herself. "Nothing. Everything. I don't know." She swiped angrily at her eyes.

She did not look at him.

"Kate?"

She drew her heavy hair over her shoulder. "It doesn't matter now." She gave a shaky half laugh. "I was so naïve." Moving as if she was exhausted, she started to rise.

This time when Bran offered his hand, she took it. The moment she was on her feet, she attempted to pull away, but he would not let go.

"Kate, what happened? If my name was used in some fashion I should know."

Finally, she looked at him. "I thought you wrote that letter. For years, I have believed it was from you." Her voice was barely a whisper.

"You went to meet me?" he prompted.

Her gaze dropped away. "I went to the church. A coach pulled up. Two men came out and told me you sent them."

"Two men in a coach? I did not own a coach. And back then, I could barely afford my dinner let alone hiring a vehicle like that."

"I'm not a fool. I was suspicious, but then they grabbed me right there on the street. It was like a scene from a play. No one cried out an alarm and those men would not let me leave. They told me you'd planned a surprise."

"And what sort of surprise did I have for you?" Bran asked with a deadly calm he was far from feeling.

"They took me to the Marquis of Hemling's country house. He told me the two of you had come to an agreement concerning me."

"I knew of no such thing. Kate, I was frantic when I couldn't find you."

Again, there was that searching look . . . and he remembered the girl she had once been, the one who had trusted easily. "Kate, what happened?"

"I told him I wanted to be returned to London. I had a performance the next day and needed to be taken home immediately."

She sounded imperial, and distant. The weight of what Bran believed he was about to hear settled deep in his gut. "And then?"

Kate leaned away from him, her gaze moving to some point in the darkness only she could see. "He raped me."

Rage shot through him. Bran turned away from her, needing to wrap his arms around the trees and pull them up, needing to shout to the heavens—

"Kate, you should have sent for me. You should have let me know. I would have *murdered him*." Happily.

But then he remembered the worst part of that summer, what had driven him to seek the farthest corner of the world away from

England to escape her, even thoughts of her. "You stayed with him. He did that and you stayed with him?" Days after that night, word went out that Hemling was her protector. He'd won the bets on the books—and the woman. She'd been with him when Bran had sailed for India almost a month after her disappearance. "Did he hold you captive?"

Her jaw hardened. She turned and began walking away.

He reached out, grabbed her by the crook of her arm and swung her around. *"Why did you stay with him?"* Bran had to know. "You could have sent for me. I would have come for you."

She jerked her arm from his hold. "Come for me? I thought you were the one who helped him kidnap me. I never heard from you. I thought I was all alone—"

"I searched for you. I couldn't believe you would leave your play without notice—"

"*I was a prisoner.* Hemling wouldn't let me leave—"

"This is England, Kate. *There are laws.* If a man imprisons you against your will, you have recourse—"

"Is that what you think?" She gave a harsh laugh. "Well, why not? You are a man in England. You have no idea what it is like to be a woman alone. The laws do not protect us."

"*I* would have come for you—"

She practically screamed her frustration in his face. "You are such *a fool.* I had nothing and no one. What? Do you think I wanted my parents to learn what had happened to me? Don't you understand the shame of it? Or the pain it would have caused my family? I kept thinking I could manage to keep everything hidden. And as for *you* coming for me, well, I am certain that all the betting books knew that Hemling had claimed his prize. I didn't see you riding up like a cavalier to rescue me. I imagined you had claimed a good share of that bounty."

The truth of her words chased the anger from him. She was right. Bran had known when Hemling had declared himself the wager's winner. All of London had known. "The Aphrodite" had chosen the marquis. And Bran's own sense of how little he had to offer Kate, how little he had deserved her, had allowed him to believe that, of course, she would desert him.

Bran stood powerless over the past, and yet devasted by this twist on what he had believed.

"No amount of gold would have persuaded me to betray you to Hemling. I thought I was in love with you, Kate. He used both of us."

Her shoulders lowered. She closed her eyes as if she didn't know if she wanted to believe him.

"However, you stayed with Hemling," Bran continued quietly. "I thought you chose him over me. I—"

Bran broke off as the truth sank in. What excuses did he have? He'd failed her. "Everyone said Hemling had offered you *carte blanche*. I never questioned it."

"Of course not." The corners of her mouth tightened as she added, "After all, isn't that what all actresses want? A rich protector?"

Yes, that was what he'd thought. What the world had thought.

"I completely disappeared from the stage. Poof! Overnight, and no one questioned it—as if I had such poor character I would do that to the company of actors I performed with. I have no doubt that Lydia Marksmore who took over my role was thrilled with what everyone believed was my decision. It was as if no one knew me well enough to wonder where I was. Or cared."

And what could Bran answer? He was guilty as charged.

"I stayed with Hemling because I thought I had no other choice," she said, her words damning. "I felt trapped. I didn't know what to do. It seemed as if the world conspired against me. He'd already taken from me my reputation. No theater owner would hire me for fear of offending the marquis. I was lost until I realized I could just walk away. When I finally found my way clear to leave him, I learned you had left England."

"Presumably with the money I'd received for your betrayal."

There was a heartbeat of silence. Then she agreed, "Presumably." She shrugged it away with one shoulder. "When I was under

Hemling's protection, everyone told me I should be happy, except he was destroying me, Brandon. I didn't like the person I was letting myself become. When I walked out, he demanded I return. He threatened any theater that might have hired me. I did receive some offers, though. From men willing to have me for a mistress. I refused." The last was delivered dryly.

And she hadn't had him to turn to.

"Kate—" he started, not knowing what he was going to say, what he could say.

She cut him off. "It is all in the past, Brandon. Hemling is dead. Funny that it matters that the man who tried to destroy me is gone. By the by, did you know my brother is a duke? You probably didn't even know I had a brother, or cared. We knew so little of each other back then. We were interested in other things, weren't we?"

He didn't like the hint of derision in her voice before she briskly moved on. "My father was a younger son. My mother was an actress and the family had disowned him but after everything is said and done, upon my grandfather's death, the title had to go to Matthew. There was no other. And, he has married an heiress. Funny how life changes. When I attended the wedding last year, I realized that I *can* return to London now. I have resources. I am not some poor girl attempting to succeed on sheer talent alone. I am wiser, stronger, and determined. This time, I will triumph because I own my company. *I* control my destiny. This is *my* company, *my* actors, *my* decisions. I'm also beyond the age where men will fall over themselves for me."

"You are still a beautiful woman, Kate. Look at Winderton."

She gave him a cool eye before saying, "That may be true, except I've changed. I'm no longer the trusting doe-eyed miss."

"That is a pity. I remember her as someone very special."

"That green girl doesn't exist anymore, Mr. Balfour. She is gone and I have no regrets leaving her behind."

He thought back to those days years ago when he'd lived for a glimpse of her either on stage or after a performance. She'd been vibrant with life. He had wanted to possess that quality that made her uniquely who she was.

"However," she said softly, "I am happy for this conversation. It made a difference. I didn't like hating you. And now, good night. Tomorrow I have to tell the troupe we have no money, and no prospects. It will be a very busy day." She didn't wait for his answer to start moving toward the tents.

He watched her go, wishing he could call her back, knowing there was nothing she could want from him—but then she stopped, glanced back at him and in a voice so quiet he could believe he'd imagined it, she said, "I thought I was in love with you, too, Brandon. I did."

And then, after that stunning admission, she hurried away.

It was over . . . before it could ever be, and he knew he'd lost someone valuable.

Bran moved through the woods toward the Dower House. He'd forgotten his nephew. Jealousy had driven him to seek out Kate and now, in its place was—what?

He didn't know.

She had believed herself in love with him . . . *and* she'd believed that he had been capable of betraying her in the vilest manner possible.

Well, his logic demanded he face the truth. What he'd shared with Kate all those years ago had been lust. Pure and simple. His overactive imagination had believed it something deeper and more meaningful. He'd been young and naïve. She'd been his first grand passion. Of course he would romanticize it.

Except, he'd never felt the same way about any other woman.

When at last he found his bed, his mind was exhausted and though he finally slept he didn't wake rested. The only way he would find any ease, he realized, would be to get Kate and her troupe to move on—far away. He had failed her years ago. Now, he owed her some restitution—and one that would not only ensure her future but safely steer Winderton away from her as well.

To that end, shortly after dawn, he dressed and went down to the stables. He instructed the stable manager to take Smythson's best wagon and deliver it to Kate. "Tell her it is a gift." He handed the man a note he'd written instructing Kate to accept this wagon and go live her dream. He felt quite noble for the gesture.

An hour later, the apologetic stable manager returned. "The lad did as you instructed, sir. The lady would not accept the wagon. She sent it back with a note of her own."

It was not sealed but folded neatly. Bran waved the man away, sat at his desk, and unfolded the missive. In a feminine hand, she'd written, *On my own terms.*

He stared at the words for a long time, aware that her response was exactly what he would have replied.

Chapter Nine

Old Andy had outdone himself on the rook pies. There were five large pies, each with a pastry crust that would have put London cooks to shame. They were cooling on a table that had been set out under the trees outside The Garland.

Bran discovered quite a crowd of gentlemen gathered for the Logical Men's Society lecture. Perhaps Ned was right and their tidy village community was ready for scientific stimulation.

Or they might have come for the free ale and pie.

In truth, Bran had almost forgotten he had promised Thurlowe that he would be in attendance. Fortunately, Mars came by to see if Bran wanted to accompany him, and he agreed, eager to do anything to take his mind off of Kate—headstrong, uncompromising Kate.

From the moment he'd received her terse reply, his thoughts had turned dark. First, there had been the sting of losing the bridge commission—and then she had walked back into his life. He needed a diversion, even if it was an academic expounding on rocks.

His sense of peace was short-lived. While riding the distance to the village, Mars, with a studied casualness, said, "Your nephew was at The Garland last night after the dance. He almost finished the keg himself."

So. That was where Christopher had been instead of saying farewell to the revelers or in Kate's bed. Bran was both relieved and unsurprised. Kate could drive any man to drink. That was certainly what she was doing to him.

He kept his thoughts to himself, however, and instead grunted as if the duke's whereabouts were of no importance to him. As if he hadn't charged through the night to be certain Christopher hadn't been with Kate. As if, as if, as if . . .

"He hasn't given up on his actress," Mars continued. "When I mentioned I might have a go at her, he was ready to put his hands around my throat—"

"*Stay away* from her." The words had shot out of Bran before he could question their wisdom.

Startled, Mars's mount took a hop step to the side. Bran kept Orion moving forward.

With a quick trot, Mars caught up with him. There was a beat of silence. Bran wanted to pretend he hadn't spoken.

Finally, Mars said, "There is more here, isn't there?"

Bran didn't answer. In fact, he was sourly realizing that Mars *could* have a go at Kate. There was nothing to stop him, well, except for both Winderton and Bran threatening murder.

"I sensed it last night," Mars said. "Something in the air."

When Bran didn't answer, his friend wisely shut up.

After a few minutes of riding, Bran recovered enough good sense to say, "I just don't want animosity over a woman to build between you and my nephew." That sounded reasonable, and he didn't mention himself.

He could sense Mars didn't believe it, however, the earl was good enough of a friend to keep his suspicions to himself.

Fortunately, they had reached The Garland and the promise of a lecture, pie, and drink.

At least twenty gentlemen were gathered around the tapped keg Andy had set up. Ned's grin was wide and welcoming as he saw Bran and Mars handing over their reins to some village boys. They crossed to the keg. Ned met them halfway.

"Is this not amazing?" he declared. "I knew there was interest in a scientific lecture but this is astounding. We have never had such a crowd. Two of the men here are interested in joining the Society as well!"

Mars and Bran both murmured something about Ned's hard work. Still, Bran was surprised. In previous years, most people who attended the Cotillion were well on their way home before noon. However, from the way the gentlemen were filling their tankards, they did not seem as if they would be traveling anytime soon.

In truth, the day was a good one for being out of doors. The sky was cloudless and blue and the temperature mild. Perhaps that was reason enough for the crowd.

"Is that our speaker?" Mars asked. He nodded toward a balding man who kept dabbing his high forehead with a handkerchief. "Seems a bit nervous."

"He will do fine," Ned answered, clapping his hands together in anticipation.

"If he is this anxious now, he might pass out when he has an actual audience," Bran suggested.

"If that happens, Ned knows more about the topic than Mr. Remy could ever have thought possible," Mars assured him and received a grin of agreement from the good doctor who immediately acknowledged a newcomer to their group.

"Hello, Reverend. It is good that you could join us."

"Especially after that rowdiness last night," Reverend Summerall said. "Ah, thank you, Andy," he said as the tavern keeper approached him with a brimming tankard. He took a steadying swallow of the brew. "I needed this. I've just had a disconcerting conversation with Mrs. Warbler."

"Is she complaining as she usually does?" Ned asked.

"No, she isn't even paying attention to what is going on over here."

"You are jesting," Old Andy said in his gravelly voice. "She always has her nose in our business. That is, when she is not lying in wait for Sir Lionel. The woman stalks him like a jungle cat."

"No, she wished to share her strong thoughts about the actress who attended the Cotillion last night. Of course, I agreed with her," the cleric said. "I'm most upset that someone would come in from the outside and start a fight the way that woman did."

Bran shifted uncomfortably. Summerall spoke in his customary loud voice and it gathered attention. Bran had to say, "I don't know that you are correct that the actress started the fight. I didn't see how it began, but I did witness the Dawson brothers take a swing at Landon Bonniwell."

Mars nodded in agreement. "And then there was the doctoring of the punch bowl. That contributed to the increased tempers."

Reverend Summerall shook his head as if weary of the world.

A gent by the keg whom Bran didn't know spoke up. "Oh, no. The tart in the striped dress started the whole thing. My wife saw what happened."

The word *tart* pricked Bran's sense of justice. Yes, Kate had dressed the part. That didn't mean he wanted to hear the appellation applied to her.

He gave the man a cool look. "The 'tart' was on the arm of my nephew and ward, the Duke of Winderton."

The man did not back down. "Young men do foolish things."

Now Bran faced him squarely. "And you are, sir? I don't believe we've met." He didn't hide the challenge in his voice.

"Reginald Montcreiffe. My uncle is Lord Dervil. I believe his property is near yours."

Of course, the man would be a braggart—he was related to Dervil, the man who had upset his chances with the bridge commission out of spite, but who had made his dislike of Bran and his friends well-known. Bran was ready to take after him, except that Summerall had picked up the theme.

"Not meaning any disrespect to your family, Balfour, I agree that the duke should not have brought her to a village event. That sort of thing should stay in London, eh, my lord?" He directed the last toward Mars, who took a step away.

"It is not my job to judge other men," Mars answered.

"Well, it is *my* job," the reverend assured them as he lifted his tankard to his lips. "Young men have been led astray since time began. Eve has always deceived Adam."

Bran himself had referred to Kate as a Delilah—however, now he thought of her being kidnapped against her will. Of her being held and used for no other reason than to claim a wager on the betting books at White's and for some man's arrogant pride. Of being treated as if she'd had no intelligence or feelings, as if she was a plaything—and he had to come to her defense. "Are we really such cowardly creatures we have no control of our emotions? What happened to logic and reason? Are you saying we are justified in behaving in a boorish manner because a dress is too low cut?"

"Ah, there, you said it yourself, Balfour," the reverend said. "The dress was too provocative for our gathering. Is it small wonder men lost all good sense?"

"Perhaps we shouldn't have bothered mounting cannon against Napoleon," Bran answered. "Apparently women in low cut dresses would have been enough to make the French stop in their tracks."

"She made me stop in my tracks last night," a gentleman murmured, a sentiment endorsed with a few guffaws from the others.

Bran struggled to control his temper. Mars spoke up, "I found Miss Addison delightful."

"As did I," Ned chimed in.

"Well, we won't have to worry about her if the women have their way," Montcreiffe announced.

"What does that mean?" Bran demanded.

"It means they are going to take care of their own," Montcreiffe said. "My wife informed me the less I know, the better. And I understand that the duke's own mother is leading the pack."

"What are you saying?" Bran asked. And what was Lucy about now?

"I'm saying that the women will put one of their own in her place. It is justice." Montcreiffe looked at the others for confirmation.

Many nodded. One said, "Yes, let the women deal with it."

"Ah, now it all starts to make sense," Summerall said.

"*What* makes sense?" Bran wanted answers.

The reverend said, "After complaining, Mrs. Warbler said she and the duchess would be attending the play, which I didn't understand after she'd told me she wanted them gone. And then, as I arrived here, I overheard one of the lads tending the horses bragging to the others that he'd sold a bag of moldy turnips to Mrs. Warbler." He looked at Mr. Remy who had wandered over. "How do you do, sir? I am interested in your edifying ideas."

However, Bran was not.

Moldy turnips and Lucy taking matters into her own hands, especially with the help of a knotty-brained gossip like Mrs. Warbler did not bode well.

He looked to Ned. "I won't be able to stay. Andy, sorry I won't have a taste of your pie." He was already moving toward where Orion was tethered.

"Well, if you are going, I'm going." Mars fell into step with him.

"I'm coming as well," Ned said. "You may need me."

They might. Bran was of a mind to throttle Lucy and who knew what her son would do?

"What about the lecture?" Mr. Remy called.

"Talk," Ned called over his shoulder. "There are those who will listen."

But that wasn't true. Most of the men now moved toward their horses and vehicles. Bran wasn't anxious for the company and yet he was powerless to stop them.

Putting his heels to Orion, he set the horse flying down the road, Mars and Ned beside him.

And a pack of curious gentlemen followed in their wake.

Once they reached the troupe's encampment, Bran was surprised at the size of the crowd. It appeared as if most of three counties were gathered, with people from all classes, young and old. The air was as festive as a village fair, with even the Widow Smethers selling pies.

Since Bran had last been to the clearing, a stage had been built, which butted against the tent to provide an entrance and exit for the actors. To his surprise, Fullerton and Sir Lionel had claimed a spot right next to the stage, where they'd set themselves up with chairs, a small table to hold their bottles, and a manservant to see to their whims.

"I had expected them at the lecture," Ned muttered.

"A provocative dress always wins out, especially with old roués like them."

Benches were provided for the rest of the audience and they were full. Those lucky enough to have nabbed a seat were not moving. Amongst them was Lucy.

She sat majestically in her black-and-purple next to Mrs. Warbler, who remarkably appeared more sanctimonious than ever. The other Maidenshop matrons were with their families or friends, but they didn't appear angry.

Still, there were a good number of them.

For a coin, two boys said they would walk Orion and the other horses.

The Irish actor, a jester's cap on his head, approached them. "Ten pence, sirs. Ten pence."

Bran paid for himself, Ned, and Mars. "We need to speak to Miss Addison."

"She's a bit busy right now." With a knowing look, he added, "You gentlemen can speak to her *after* the performance."

"No, we need to talk to her now—"

"*Uncle,*" Christopher's glad voice boomed out, interrupting them. He came out of the tent where he had obviously been with Kate. "You *did* decide to come," the duke said. He nodded to Ned and Mars. "What? Is the lecture over? Lucky you. I trust you will be well pleased with what you will see on that stage. London couldn't boast finer."

He acted as if he was the manager of this company . . . and Bran remembered a time when he'd felt somewhat that way. He'd watched so many of Kate's performances, he could have mouthed her lines. He had taken an interest in all of it.

Seeing his behavior mirrored in his nephew, he realized he'd been an arrogant sod.

He also had a stab of jealousy that was crippling.

"Come, the performance is about to start," Christopher said. "We will have to stand over to the side. We will see better. Can you believe my mother is here? Maybe this is what she needs to move past Father's death—"

"Christopher, we must talk to Miss Addison. It is imperative—" Bran started.

Anything else he could have said was overridden by the banging of a drum. An old man came out in a cloak with strips of material. He wore sandals on his feet and a half circle of myrtle leaves upon his head.

The crowd instantly silenced.

"Here we are, poor players," the actor began. "Gathered for your enjoyment. Do not believe our tales have no meaning. As you shall soon see, what we share is as old as mankind. I am your guide. The humble Aesop."

The mention of the name commanded Bran's full attention. The actor began talking about his life as a lowly servant with the gift of story.

Winderton moved closer toward the stage.

He was not the only one. Child and adult alike jostled their way for a better view.

But Bran was stunned by what he was hearing. These are the stories he had told to Kate. She had taken them and cleverly woven them into a delightful play of vignettes strung together.

The first was that of a greedy fox who wanted all the grapes. That story quickly rolled into another where Mr. Crow had a piece of cheese. The fox tricked the bird by playing on his own greed so it could be stolen.

Each vignette had a recognizable message that the good folks watching easily embraced. There were even changes of costume as different cloaks turned the actors into a cast of animals.

The audience laughed knowingly as the hare thought too much of himself and napped, giving the race over to the slow, steady tortoise. A child shouted from the crowd for the tortoise to hurry and everyone started cheering on their favorite, knowing full well the outcome.

After the race was won, Aesop came to the front of the stage. "The best stories are of the gods and goddesses. To tell them, may I present the lovely Juno."

The flap of the tent was dramatically pulled back by animal/ actors to reveal Kate standing there—and she *was* a goddess.

Her gown was of Grecian cut and sleeveless. Her hair was piled high on her head and held in place with gold cords. The gauzy white dress clung to her curves and her feet were bare save for a single gold ring on her toe.

Bran's focus flew like an arrow to that saucy gold ring. He was not the only one who was stunned by her beauty. Beside him, Mars released his breath with a low, "Dear God."

And Bran was reminded of how it had been all those years ago. Whenever Kate took the stage, it was as if she was the only one of importance upon it. She was Circe, the enchantress, because no man, once laying eyes on her, could turn away. What Bran remembered was that her eyes seemed to shine with an ethereal light when she was on the stage, as if she was exactly where she was supposed to be in life.

Today, it was still true. Her beauty was undiminished by her age and her presence alone commanded attention.

The crowd had gone silent, as if holding their breaths to hear what this stunning creature had to share. Kate raised her arm, preparing to introduce herself—

The mood was suddenly broken by a woman's shout, "*Doxy.*"

Something was thrown at the stage. The aim was poor and the throw weak. The item hit the edge of the stage front and bounced right at Winderton—who caught a moldy turnip.

Before Bran could pull his brain from the vision of Kate as Juno to what was happening, several turnips were launched from different areas of the crowd, the areas where the Matrons of Maidenshop had been sitting.

Some hit their target. Kate gave a soft cry as one bounced off her hip. She ducked another. "Tart," came a cry. "Bitch," yelled another.

And there was laughter. Husbands, gentlemen, farmers, yeomen, stable hands—they all thought it was great fun.

Aesop and the crow came running out. However, before they could get there, Winderton jumped up on the stage like Kate's savior.

"Stop it," he commanded. "Stop now." His young voice rang with authority through the air.

There was a pause in the throwing—until a turnip hit him right in the chest. Christopher fell back, his hat falling off his head. People were shocked and yet there was nervous laughter—

Another turnip was thrown.

"This is out of hand," Mars muttered, surging forward but Bran was already ahead of him.

"You grab the man who threw that turnip at Winderton. I'll take care of Kate."

However, just as he was ready to jump up on the stage, Kate stepped forward. She had helped Winderton to his feet and pushed him toward the safety of the tent, but she had not run herself.

Instead, shoulders back, she faced the crowd, bravely warning with her hands for her actors and even Bran to stay back.

Lifting her chin, she began, *"The quality of mercy is not strain'd, It droppeth—"*

A turnip hit her shoulder.

There was laughter. She did not back down. If anything, she stood straighter, making herself a perfect target, and continued, her voice strong and carrying, *"It droppeth as the gentle rain from heaven upon the place beneath; it is twice blest; it blesseth him that gives, and him that takes."*

A turnip missed her. It hit the stage and rolled.

Kate gave it no mind.

In fact, it was as if she had gone into a different world. One could almost imagine a light from heaven shining upon her.

Her actors gathered at the back of the stage, watching as if they were witnessing something rare and wonderful . . . as did the crowd.

Kate continued Portia's speech from *The Merchant of Venice*.

She was regal, mesmerizing.

Her expression had turned serene. *"That, in the course of justice, none of us should see salvation: we do pray for mercy; And that same prayer doth teach us all to render the deeds of mercy."*

The turnip missiles had stopped.

Everyone, even the children, listened and Bran knew that it wasn't just her performance, but also her incredible courage that held them spellbound.

They could have hurt her. They wanted to run her off.

She was letting them know she was unafraid.

Her last words hung in the air, fading into a proud silence.

There was a thunderclap of applause.

Even the most boorish rustic in the crowd knew they had witnessed an uncommon talent. Kate had swept them away. She had captured their imaginations, and changed them from within.

She fell into a deep curtsey, acknowledging their praise, and they clapped louder, stomping their feet.

Mars spoke beside Bran. "She is magnificent."

She was. The Aphrodite of London had risen again.

And there wasn't a man around who didn't agree with him. Even Montcreiffe and the Reverend Summerall were applauding enthusiastically.

Taking charge, Kate signaled for quiet. She ordered her actors to their places, and finished out her play. It was brilliant. Her performance as Juno was no less riveting than her presentation of Portia's soliloquy. She *did* belong on the London stage.

Afterward there was a surge toward her. She was surrounded not only by male admirers, all wanting to be closer to her, but also female ones, including the matrons. Mrs. Warbler in her bad wig acted as if she had not instigated the assault on Kate. She oozed compliments.

Even Lucy praised Kate's performance. Her lips tightened at the sight of her son standing so close to the actress, and yet she kept her peace.

Mars and Winderton both flanked her protectively. The young duke understood that he had to stake his claim. He frowned at Mars, then sent a glance at Bran as if ordering his uncle to grab the earl by the scruff and toss him away from Kate.

Which was something Bran was tempted to do, except he wanted Winderton gone as well.

And just that simply, history was repeating itself.

He remembered those evenings of waiting for Kate and having her attention claimed by other men. The bite of jealousy was just as mean now as it had been then—especially when he realized he had no right to feel it—

"You are the one Kate spoke to last night, are you not, sir?" a man's voice said close to Bran's elbow. He turned to see he was being addressed by Aesop. The actor was a good head and a half shorter.

"Last night?" Bran decided to play ignorant.

"Out in the woods."

Bran could have sworn. He had hoped that his nocturnal visit had not been noticed.

"You sent the wagon this morning as well," Aesop said. "You made her angry."

"That was not my intent."

"Oh, you knew what you were doing." The man held out his hand. "My name is Silas Leonard. I have been with Kate for all of fourteen years."

Wary, Bran took the man's hand. Silas had a firm grip and he held Bran's hand fast so that to free it would be a bit of a struggle. They stood close to each other.

"I want to warn you away from Kate, sir. I don't know all that happened last night, but I love that woman as I would my own daughter. I'll not let the likes of you after her any more than I would the likes of Nestor."

"I don't know who Nestor is." Bran kept his face expressionless.

"You don't need to, sir. What you need to do is heed my words."

"What of Winderton?"

Leonard made a dismissive sound. "I've no fears."

"And what makes you think *I'm* the danger to Kate?"

"I saw the look in her eye when you sent that wagon."

That was interesting news. "If she accepted it, she could be gone from here by now."

"She could have. That is why I'm warning you away. Leave her alone. She's happy in her life." He released his grip on Bran's hand and walked away as if the matter was solved.

Bran glanced at Kate. Her attention was on the squire's wife and Miss Taylor who were beaming with their enjoyment of the performance.

Kate probably didn't even know he was here. Instead, she was reveling in her success. She'd changed everyone's opinion of her. She had that power. It was her gift.

And what did he have?

The question haunted him as he found his horse and returned to The Garland.

Ned had already come back. Mr. Remy was still talking about rock formations to the two men who had stayed behind and Old Andy. Natural science was something that interested Bran, but not today. Bran didn't even know why he was there except that he had no place else to go. Kate certainly didn't need him, and when she had, he'd not been there for her.

Bran didn't remember much of what he said or was said to him the rest of the afternoon. He did not taste Andy's pie. He didn't want to drink.

No, instead, his mind was on years ago when he'd assumed the worst and had thrown away someone who had been more important to him than he could have imagined.

Even this morning, he'd wanted to insist it had been lust between him and Kate, because, apparently, he had a skill for lying to himself.

He understood why she had felt betrayed. He also believed she was right.

Later, instead of returning home, he found himself standing in the woods surrounding the actors' encampment. They were gathered around a fire and excitedly talking about the success of the day in that way actors had.

Bran listened, but he could not join them.

Regret was a bitter medicine.

Whether he liked it or not, Kate was lost to him. He was not worthy of her.

HE WAS *close.*

Kate sensed his presence. She'd known Brandon was there the moment he had arrived.

And she remembered hours of whispered promises, breakfast dishes, and the wild, sweet glow of having found love. She remembered having him inside her, his breath against her ear, and believing it was the most marvelous feeling in the world.

This afternoon, while the duke and the Earl of Marsden had battled for her favors, Brandon had stood apart. He'd not told her what he thought of the play. Or her performance.

Had he recognized that many of the stories she'd used on stage had been the ones he'd once told her?

Now here he was, out in the woods like a silent sentry. He did not seek her out. Not this night.

She wondered what he was thinking. Did he have the same regrets she did? The same questions?

Years ago, she had wanted him to rescue her. Instead, she'd had to learn how to rescue herself. And yet, there was something deep and empty inside of her, a place that only he had been able to fill.

She caught herself playing "what if?" What if he'd been there for her? What if there had been no Hemling? Or if she had not been so trusting as to go to that ill-fated meeting spot?

How different both of their lives would have been.

Would they have been happy?

The questions kept her up for most of the night.

Chapter Ten

"$\mathscr{I}$ write." Mrs. Warbler spoke to Kate as if she was delivering a dark secret.

Three days had passed since that first performance. Now Kate was sitting in Mrs. Warbler's house, in a lovely room with windows all around overlooking a quite substantial rain-soaked back garden. The house was modest and yet, well-appointed. "My husband was a man of some means," Mrs. Warbler had said proudly when Kate admired the furnishings.

A maid had served them sherry and biscuits before busying herself elsewhere.

In truth, Kate had found the invitation for a visit from the matron rather surprising, considering the widow's earlier animosity. The matrons' attack had been the first time Kate had ever experienced vegetables being thrown at the stage. It had happened to other actors, and for some with great regularity, but it had never happened to her.

And she had stood her ground. She was very proud of her courage because it had required *all* of it. Since that performance, the crowds attending her play were larger than she'd ever had before. The troupe's coffers would soon be replenished.

When the invitation had been delivered inviting Kate to call on Mrs. Warbler, Silas hadn't wanted her to accept it. She felt she must. She'd learned that Mrs. Warbler was a close confidante of the Dowager Duchess of Winderton. The duke still followed Kate everywhere. No matter what she did to discourage him, short of ordering him away, he refused to see that she was not interested in his attentions or his gifts, and definitely *not* his opinions.

She didn't quite know what to do next. His youth made him irritatingly persistent. It was as if he considered her fortunate to have his presence in her life . . . while the man she actually wouldn't mind seeing a bit more of was annoyingly absent.

Brandon Balfour had gone on about his business with apparently no thought of Kate. After that one night when she'd sensed his presence in the woods, she'd not felt him at all. For the second time in her life, he seemed to have vanished.

Except she knew he was in Maidenshop.

Of course, what Mr. Balfour did should be of *no* interest to her. She was a woman with big dreams. She was returning to London. How many times did she need to be reminded that men only complicated matters? It became their will, their desires.

Kate did not have time for such rot.

She hoped today to reassure an anxious dowager by way of her friend that she was not a threat to her precious son. Silas was certain she was walking into a trap, and Kate was wise enough to be wary—but what she'd not expected to hear today was a confession.

"You write?" Kate repeated.

Mrs. Warbler was pouring a healthy draft of sherry into Kate's glass. "I do," she said, putting down the bottle after topping off her own glass. "Poems." Lifting a hand to her chest, her wig ever so slightly askew, Mrs. Warbler started quoting, *"Dew upon a blade of grass, a maiden's hopes and dreams. A lock of hair, a memory there, and sadness to all extremes."*

She sat back in her chair and smiled hopefully at Kate—who understood her role here. A fortifying drink of sherry gave her a chance to think. "Why, that was astounding. Truly, I've not heard anything like it."

"My mother was a poet as well," Mrs. Warbler answered with a pleased blush. "Father never approved. He discouraged both of us. I vowed the man *I* married would not be so dictatorial. I never understood what was wrong with stringing words together."

"And did you marry the right man?" Kate asked. She'd known she'd been fortunate that her father had been one who appreciated intelligence and talent in women.

"Ah, the colonel. He was rarely home." For a moment, her pigeon-bright eyes dimmed. "I had all the time I needed. I stopped writing, well, except for letters to my husband. I don't know that he appreciated my small observations of life in Maidenshop. I would tell him the goings-on and include a little poem. Something cheery. He never mentioned them and only sent back the tersest of replies. *Dear wife, I am well. Your husband, Peter.*"

She lifted her glass in an ironic salute and drained it halfway. "Not romantic."

"Some men are not that way," Kate offered, responding to the loneliness in the older woman's voice.

Mrs. Warbler poured more sherry into her glass and offered some to Kate who shook her head since she hadn't touched any of it. "I sent one of my poems to a publisher once." Mrs. Warbler looked shocked by her own audacity.

"What happened?"

"I received a letter from him stating that no woman can write even passably well."

Kate jumped to her defense. "That is not true. There are a number of very good writers who are women."

"But are there any poets?"

That question stopped Kate. She could not think of one—in print. "I'm certain that there are dozens," Kate said with conviction. "I do understand your doubts. I'm often chastised for being too independent," Kate confessed. "I've even had men, always men, rarely women, inform me that I could not have possibly written my plays. They claimed they are too intelligent to have been penned by a woman."

Mrs. Warbler huffed her disgust. "Why do they dismiss everything we do?" she asked, sounding more than a bit tipsy. "Anything that is fun, or interesting, or challenging, they tell us we must not do."

"We don't have to listen to them."

Her eyes widened at Kate's suggestion. "You never do, do you?"

"I did at one time," Kate answered. That had been a very dark time when she'd failed so miserably in London and her parents had been dying. She'd truly lost sight of herself. "I finally came to realize that I had this need inside of me to perform and to share stories. To make people believe that what they see on the stage could be real. To forget their troubles, or their doubts, or their fears. You see, I believe stories, like poems, are important. They make us think. They make us feel."

"You are very good." Mrs. Warbler uncapped the sherry decanter but did not pour. Instead, she asked thoughtfully, "But are you happy being alone? Is it not hard, especially since you don't follow convention?"

"The better question is—am I happy not having a husband who leaves me behind and only sends me frustratingly short letters?" Kate shivered. "Of course I am. I also don't conform to convention. I'm not the only one in my family. I have a sister who is a wife, a mother, and a chemist. Her husband taught her everything she needed to know and they own their shop."

"She works?"

"Every day. I admire Alice more than any woman I know. She's intelligent and her husband refuses to let her hide her intellect 'behind her skirts,' or so he says. He is the perfect man."

"I can't imagine my Peter speaking of me that way. When he was home, he called me Bird and liked patting me on the head, but he rarely heard a word I said, unless he wanted a bit of 'you know.'" Mrs. Warbler pulled a face of distaste and pushed her glass an inch to the side, her brows drawing together. "So messy and very unenjoyable and yet we can't help but long for someone in our lives. Someone to make me feel useful."

To feel useful.

Kate understood exactly what the older woman meant, and in that moment experienced a bond between them.

One of the reasons for her crusade to return to London was to stave off those feelings of uselessness. Life had started to become a drudge. Kate had felt age creeping upon her. She'd needed a new challenge, or at least that seemed to be her nature. Alice and her other sisters seemed content. Kate envied them their peace in their homes, husbands, and children, telling herself that wasn't for her.

And it wasn't. She wanted more . . . except she couldn't define exactly what "more" was.

"Perhaps I would feel differently if the colonel and I had had children," Mrs. Warbler said. "Do you regret not having them? I'm certain you have had plenty of men in your life?"

Immediately, Kate's guard went up. She drew back and Mrs. Warbler made a sound of genuine alarm. "I did not mean to insult you, Miss Addison. I was just . . ." Her explanation trailed off.

"Prying?" Kate suggested tartly.

"No, no. I rather admire you. I invited you here because I owe you an apology. My behavior the other day was appalling. I don't know what I was thinking. I can be judgmental. That is true. However, to throw things, especially a turnip, well, I am appalled at my behavior. I'm sorry for attacking you."

Kate studied her a moment. She'd been given false apologies before.

The image of Hemling the last time she'd seen him rose as a specter in her mind. His mighty lordship on his knees begging her to return to him. He'd honestly believed he was making an offer she couldn't refuse.

She also remembered how his contriteness had turned vindictive, how he'd done all in his power to ensure no theater in London would take her in.

But Mrs. Warbler wasn't a powerful lord or even angry. Yes, she had been spiteful. Then again, Kate had often wondered how many women's judgmental attitudes and general vindictive pettiness, especially toward their own sex, was because they felt a need to exert a bit of authority in their lives. There had been times when she'd caught herself wanting to lash out because she'd felt powerless. It had been just such an incident that had pushed her to start her own troupe. She'd grown tired of feeling as if her opinion did not matter.

"I'm sorry for the incident myself," Kate answered. "I had not realized the impact my appearance would have on the social gathering."

"It was the dress," Mrs. Warbler assured her. "You looked magnificent, and there wasn't a man in the room who didn't notice. Or woman. We pay attention to those things more than the men do."

Kate had dressed to tweak the nose of *one* man, and it hadn't made *any* impression that she could see on Brandon Balfour.

Mrs. Warbler took in Kate's simple muslin day dress with its modest décolleté. The material had small flowers woven into it. "You are the very image of a genteel lady today."

"I always thought it was manners that made a woman genteel."

"You know that is not true. It has to do with who her husband is or if she has male family members to protect her."

Kate raised her sherry glass. "Mrs. Warbler, that is the most astute observation I have heard for some time. I also believe you should write."

"I'm too old—"

"Men write when they are old. What is to stop us?"

"Ourselves."

"Exactly. There is no excuse."

Her hostess lifted her own glass. "You are right. Absolutely right." She downed her sherry.

Kate took a small sip and then asked the question that had been on her mind since she'd first met the lady. "Why do you wear a wig?"

Mrs. Warbler touched the hairpiece. "It was the fashion when I was young. Because I look better. Is there any other reason?"

"Let me," Kate said. She leaned forward. Was it the sherry making her so bold? She lifted the ancient wig off of Mrs. Warbler's head. The hair beneath was matted to her head and white. Mrs. Warbler closed her eyes as if ashamed. She even seemed to grow smaller.

Gently, Kate touched the hair and it sprang to life. It was actually very good hair. After years in the theater creating hairstyles for characters, she knew quite a bit about hair. "Do you have scissors?"

"What? *No.*" Mrs. Warbler brought her hands up to protect her hair. "I'm losing it. I don't want it cut."

"Trust me," Kate said. "If you don't like it when I'm done, then you can put the wig back on." Mrs. Warbler's brows came together. Gently, Kate said, "The wig seems to swallow your face. It overshadows your character."

Ever so slowly, Mrs. Warbler lowered her hands. "Do you think?"

"I know. I have a good eye." Now that she'd started, Kate was anxious to see if her hunch was true. "Trust me?"

Perhaps it was the sherry that lowered Mrs. Warbler's inhibitions, but she did ring for the maid. "Scissors, Janie. Fetch the scissors."

The moment Kate cut a lock of Mrs. Warbler's hair, she knew she had the right of it, in spite of the maid wincing at the sight. The hair curled as if set free. Kate kept at it, trimming the hair until it was a mass of small, bouncing curls that framed Mrs. Warbler's face in the most becoming manner and gave her a youthful, and modern, expression.

"Oh, miss, *miss,*" Janie said.

"What?" Mrs. Warbler said in alarm. "Is it terrible?"

Instead of answering, the maid said, "Let me bring you a mirror."

"And a scarf," Kate called.

"Do I look horrible?" Mrs. Warbler demanded, panicked.

"You will see."

Janie returned with the hand mirror and, with great ceremony, Kate flipped it so that her hostess could see her reflection.

Mrs. Warbler gasped her surprise. "Is this my hair?"

"Undoubtedly," Kate answered, very pleased with herself. "It looks like a London style. You could pass for the goddess Artemis."

Holding the hand mirror, Mrs. Warbler angled her head this way and that. "My head feels lighter, as if I'm undressed." She put a hand beneath her chin, smoothing it back. "But I do look younger, don't I? Wait until the duchess sees me. She'll be shocked. She thinks I look much older than herself . . . but not any longer." She gave an impish smile to Kate. "Excellent work."

Kate wondered if she had done herself any favors, and yet she didn't regret Mrs. Warbler's delight in the style. She began wrapping the scarf like a turban around the curls, letting them peep out beneath the purple material. "You could go anywhere in society like this." When she'd finished, she picked up her sherry glass that had miraculously been refilled.

"I could." Mrs. Warbler sounded almost giddy. She almost kissed herself in the mirror, until a movement outside the window caught her attention.

Taking a drink, Kate followed the other woman's gaze and realized The Garland, the village tavern, was right across the road. The Earl of Marsden was leaving. He wasn't alone. Brandon was with him.

Now, it was Kate's turn to drain her glass.

"There they are," Mrs. Warbler said with great forbearance, "the gentlemen of the Logical Men's Society."

"Logical men? Do you mean the bachelor society?"

With a sharp bark of agreement, Mrs. Warbler said, "I know, it doesn't make sense." She poured herself another glass of sherry. "Men carry on about their rational thinking. In truth, they are all tiringly predictable. They all like their meals served on the table and 'you know' in their bed. The rest is all filler in their day."

Her bluntness got a surprised laugh out of Kate.

Pleased with herself, Mrs. Warbler leaned forward. "The Earl of Marsden is their leader of sorts, although our good doctor seems to be the chairman. Marsden's grandfather started the society."

"And the purpose of it?" The earl and Brandon stood discussing something quite earnestly.

"Silliness," Mrs. Warbler said. "At least that is what the ladies and I think. They vow to have no interest in marriage, but as you can tell their numbers are small and there is even a gentleman I am quite fond of who is a member. But my hope is he won't be for much longer."

"There is?" Kate's skepticism was clear.

"Oh, the members aren't all young men. Widowed man can rejoin. I have my eye on Sir Lionel. He served our country honorably in Italy. His wife died around the same time as my Peter. However, he claims he is devoted to the society. He has resisted all my entreaties."

"Perhaps he was deeply in love with his late wife?"

"It's been five years. Why wouldn't he want more from life?"

"You have tried to coax him out?"

"Every chance I can."

"Perhaps he will notice your new hairstyle."

Mrs. Warbler touched her soft curls. "He might. Unfortunately, the Widow Smethers fancies him as well. She's younger but I have more money. Then again, she cooks."

"Competition is not bad for any of us." Kate realized she hadn't taken her eyes off of Brandon. She forced herself to bring her focus back into the room. Janie had brought in a broom and swept up the hair. The sherry glass was full again.

"The earl has his eye on you."

Kate gave a start. "Does he?" Now she was wary.

"They say he is a generous benefactor."

"I'm not interested in a benefactor." Kate started tidying up the table. She moved the scissors over, then the hand mirror—

Mrs. Warbler reached out and stopped her hand. She gave a heavy sigh and admitted, "The dowager is very nervous about her son's infatuation with you. You'd be wise to leave him alone."

"I am not encouraging him," Kate could say honestly. "If any-thing, I am avoiding him." Which had been another reason for accepting the invitation this afternoon.

"I know it isn't you. We all do. Even the duchess will acknowl-edge this once she calms down and thinks clearly. Winderton is very young and, yet, he has always been anxious to settle down. The duchess has had her hands full trying to keep him from jumping in where angels should fear to tread."

Kate sat on the chair she'd vacated. "Her Grace has nothing to worry about from me." Her glance had to return to the doorway across the road. Brandon had started to walk away but the earl grabbed his arm and was speaking seriously with him.

"For my money, the man who is the most interesting is Mr. Balfour," Mrs. Warbler said.

Now she had Kate's attention. "Why do you say that?"

"He's handsome and there is a mystery about him."

"A mystery."

"Yes, he so rarely smiles. He is always serious. He is an archi-tect. He was working for the East India Company when Winder-ton's father died. They say he didn't want to come back to England and only did so for duty."

"How long ago was that?"

"About three years ago. He has complete say over the duke's affairs until he turns one and twenty, which is very soon. It is unfortunate the duke's father didn't make the age of his major-ity much higher. Winderton could use more seasoning—" She stopped abruptly. "Perhaps I shouldn't be saying this to you? The dowager would be furious."

"It is not a problem. Whatever we say here won't go further than this room."

Mrs. Warbler looked outside. Brandon and the earl were still in their deep discussion. "I know Mr. Balfour will be relieved when he can discharge his duties to his nephew. He has had a hard time adjusting after being gone so long. He struggles to reestablish himself. It must be difficult for him to live in the Dower House."

"The Dower House?" Kate hadn't really thought about where Brandon lived. She'd assumed in the redbrick manse the duke owned.

"Yes, on the estate."

"Of course, that makes sense." Kate remembered the room that he'd had in London. Student's quarters . . . and yet, they had been a magical place in her mind.

"The duchess worries about him. And then, of course, there is the tragedy of his life."

Kate swung her attention away from the gentlemen. "Tragedy?"

Mrs. Warbler moved her chair closer. "His wife died. Very sad."

Brandon had been married?

For a second, Kate's mind froze. All earlier charitable thoughts vanished.

Had he been married when she'd known him? Or had he gone on to marry?

And why hadn't he said something? He could have spoken up the other night. He didn't.

"The duchess tries to do what she can for him," Mrs. Warbler was saying. "All the matrons have been thinking of suitable parties for him to wed. I mean, the nonsense of the Logical Men's Society aside, men need to be married. Don't you agree?"

The earl and Brandon finished their conversation. Marsden untied his mount and rode away. Brandon started down the road. On foot.

Married?

Kate had a sudden need to talk to him.

She came to her feet. "This has all been very nice, Mrs. Warbler. Unfortunately, I must take my leave."

"Oh, yes, you have a performance this afternoon."

"Exactly. Thank you for your hospitality." Kate hurried as quickly as she dared for the door. She picked up her green velvet cap off of a side table. It was a stylish chapeau that she had made herself from a description someone had given her of what they were wearing in London.

"Janie will see you out," Mrs. Warbler offered.

"Not necessary." Kate set her hat on her head at an angle and opened the door herself. "Thank you very much."

"No, thank you. This has been the nicest visit."

Kate started to leave but noticed two aged gents leaving The Garland. She looked back to her hostess. "Is one of those Sir Lionel?"

"Yes, the one on the right."

The man appeared ready to fall on his face from drink. His friend held him up, or perhaps they were holding each other up. He was not the sort Kate would want. Mrs. Warbler was welcome to him. "Good day," she said in a quiet voice and slipped out the door.

At Mrs. Warbler's gate, she looked up and down the road. Brandon was walking with a long, purposeful stride toward the sprawling buildings of the wainwright. What business could he have there? Unless he was prying into hers?

Since she'd rejected his gift of a wagon, perhaps he wanted to hurry the repairs on her vehicle, a thought that she found surprisingly hurtful. Just as it had bothered her that he had not attended any other of her performances.

And the idea that he'd married—and had not said a word to her?

Kate set out after him.

Chapter Eleven

$\mathcal{E}$arlier, on Bran's way into the village, Orion had thrown a shoe. Rather than wait until he returned to Smythson's stables, Bran had chosen to spend time over a pint at The Garland and have Fred Burnham, the smithy, shoe his horse.

His decision would annoy Jim, the Smythson stable manager. The man was picky about how the horses' feet were done. His suggestion would have been for Bran to return to the estate. However, Bran never felt comfortable riding his horse shoeless, even for a short distance. Orion was temperamental enough when all things were good.

Unfortunately, when Bran returned to the smithy, Fred hadn't had a moment to see to Orion yet. "Had to do a plow for Squire Nelson. I could have one of my lads shoe your horse, but I know how partial you are to the animal. I'll see to it right now."

"Thank you," Bran said, because what else could he say? Both plow and horse must be done.

He could wander back to The Garland, but truth be known, he was done drinking. He'd been indulging too much over the past several days. He thought about what Mars had told him in front of The Garland: the commission for the bridge was supposedly still in play, and that he should return to Town to personally see how the wind was blowing.

But ever since Kate's performance, he hadn't given a damn about the bridge.

No, instead he'd spent his waking moments trying to not think about her while also keeping tabs on everything she was doing, which was easily done since every servant at Smythson along with everyone in the village had attended one of her performances. Even Andy had pulled himself away from the tavern to attend.

Bran was tiring of Aesop's famous proverbs being spouted all over the county. It was said that Reverend Summerall was plotting ways to weave the morals of those stories into one of his sermons.

Apparently Kate, "quite wisely" according to his still lovesick nephew, had several plays going, all on different Aesop themes, making it possible for someone who attended the play one day to see a different one the next. "Brilliant idea," Winderton had proclaimed. "And she mixes up the pieces so even though someone may have seen a particular story, it is still new because the tales around it are different."

It was a very clever idea.

Bran didn't wish her ill. He just wished he could exorcise her from his mind. That he could cut out that piece of his brain that mourned the past. Drink hadn't done it and since she showed no signs of packing her troupe and leaving the area the only thing left to do was avoid her and all mention of her—and that was hard.

Kate was the topic of conversation wherever he went. The rowdy Crisp was said to be at every performance. Even the Dawson lads had taken to the "theater." And the duke attended daily, which led Lucy to daily hunt Bran down to wring her hands over the actress's continued hold over her son and how Bran must do something about it.

So here he was, putting himself through the misery of knowing Kate was near and yet wishing she was not.

A man could go mad—

Beyond the forges, next to an old shed, his gaze caught sight of a large wagon propped up on barrels instead of wheels. The smithy's brother, Tom, oversaw the wainwright services for the village, and though he wasn't in sight right now no one had ever accused Tom of working hard. He was likely snoozing somewhere.

The wagon wasn't particularly attractive with its sides weathered by age, but it appeared functional. Bran had no doubt that it could easily haul the tents, wood planks, costumes, and several actors over the countryside.

"What is wrong with that wagon?" he asked Fred.

Having finished the plow, the blacksmith had tied Orion up and was preparing to have him lift his leg. He looked over to see what Bran was talking about and said, "Oh, the actors' wagon. What *isn't* wrong with it? Tom is having to fashion a new axle and it has been hard. We didn't have the wood for it. The back wheels were cracked in two when the wagon fell. The spokes on the front were ready to break as well."

"When will you have it finished?"

"Next Tuesday or so." *Six days away.*

Orion impatiently pawed the ground and Fred gave his attention back to the horse. "Your front shoe is loose as well."

"Do all of them."

"Yes, sir."

Bran strode through the shop toward the wagon. There were several other broken vehicles around it. One was an aging phaeton that Fred bragged he dreamed of repairing and driving. Thurlowe was certain the heavy blacksmith would kill himself on it. Bran knew Fred didn't own the horseflesh to make the vehicle go fast enough to be a danger.

He studied the wagon. Kate would be lucky if it was finished in six days. So many things could go wrong when parts were hewn by hand, which was the only way the Burnham brothers worked. Like so many, they did what their fathers had done and their fathers before them.

Bran leaned to inspect the undercarriage. It was a matter of male curiosity, if nothing else. There was rust on all the metal trappings.

He wondered how Kate traveled. Did she walk beside this wagon? Her resilience would put soldiers to shame—

"Why didn't you tell me you were married?" Her low, very angry voice came from behind him as if he had conjured her to this place.

Still stooped, Bran looked up. She stood no more than three feet from him, her head high, her shoulders back, the lines of her mouth tight. She had a pert cap on her head and her graceful day dress extenuated every important line of her figure.

And he wasn't certain he'd heard her correctly.

She took a step toward him. "Were you married that night we were together?"

He rose so abruptly in surprise at her question, he almost bumped his head on the wagon. Kate had never been one to mince words.

"Answer me, Brandon, or I swear—" Her voice stopped as if what she had in mind for him was too terrible to say aloud.

And his own temper ignited.

She charged in out of nowhere to accuse him of unfaithfulness? Him? The man who had pined for her all these years and was now doing all he could to let her go?

"What? What will you swear?" he challenged. "And why would you even care? Everything between us was in the past. You were very clear the other night on where we stood with each other."

"As it should be," she snapped. "So answer me. Did you marry? And when?"

Her impertinence annoyed him. "I do not believe I have to answer. Good day, Miss Addison." He would have grandly walked away but she practically jumped into his path, a gloved hand raised to block his way.

"I trusted you," she said. "And I must know if I was wrong. I gave so much."

"Kate, I have never given you cause to distrust me. I thought we cleared the air between us the other night."

"Then answer the question."

"Why is it so important?"

"Because I believed you were different from other men."

"I was not married when we knew each other in London. And *what if* I married after we parted? What gives you the right to have a say?"

She blinked as if surprised by his reason, and then demanded softly, "Did you?"

A part of him was unreasonably angry. They hadn't spoken since the other night when she had let him know she was done with him. What was this attack about?

Another part of him was overjoyed. Kate had come to him. Every membrane, every fiber of his being honed in on this moment. Even the air around them seemed to change and insulate them from the world.

"There was no wife. I've never had one."

Kate looked away, troubled.

"You don't believe me?" Bran shook his head. "Who told you I had married?"

A flash of fire came to her eye. "Mrs. Warbler. She is a good friend of the dowager duchess."

"You don't have to explain who Elizabeth Warbler is to me. I know exactly whom she is, and a bigger gossip has never existed in all of time."

"She wouldn't make up that you married."

"You haven't been in Maidenshop long. There are all sorts of stories circulating about me. Very few of them true."

"Then you should correct the record." She sounded charmingly prim.

"I don't have time for that. And I thought you were more intelligent than to believe secondhand tales. Besides, I ask again, what is it to you if I had been married?"

Her brows came together. Her gaze slipped away. She looked around, as if uncomfortable and then asked, "Why were you looking at my wagon?"

"Curiosity. Nothing more and nothing less, Kate."

"I would prefer that you not interest yourself in my affairs."

"Well, then, I shall hide my gaze from your wagon." He held up a hand, mocking her presumptuous attitude.

Her hands curled into fists. "Stop that, Brandon."

"No, you stop it, Kate." And then, in the abrupt silence, in frustration, he added, "Damn it all," because this conversation was not going in the direction he wanted. He looked over to where Fred was working on Orion. No one appeared to be paying attention to them, but just in case, Bran took her arm and guided her to the other side of the wagon, away from view.

To her credit, she did not fight him.

Once he felt they were safe, he let go of her arm, but he did not step back. "What is going on here? Did you honestly track me down because of something Mrs. Warbler said?"

Her lips pressed together and then she said, "I had to. We barely knew anything about each other back then. Not really. You could have been married."

"And then?"

"Then what?" she challenged stubbornly.

"We would go back to relive those days? I was not married, but if I had been, well, the damage would have been done."

She did not like his common sense, so of course, he had to press the matter further. "And while you claim to recall little of that time, you did remember the stories I told you. You made them into your plays."

"*Aesop's Fables* are popular stories."

"Some are. And some I shared with you were not well-known at all. They are part of your performances."

She hadn't moved away from him. Her troubled gaze met his as if she was just recognizing the connection of her plays to him.

"As for the Maidenshop gossip," he said, "I have no doubt that Lucy probably spread some story of my having married. She cares about what people think and likes to speculate. She has drilled me several times over whether I was hiding a wife back in India. It's her flair for drama coupled with her nosiness." He frowned. "Did Mrs. Warbler say what happened to my 'wife'?"

"She died." Her words were barely a whisper.

"Ah, how convenient."

They stood very close to each other without touching and the world around them could go to hell as far as he was concerned. She was beautiful in her gown of soft green and her dark curls beneath her velvet cap framing her face. There were tiny flowers in the pattern of her dress and when she moved, he caught the scent of violets. Lovely.

He leaned closer. "I've given you no reason not to trust me, Kate. Others conspired against us. It wasn't me. I would have killed Hemling for what he did to you, if I had been aware. Instead, I thought leaving you alone was what you wanted."

She swallowed hard at the mention of her attacker. He could feel the heat between their two bodies. Her gaze dropped to his neck cloth. "And yet our lives have gone on," she said. "You could have married."

"I meant to. I thought I would. However, the truth is, you spoiled me for other women, Kate. I kept comparing them to you." *Always you.*

Her lips parted in surprise, her brows drawing together as if she didn't quite believe him, and he had an insane desire to kiss her until she trusted him. All he had to do was lower his head—

"Ah, there you are, Mr. Balfour," Fred's hearty voice interjected. "Your horse is ready . . ." He trailed off as he realized that he might have interrupted something. Both Bran and Kate stepped back as if his voice had made them aware of how close they stood. "Beg your pardon, sir."

"It is fine. Thank you, Fred." Bran looked to Kate. Should he have been as honest as he had been?

Her color was high. She didn't look at him. In fact, it was obvious she was trying to look everywhere but at him . . . and there was his answer.

However, he'd had his say. She might hold the past against him forever, and how could he stop her? Kate had an iron will and apparently knew how to nurse a grudge.

"Goodbye, Miss Addison."

She didn't respond.

He turned on his heel and went to collect his horse.

OTHERS CONSPIRED *against us. You spoiled me for other women.*

The words trailed in the air behind him.

Kate placed her hand against her belly, trying to steady herself. There had been a moment between them just now when she'd wanted his arms around her. Had *needed* to feel his body against hers. Her mind, her reason could argue and yet, her body remembered. Everything deep within her responded to him.

"This is not what I want," she whispered as if saying the words aloud could make them true. She was going to London. She planned to reclaim her place in the world.

Kate did not need the complication of Brandon Balfour in her life. Or any other man, she quickly reminded herself. Men mucked things up. She'd lived it and witnessed it in other women's lives. She liked her life uncomplicated. Her sights were set on her future.

So, why did she feel overheated and completely discomfited?

Why had she reacted so strongly to Mrs. Warbler's gossip? If Brandon had married or not wasn't her business, as he'd pointed out.

She had been making her own decisions for quite some time. She knew what was best for her—and Brandon Balfour was not necessary to her life. Especially right now when she had a performance to give in an hour's time.

The last thought moved her forward. She tried to ignore the glances of the smithy and his workers. They were obviously curious about what she and Brandon had been doing behind the wagon. She smiled, nodded, and kept moving.

However, something had changed about the day. Every step she took seemed to be on unsteady ground. Brandon's words, the information that he might still care, rattled her.

Mary noticed that something was not quite right with Kate. They had just finished dressing in their costumes. Half the benches outside were already filled. There were clouds in the sky but they did not promise rain, at least, not anytime soon.

Actors were running back and forth, either to don costumes or to carry out their duties in preparing the audience. Robbie was an excellent juggler and Jess had taken to pretending to make him lose his concentration with her saucy ways. The crowd loved it.

"We are going to have another full till," Mary predicted.

"Yes," Kate said, giving her only half an ear.

"We will still be leaving soon, no?"

"Yes . . . I just saw the wagon. The wainwright promises it in six more days. Possibly five."

"Do you believe him?"

Ah, there it was—a question of trust. "Of course," Kate answered a bit too brightly. "He wants to be paid." She piled her hair up on top of her head and began poking pins into her curls to hold them in place.

Mary watched her a moment before taking the pins from Kate's hand. "Let me do this."

Gratefully, Kate did. She felt tired. And a touch annoyed at the responsibility of everything.

"What is it?" Mary asked.

"It?"

"You are distracted." Mary pushed the last pin into Kate's hair. "Is it the duke?"

"The duke?" Lord, Kate had barely given him a thought. "Has he been around today?"

"He is out there right now. He was most put out that you were gone when he arrived a few hours ago. He actually stomped around."

"Oh dear." She closed her eyes, willing herself to keep everything in perspective.

"Jess teased him and he brightened a bit."

Kate rose and shook out the skirts of her Juno costume. "Perhaps it is a good thing she did. I'm trying to discourage him but he is remarkably persistent."

"You might talk to him."

"Do you mean be blunt? And how do you believe that will play out, Mary? I've suggested every polite way possible that we aren't suited." She shook her head. "One does not offend a duke. Even such a young one. Hopefully, we will be leaving shortly and then that will be that. I just have to fend him off as best as I am able."

"So, you don't mind that Jess has been doing a bit of flirting with him?"

That gave Kate pause. "Is it a problem?"

"What she does flatters him."

Kate shrugged. "If his attention is on her, then he will leave me alone." Besides, Jess had once been a simple milkmaid. She couldn't possibly keep Winderton's attention for long.

With that thought, she turned her focus on the play and her performance—except, things felt different. Kate truly hadn't made a connection between her use of *Aesop's Fables* and the charming stories Brandon had once told her.

When her part was finished and she was watching backstage . . . she found herself remembering the warmth of his skin, even the scent of it. She'd nestled against him after their lovemaking. She'd been a virgin. Shy, awkward, and amazed. His body had taught hers what it meant to be fully alive. What had happened between them had seemed preordained.

There had been one second when she'd been almost overwhelmed by regret. That was when she'd thought of her mother—who had warned her to be wary, to guard against just this sort of thing. *They will ruin you, if you aren't careful* . . . and Kate had assured her she was made of sterner stuff. She could resist temptation—and she had, until she met Brandon.

Then, all of her fine promises of chastity had crumbled. She'd wanted him as much as he had her. She'd been drawn to him from the first moment their gazes had met. He'd made her laugh. He told her stories. She'd experienced no shame in giving herself to him or making that leap outside of marriage. Well, not until Hemling had ruined her life.

Now, every vignette on stage had a deeper meaning. Others had fought for her attention with flowers and gifts . . . but Brandon had offered his imagination. She found herself thinking about what might have been.

The performance went well. Afterward, Winderton pouted, apparently offended by her casual disregard for him. She was unable to keep up even a pretense of interest in his babble. He left shortly after the performance, and Kate was relieved.

She organized for the next day and joined her troupe for a meal she barely tasted. Her mind was on other things—

No, her mind was on *one man*.

Others conspired against us. You spoiled me for other women. She wanted to forget his words, and could not.

Feeling a stranger in her own life, Kate went to her tent early. She lay in the dark thinking until Mary and Jess came to bed. Only then did she manage to sleep an hour or two.

Her dreams woke her. She was surprised she was on her cot. Her dream had been very real. In it, she'd been back in Brandon's tiny room—a student's quarters. There had been the table and the chair, the bookshelves, and even the dingy curtains. In her dream, she'd wanted to be in the bed but the sheets seemed glued together. She couldn't pull them down no matter how hard she tried. *He was coming*, she told herself. She wanted to be in his bed before he arrived, and yet, she was afraid for him to find her there. She could even hear him outside the door just before she woke with a start—

Kate lay in her cot, her heart pounding. She understood the dream. There was so much left unresolved between herself and Brandon. She'd find no peace until she came to terms with whatever it was churning inside her.

Kate had learned to go after what she wanted. She had discipline and was willing to sacrifice what she must to see her way clear.

She also did as she wished and what she wanted right now was to see Brandon. Until she did, she would have no rest.

Others conspired against us. You spoiled me for other women. She needed to hear him say those words again.

Mary and Jess were sleeping deeply when she rose from her cot. Kate put on the dress she had worn that day and covered it with a cloak. Her hair was in a loose braid and she didn't bother to pin it up or to put on a bonnet.

She left the tent. The embers of the fire were dying. The snoring from the men's tent could have woken the dead. No one was roaming around. She wasn't certain where the Dower House was, but she had an idea. After all, they'd already spent the good part of a week on the Winderton estate.

What moonlight there was lit her way and the paths were well marked. She knew where the main house was. Without too much trouble, Kate came upon a broad lawn around a whitewashed, two-story, brick manor house. It had a domed roof and a broad portico.

The main house had a torch burning by the front door all night according to the duke.

Not so here. No light shone from its windows. She could almost imagine that the place was abandoned.

She also didn't feel comfortable going to the front door. A servant could be posted there and she definitely didn't wish to be seen— and that was the gist of it, wasn't it? Kate's parents had been poor but genteel. She knew what was expected of a lady, even though she broke the rules at will when they didn't serve her purpose. That attitude was what her mother had feared, what had disappointed her.

Kate walked around to the back, her feet sinking into the thick grass. All was dark here, too.

Surveying the back of the house, she wondered which window might lead her to Bran. How had he woken her that night? Had it been just the force of his presence? Could she do the same?

Kate focused on the house and closed her eyes. She summoned all that was in her and reached out to him. If it didn't work, she'd have to knock on a door—

"What are you doing here?"

At the sound of his quiet voice, she popped open her eyes, except the sound had not come from the house. No, it came from behind where she stood.

She whirled around.

Brandon was several feet away from her. He walked toward her until he was almost as close as they had been earlier that afternoon by the wagon.

He held his hands out as if he could not believe she was here. "Kate?"

Suddenly, the past did not matter.

There was only here and now. This moment.

"I'm tired of being alone. So tired." And then she cupped his face in her hands, his whiskers rough beneath her palms, and kissed him.

Chapter Twelve

𝒦*ate was kissing him.*

Brandon had never realized what a kiss could communicate.

There was anger in her kiss—and disappointment, resentment . . . and a sweet, sweet plea for him to understand. For him to be here for her.

He wrapped his arms around her, pulling her into the haven of his body. He didn't hold her as close as he wanted. He would crush her to him if he could. His every base impulse had already come to life. He wanted to take her to the ground, to bury himself in her—and he knew that would be wrong.

Kate had come to him. This very independent, very proud woman was offering him her trust. That made this kiss almost a sacred act. He'd failed her once. He did not wish to do so again.

He'd been at the stables. He'd not been able to sleep. Thoughts of his argument with Kate, with what he should have said, preyed on his mind. Finally, he'd taken himself off in the opposite direction of her tent. Brushing Orion and being out in the night air had helped to calm his restless energy.

Well, that and having his nephew come upon him in the stables and begin to carry on about how he worshipped the actress and felt she didn't understand him. "She thinks I'm too young to know my own mind. And here I am, ready to offer her everything."

Christopher's declarations of undying love had not sat well with Bran. What if Kate did choose the duke? He'd offer her a security of which she could only dream—and one that Bran had helped rebuild. Kate was ambitious. She had learned to take care of herself.

True, years ago she had singled Bran out. However, they were now different people. Life had tempered them. He could offer her wealth, but did *he* want *her* if that was all she desired?

In India, his work had been respected. In England, it seemed as if he couldn't find a foothold. There were times he doubted if he'd ever make his mark in the world. Yet miracle of miracles, Kate was here, *with him*.

She broke the kiss, her hands warm against his jaw. Her curves pressed against him. The moon caught the sheen of tears in her eyes. "I shouldn't be here." Her voice was raspy as if she struggled with herself.

"Kate, if I could go back and relive everything, I would not have—"

She silenced him with her fingers over his lips. "It isn't the past, Brandon. It is not that."

He took the opportunity to kiss the tips of her fingers. She pulled her hand back. He captured it, lacing their fingers together. "Then what is it? Why are you here?"

Her eyes had always been expressive. They searched his face a moment before she said, "I want you."

His answer was to sweep her up. He began walking toward the house. Her arms locked around his neck, her breath against his throat.

Years ago, they had spent one day, less than twenty-four hours, as lovers. Bran had been unaware of how precious those moments had been at the time. How treasured this woman in his arms was. He'd assumed that life would take them their separate ways, and yet, here they were. The Fates, those mythical creatures who knew the future, had woven he and Kate together.

He carried her toward the house. He'd left the back door open and easily let them both in.

"Is anyone awake?" she whispered.

"I live alone."

"Servants?"

"No, Kate." His valet was in London in a house he owned there. "It is just us."

She gave a soft sigh and rested her head on his shoulder. "Like years ago."

He climbed the stairs to his room. Neither spoke. His suite of rooms was at the end of the short hall. The door was ajar. Bran shoved it open. He crossed over to the bed. It was a four-poster with a plain white coverlet. The drapes were open and the dim, silvery moonlight gave the bed a soft glow.

Bran sat her on the mattress. He knelt on the floor in front of her. Strands of loose hair curled around her face. He gently pushed them back and kissed her.

Her arms slipped around his neck as if it was the most natural movement in the world for her. Her tongue met his and Bran experienced that timid touch all the way to his soul, and the kiss deepened.

He untied the string of her cloak. Her hands slid into his riding coat and pushed it back over his shoulders. Their kiss broke, giving them a chance to undress in earnest.

Bran realized his hands were shaking. It was as if his body had been waiting for her. He pulled her dress over her head and laughed to find she wore that impossibly thick nightdress.

She was more successful with his shirt. She placed her hand against his bare chest, right over his heart. "It races like mine."

His answer was to kiss the sensitive skin at the line of her throat. He tasted her skin. Her breasts flattened against his chest and he ran his hand down along her rib cage, feeling the curve of them.

Reluctantly, he rose. He began unbuttoning his breeches—and for a second, he wasn't in this room in the Dower House. No, he remembered that other night when they'd both been as eager.

The difference this time was that they each knew what they wanted. Bran made quick work of taking off his boots. He pulled down the leather riding pants. Kate watched with solemn eyes as if memorizing his every movement.

When he was naked, when his desire for her was obvious, strong, and demanding, he said, "Stand up, Kate."

Like an obedient child, she came to her feet.

He took hold of the skirt of her nightdress. Finding her lips, he kissed her as he slowly gathered it in his hands.

She smiled, the movement tickling him. She lightly bit his bottom lip before soothing it with her tongue and intensifying the kiss between them. Her lower body was naked and pressed against him, his arousal against her flat belly.

A growl of desire rose in his throat. He sucked hard on her tongue and released the kiss. He raised the nightdress over her head. She made it easy for him by holding her arms up. The room's wan light highlighted her glorious breasts with their dark points and Bran was undone.

He threw the nightgown aside, hungry for her. Her core against him was hot and wet.

Fifteen years had passed. Fifteen years of nursing hurt and resentment. He did not want to waste a second more.

FROM THE moment Brandon had lifted her up in his arms, Kate felt as if she was in a dream.

She was tired of living with the ghosts of her past. Tired of being the responsible one. Tired of protecting herself.

Years ago, she'd believed herself in love with this man. He'd loomed large in her life even during their years apart—either as a shameful memory or the focus for her anger. To realize that she had been wrong about him, that he had *cared*? If the sun had suddenly shone in the middle of the night, it could not be a greater miracle.

His arms felt good around her. Solid. *This* she remembered. She'd been safe with Brandon. There had been a wholeness to this act between them that had once made the world exactly right, and she yearned to experience it again.

Their kiss took on a stronger purpose. His hand rested on her hip, its stillness an assurance that he waited for a sign from her.

Yes, this was the lover she remembered, and she lowered herself to the mattress, bringing him with her.

Back then, Brandon had been gentle and somewhat clumsy—as she had been herself. Neither one of them had really known what they were doing, she realized.

Her braid was caught beneath her. She turned her head and pulled it out. He stretched his body beside her and traced her jaw with one hand.

"You haven't changed," he whispered. "You are as lovely as when I first saw you. You were Juliette on the stage and I was lost."

She rolled on her side, the better to confront him. "You've changed." She ran her hand over his shoulder. "You are stronger, bigger . . ." She drew her hand down along his waistline to his hip. "They are all good changes."

His answer was to kiss her as if breathing her in. He rose above her, guiding her onto her back. His weight settled upon her.

Ah, yes, this she remembered. They fit together, especially when she bent her legs and cradled his hips between her thighs. Her hand smoothed over his buttocks. The heat of him was pressed against her—

And she found herself struggling to breathe.

Every muscle inside of her tensed. His weight that had seemed comforting, now threatened to suffocate her.

Kate lifted her hips to buck him off, suddenly not wanting anything to do with him.

Brandon moved off of her. "Is something the matter? Kate?"

She scrambled to sit up and crawled backward toward the headboard. Leaning against it, she willed herself to calm down, her hand covering her mouth. "I don't know. I don't know . . ." She looked wildly toward him. His face was in the shadows. "I can't see you. Brandon, I can't see."

"It is all right," he said soothingly. "Let me light a candle."

She closed her eyes. She heard a scratching noise on a bedside table. There was silence, and then the sound of flint being struck.

"I've lit the candle. Stay here."

She nodded, not opening her eyes. The mattress dipped as he rose. Her breathing grew normal. She didn't understand what had come over her. The intensity of what could only be described as fear overwhelmed her. Slowly, she opened her eyes.

The candlelit room was sparsely furnished. There was the bed and a washstand. There were no chests or cabinets for clothes. It was almost as if no one lived here.

Steps sounded in the hall. Brandon appeared in the doorway. He held a glass in his hand. He wore his breeches and nothing else and she was very conscious that she was naked. She reached for the bedspread to cover herself, tucking the coverlet up and around her breasts.

He made no remark. Instead, he walked to her side of the bed. He sat on the edge and offered her a glass of dark liquid. "Have a drink."

"What is it?"

"Port. That is all that was in the cabinet."

"I don't think—"

"Kate, drink it." He wasn't stern and yet he had a tone that warned her he expected to be obeyed. She'd used that tone several times herself.

She took the glass, gave it a sniff, and sipped the heavy liquor.

"More," he ordered.

She mugged a frown. His response was a nod of his head that she was expected to take it all in.

Closing her eyes, Kate downed it. She lay back. The heavy wine seemed to flow right to her belly. There was a moment of intense heat and then a gradual warmth spread to the rest of her.

"Good?" he asked.

She opened her eyes and glanced at that portion of Brandon's breeches that should have been quite tight from his erection. He noticed. A deprecating half grin twisted his mouth.

"Is he completely gone?" she asked.

Brandon shrugged. "Let's say he is hopefully lingering off stage."

The description startled a giggle from her. She covered her mouth with one hand in embarrassment and then was horrified as that giggle changed into a sob, followed by another.

Before she understood what was happening, she was bending over, lost in deep, humiliating tears.

Brandon climbed up to the headboard to sit next to her. "Kate, what is wrong?"

She put out a hand to block him from touching her, unable to speak. She also didn't have an explanation. A tumult of feelings had overtaken her.

"Is it me, Kate?"

She shook her head. She didn't understand herself.

This time when he offered his arms, she fell into them, burying her face against his chest and letting the tears flow. She gasped for breath, trying to control them, and failed.

"You don't have to be strong all the time, Kate. You can trust me."

Trust? She didn't think she knew what that word meant.

Then again, he was right. She was tired of being in control. Exhausted by things so deep inside of her, she'd not even known they were there.

He let her cry until she was spent, until she could do nothing more than put her arms around his torso and be still, resting her head on his chest. He smelled exactly as she remembered—of clean soap, warm man, and a hint of fresh air and horseflesh.

The peace of silence settled upon them. She listened to his heart beat and felt the stirrings of trust again. And a desire for him to understand. Years ago, their time together had been too brief for confidences. The details of their lives had seemed unimportant compared to the attraction they'd felt. No wonder they had misread each other's motives.

Kate wanted now to be different.

She spoke. "Jeremiah Earls was a family friend. My mother knew him from her acting days. When I announced that I was going to be an actress, my mother was the first to inform me I would not, and yet I had my heart set upon it."

"So she let you go?"

"She had no choice. I have a strong will."

With a short laugh, he signaled his agreement.

She tightened her hold around him. Her memories were clear and vivid.

And that was how she'd been living, she realized, with memories. Only memories.

No wonder her recent decision to finally take action for herself and return to London was so important.

"Father didn't want me to go either, although he could see my mind was set. So, I went to London with Mr. Earls. Before I left, Mother informed me that she had high expectations for me. She warned that choosing this course in life would put me on the outside. There would be many who would think the worst of me." Brandon cradled her closer. She snuggled against him. "I was brave then. And so young. I didn't think anyone could harm me. Except, I was foolish."

"Kate, naïve maybe but it isn't foolish to want to make something of your life."

She silently disagreed. She knew who she was. She jumped into the story. "When I was met with success so quickly, I thought I was invincible. I also had made a promise to my mother that I would stand for the high morals of my family. She told me a lady had nothing to do with status or position. A lady is a woman who thinks highly of herself."

"Which you do."

She shook her head. "I don't know."

He gave her a reassuring squeeze. "Kate, you *are* a lady."

"Says the man I am naked in bed with."

Brandon made a dismissive sound. "Now you are being foolish. All this protecting virgins and living a cossetted life is nonsense. It certainly hasn't helped my sister."

"But it does brand me. Oh, dear God, it has. You've heard the names they call me. Most times, I can ignore the unkindness of others . . . except for those moments—" Her voice broke off.

"Moments?"

"When I *am* ashamed." The truth of those words almost robbed her of breath.

He gathered her closer. "And what have you done that should make you ashamed?"

"Brandon, you don't understand—"

"Maybe I do. Answer me, Kate. Let's have it out."

Her throat closed, blocking anything she could have said. In the depths of her belly was a resistance that seemed as hard as rock.

Brandon shifted his weight, giving her a bit of space, before he said, "I never thought of you as a woman of easy virtue. I remember what happened between us as being joyous. Freeing."

"It was." Oh, God, why was this all so muddled? "And yet, it was wrong," she insisted.

"Because?"

"I promised my mother . . . she warned me."

"About *us* specifically?"

Kate came up on one arm, a truth becoming clear to her. "Of course not. She never knew about us. I didn't tell her. She did know about Hemling. It seemed as if all the world did."

"But she didn't know everything. She didn't know that he forced you, and then made you afraid to leave. And he bragged about what he'd done."

She placed her hand on his chest. "I promised my mother I would not give in to the temptation of the world. She was so worried about me and I assured her over and over that I understood that I was an Addison and that, as she often said, 'the blood of kings and queens flowed in my veins.'"

"That is true of most of us, isn't it? Kings were indiscriminate in where they procreated. There is probably many a yeoman or cowherd with the blood of kings in his body."

"Ah, but no one questions a king for his indiscretions, while his queen might find herself pilloried." She pushed her heavy hair back over her shoulder. "I meant to keep that promise. I understood what my mother was saying. I was raised with high standards and I felt blessed that I could be on a stage. I wasn't even tempted—until you appeared."

"I have no regrets."

She nestled down into the haven of his arms again. "I had no regrets either, although I'm clear-eyed about what it was."

"And what was it, Kate?"

She didn't hesitate. "We belonged together."

Brandon ran a curled finger against her lower lip and pressed a kiss against her forehead. "Kate, the bedrooms of London are filled with people who are not married to each other. No one can hold what we felt against us."

Or could have stopped them.

"However," she bravely went on, ready to confess all, "with Hemling, I lost sight of who I was. I stayed because I was afraid of what he might do when I tried to go—that this was what I deserved for my own foolishness. And I was angry, Brandon. I believed you had betrayed me, that I was abandoned. I was too proud to go home. I'd come to London to act and now, I was a prisoner, even with my own coach. Everyone thought I was fortunate to be kept by a marquis, but it was hell. I was an outsider. No matter how well I behaved, he saw me as almost less than human and not deserving of any dignity . . . and society felt the same way. The turning point came when I decided to take dignity for myself, when I left Hemling." She shook her head. "He paid the theater managers to keep me off the stage. People thought I was rash to leave such a rich benefactor. They didn't know how he really treated me. Nor did they care."

"What did you do?"

"I went home." Suddenly, his body heat was too warm for her. She rolled onto her back and stared at the ceiling, wishing she could blot out those days. "I had been so involved in myself, I had no idea what was happening at home. My parents were dying. It was the fever. Mother nursed Father and then she started to feel poorly. My sisters were doing all they could . . . it was a terrible time. They died within days of each other. In the middle of it, on her deathbed, Mother confronted me about Hemling. She'd heard the rumors." Again, her throat threatened to close. She'd never told anyone of this. She forced herself to speak. "She said I shamed the family. Those were her last words to me."

Hot tears flooded her eyes. She tried to will them back. She'd already cried more than she had in all her years combined.

Brandon came up over her. "Kate, stop this." His voice was stern. "Your mother was ill. Your family in desperation. You can't hold on to the words she said during that time."

"She knew what she was saying—"

"Yes, but did you tell her Hemling had forced you?"

"I couldn't."

"Kate, you must listen to me, *you were not at fault for what happened.* Do you understand?"

"I should have left immediately. You even thought that—"

"Because I was jealous and jumped to a conclusion that wasn't true. I was wrong, Kate. I was holding you to a different standard than I would have held myself. Hemling was evil. You were not at fault."

Kate stared at him in disbelief. "I could have left. I did leave—"

"The man held you emotionally, if not physically, hostage. It was not your fault," he repeated the last as if wanting to imprint the idea in her brain.

She started to protest again, and once more, he denied her. "You coped the best you could. You survived. You found yourself again. Can you forgive yourself, Kate? Hemling was wrong. He should have been lashed and quartered for what he did to you.

And I am to blame as well. I left. I should have had more faith in you."

Something that had been tightly wound inside her began to loosen. "I was not at fault."

"No. You were trying to do the best you could. The world is a confusing place and sometimes, we don't know the right answers immediately. Look what I did when I thought you chose another. I left the country. I upended my life."

"No, Hemling upended your life, just as he did mine."

"But now, we have a chance to reclaim what we once thought lost. You are on your way to London . . . and I'm holding you again." He pressed a kiss on her shoulder.

"I hate the thought that she died believing what she did about me."

"She knows the truth now. She probably knew it the moment she passed."

At the doubtful look Kate gave him, he said, "Come now, have you not ever felt your mother's presence in your life after her death?"

"She is gone, Brandon."

"Don't close your mind, Kate. Do you truly not ever feel her spirit?"

Kate looked at him with new eyes. "Sometimes," she admitted. "When I am about to step out on stage, I'll be nervous and I'll say a quick prayer . . . and then I pretend I can sense her. Actually, what I'm really doing is being superstitious."

"Because?"

"Because ghosts aren't real."

"I'm not claiming she is a ghost. That is superstitious. But don't you feel her influence?"

That was true. Kate rolled onto her side to face him. "Are you going to tell me a story that explains this?"

"I could. The world has many of them. In India, there is a sense that our ancestors are always with us. That people we love or respect and admire never die but live within us. I can see you don't quite believe me, so think of it this way—if you were your mother and you knew the full truth of what had happened to your daughter, would you blame your child?"

His reasoning astonished her even as the sense of his words settled inside her. He was right.

He was right.

Over a decade of recrimination and regret, of holding herself to a standard she believed she had failed, evaporated.

"She wouldn't have blamed me. My sister Alice knows the story and doesn't hold it against me. I've not heard a word from my other siblings. And if I did, well, we have all learned such hard lessons in life that I don't believe they would accuse me of being wanton. They haven't."

"Says the woman who is naked in my bed," Brandon answered, and Kate laughed at his parroting her words back to her.

"I *am* naked in your bed," she answered, pointedly. She moved toward him. "I am naked, and it has been a long time, Brandon."

"Too long," he answered and started to bring his lips down on hers in a kiss—however, before he could, she stopped him.

"Thank you," she whispered. "I needed someone to help me understand. I—"

He cut her off. "No more recriminations, Kate. Never apologize for surviving. Or wanting to live life to its fullest."

His lips found hers.

Chapter Thirteen

$\mathcal{T}$o all the world they were both strong souls—a grand lie, Bran realized.

He was as guilty as Kate of protecting his heart by not letting anyone close. Suddenly, he was tired of the pretense.

He had Kate in his bed. It was all he'd ever wanted.

Bran leaned her back onto the mattress, his lips finding hers. Her arms wrapped around him. Her legs opened, welcoming him.

He slid his arm beneath her, lifting her hips. He kissed her ear, her cheek, her neck. Her skin was velvet soft and tasted of rose petals and promise. He settled against her core, gently nudging to let her know he was there. Her hand smoothed over his buttocks, pressing him to her.

Their kiss became hungry and demanding.

Years ago, he'd not been an experienced lover. He'd been clumsy at best and overwhelmed by his own pleasure. It was a miracle that Kate remembered their time together with any fondness at all.

Now, he was going to make up for it. He slid into her. She was tight. Those muscles threatened to unman him. He caught his breath, holding himself as he felt her ease around him. She rocked her hips up, letting him sink deeper. Her quiet shudder of pleasure let him know he was exactly where she wanted him.

He began moving, and he was surprised to realize that his memory had not been wrong. There was something special about Kate. She was like no other.

She matched his rhythm. She was no practiced courtesan. Her movements were instinctive and yet, they drove him harder than he could drive himself.

Conscious thought left him. Primal need focused on the beautiful woman he held in his arms.

This was Kate. *His* Kate.

She had one arm around his shoulders. The fingers of her other hand curled in his hair as if she'd not let him escape.

He tried to hold back. He wanted this to be about Kate, and it was damned hard to keep his need at bay—

He felt the quickening in her. She tightened, arched. *"Bran."*

Her release was powerful. It radiated through her like ripples of water, carrying him with it. He was lost in the shimmering warmth until his own desire eclipsed it. With a hard thrust, reaching as deep in her as he could, he found his release.

Time halted. The force of life flowed between them.

He had no idea where he ended and she began. They had truly melded into one being. The whole world came down to this woman in his arms, and nothing else mattered. He held her as long as he could before the world intruded once again.

The chill of the night air skittered across his skin. Bran collapsed. Her legs were hooked around his hips, holding him to her. He could spend his life right here, and yet reality always had its way. He had to be crushing Kate. He eased off her, pulling her with him onto her side. He reached for the coverlet and flipped it over them.

She lay where he had left her. She appeared serene and peaceful, her lashes forming dark half-moons against her cheeks. He watched, thinking she was completely perfect.

Her eyes opened. Her gaze met his. "Dear Lord," she whispered reverently.

Bran grinned, pleased with himself. "We are good together, aren't we?"

"I'd forgotten."

"I had as well," he confessed.

In the haven of the coverlet, she turned to him, her hand resting on his chest. She wet her lips. Her every movement was fascinating to him.

And then she kissed him. Deeply, fully. Her telling kiss a ringing hosanna of praise.

With Kate in his arms, he fell asleep.

KATE'S BODY hadn't stopped humming from their lovemaking. She was unwilling to move or do anything to destroy her perfect sense of well-being.

It was as wonderful as she remembered. More so.

Hemling had almost destroyed her memories of that night in Brandon's bed. In truth, the aging marquis had rarely touched her after the rape. He had preferred parading her around as if she was some pet.

She ran her hand down over Brandon's arm. Her leg rested on top of his and she reveled in the intimacy of their position. She'd never felt shame being with him.

Brandon's large body took up most of the space on the bed. Her heart filled with tenderness as she watched him sleep. She would adore nothing more than to sleep beside him, and yet the time had come to leave.

She didn't want her actors to know of this. They would tease her unmercifully—they would see this as weakness. A man could take on lovers. A woman was held to a higher standard if she wanted respect.

Over the years, Kate had witnessed many independent-minded women who set their own rules, and there was always a price. Those who pretended to be widows usually fared well in the long run, even if they had many lovers.

Then there were others—never married—who didn't give two snaps of their fingers what people thought. Some acted in secret and others boldly, almost defying anyone to judge them. The bold ones always struck Kate as coarse. The secret ones made her wince at their weakness.

She had chosen a different path, an honest one to her way of thinking. She'd been celibate. She had never wanted to be seen as weak or coarse or to be pitied.

Of course there was speculation and gossip, but Kate lived in her own truth.

Nuzzling up against Brandon's warmth, she accepted that this was a new truth with which she must live.

Then there was the problem of the duke. She had no doubt he wouldn't take her choosing his uncle over him well. Perhaps the best course was to say nothing to Winderton, at least until she and Brandon could sort out what truly was happening between them. If he found out, he might impetuously throw his uncle out of these quarters and, while Kate had no doubt that Brandon could fend for himself, she didn't want to be the one to cause problems.

She leaned forward and kissed his cheek at the corner of his mouth. His lips curved into a sleepy smile. His arm draped around her waist, keeping her close to his body heat. She was tempted to stay right here forever, except she was a realist.

Gingerly, Kate slid out from under his arm, inching to the edge of the bed. She put a foot on the cold hardwood floor. They had thrown their clothes here and there. Fortunately she had not worn much. Still, it did take her a few precious minutes to locate her shoe from under the bed. She was thankful for the candle.

Brandon rolled over, gathering a pillow to him as if holding her. His sleep was deep and peaceful. She fought the urge to give him one last kiss.

She left the room. She did not look back.

The hall was very dark. With one hand on the wall, she felt her way to the staircase. Downstairs was as sparsely furnished as the upstairs. It was as if no one was living here. She passed a dining room with a table and chairs and yet there was nothing as a centerpiece. She wondered if that meant that Brandon wasn't here very often. She would have to ask him the next time she had an opportunity. She let herself out the back door.

The walk back to the tents did not take long. There was maybe an hour left before dawn although Kate was far from tired. In fact, she felt like dancing. She could have performed a reel right there in the middle of the forest and managed a few steps to prove her boast—

"It isn't like you to sneak around, Kate."

Silas's voice made her jump. She had just passed the line of trees and her tent was in sight. She slapped her mouth to keep from screaming. Kate whirled on him, her voice low. "You gave me a terrible fright. Why, I must have passed right by you without seeing you. What are you doing up?"

"I couldn't sleep. Not after Jess woke me to tell me you were missing." He kept his voice equally low. "Apparently she discovered you were not in your bed."

"Where is she now?"

"I assume in the tent, but she is probably listening for you. Thought you should be warned. She'll want to know where you have been."

"Thank you for that."

She started to turn except Silas asked, "Where *have* you been?"

Kate straightened. So, now the lying begins. "I couldn't sleep. I went for a walk. However, now, I find myself very tired. I'm for my bed. And you?"

He answered, "Kate, do you know what you are doing?"

"I don't know what you mean."

Silas took a step closer to her. "You do. I don't know where you've been. However, I have an idea of what you've been up to. Young men take on crazy ideas. They don't know boundaries. You are usually careful about such things."

He thought she'd been with Winderton. Kate decided not to correct him. Brandon was her secret.

It wasn't that she didn't trust Silas. It was that what she had experienced tonight with Brandon was very new and fraught with many potential hazards. Kate was a master at the art of being wary.

"I went for a walk, Silas. I appreciate you and Jess being concerned." She silently dared him to challenge her.

Seconds passed like minutes and then he stepped back. "Very well. As you say. A walk. I beg pardon."

"Thank you. You also need your sleep. We have a busy day ahead of us."

"Aye." There was a pause and then he said, "We will be going to London soon, won't we?"

"Of course."

He nodded and his features relaxed slightly.

"Come, let's go to bed." She spoke quietly and his shoulders suddenly sagged as if he, too, carried a great deal of worry.

Chances were he did. Silas was ever present. She didn't know how she could have made it over the past years without him. She tucked her hand in his arm and walked with him to the tents. At the door of the women's tent, she gave him a peck on his furrowed forehead. "We both worry too much, Silas. The plans have not changed. There is no duke in my future. And I am grateful for your care and concern." Those were the right words. He gave a short bow of his head and made his way to the men's quarters.

Kate went inside her tent. A cave could not be darker. Mary snuffled softly in her sleep. Jess appeared asleep, although who knew? Kate removed the cloak and pulled the dress over her nightgown. She climbed into her cot. It was a far cry from Brandon's mattress.

Her skin smelled of him. She stretched, recalling how it felt to have his body against hers, indentations that matched her own . . . the feel of him inside her.

And that was when she knew Jess was not asleep. She could feel the girl staring at her.

Her response was to turn on her side, giving Jess her back. In a blink, she fell into an easy sleep.

Bran woke surprised to see his bedroom was full of light. Usually he was up before dawn to give Orion a workout.

In truth, for the first time in what seemed ages, he felt fully rested—and then he remembered. Kate.

He was alone in his bed. There was even an indent in the mattress where she'd been.

Bran jumped up. His clothes were still on the floor; hers were gone.

A knock sounded on the door. "Who is it?"

"Randall, sir. Her Grace would like for you to come at your earliest convenience."

"Oh, bother," Bran said under his breath.

"Also, I brought over hot buns that Cook served at breakfast. You were missed this morning."

"Thank you," he said to the door. "Tell Her Grace, I will be over in the hour."

"Yes, sir."

Bran wasn't interested in what his sister had to say or the buns. He wanted to see Kate. Now that he was waking, he worried that she was upset with what had happened. After all, who knew the minds of women?

It didn't take long for him to dress. Chewing on a hot bun, he made his way to the main house by way of the stables where he asked for Orion to be made ready. This would give him a reason to excuse himself from Lucy.

His sister was waiting for him in her private quarters. He'd barely shut the door before she launched into him. "Christopher was out very late last night. Brandon, I'm worried. He seems more enamored of this actress than before. She has her talons in him. Worse, my friends, including Mrs. Warbler, have taken *a liking* to her."

"You needn't worry about Miss Addison and Christopher. There isn't anything there."

"Then where was he last night?"

"I don't know." Bran shrugged. "Perhaps at The Garland? There are usually lads over there."

"He is so secretive."

"Lucy, if you had been my mother, I would have been secretive as well."

"You sound as if I am doing something wrong. He is my son. He is the duke," she blustered. "He has responsibilities—"

"He is a young man. He will go after young men's pursuits."

"As long as it isn't *that* actress. You act as if you think me silly for my worries. Let me tell you, these things can become very messy. I'd rather have the matter under control *now* than deal with a by-blow later. We'd have to find someone to raise the child and, well, it is untidy. You know how bastards are."

"Not having had one, I will take your word for it."

"All you need do is look at Miss Taylor."

"Lucy, be kind. However, I can tell you with complete assurance that Christopher is not dallying with Miss Addison."

She pursed her lips at him, her brows rising. "I trust you, Brandon, except every one of my mother's instincts warns me that my son is in trouble."

"Then why don't you take him to London? He should be there this time of year. Let's utilize a geographic cure. Take him to the city as part of his duties and separate him from your concerns."

The purple ribbons on Lucy's black lace bonnet bounced as she shook her head. "Neither of us will go. I don't know if I can stand London anymore. Christopher is very much like me. He prefers the country."

It was on the tip of Bran's tongue to tell his sister to throw off her mourning, wear color, and move back into the stream of life. He also knew his words would set her off into a tirade about how unfeeling he was, and he did not want to put up with that this morning.

So, he tempered his voice and said, "Your fears about Miss Addison are groundless. Beyond that, there is little more that I can do." He took a step toward the door.

Lucy rose. "She has bewitched you as well, hasn't she?"

Bran didn't flinch from the accusation in her tone. "I admire Miss Addison."

"That is not how you spoke about her in the beginning."

It hadn't been. "You are working yourself up over nothing."

"One would think that people with good common sense could see what she is doing to Maidenshop. Everyone is lowering their standards."

"We lack your gift, Lucy," Bran said placatingly. "However, buck up. All will be well. And I must go. My horse is waiting for me."

"Oh, we can't let your horse wait . . . not when my son's immortal soul is at stake."

"When did you take on religion, Your Grace?"

That question caught her off guard. "I—I've always been of a serious state of mind."

"No, you are using everything you can to worry about your son. He will be fine. Furthermore, I am his guardian, and I am not worried. You have very little say here." On those words, Bran made his escape.

It was already late morning. An anxious Orion was being walked by a groomsman in front of the house. Bran mounted and set off for Kate.

He couldn't wait to see her. They needed to talk. He was curious as to why she left. He was also going to discuss with her the danger of walking around alone in the middle of the night. Maidenshop was one of the safest places in England but every woman should be careful, especially one as lovely as his Kate.

His Kate.

The title sang through him.

Given his head, Orion's hooves gobbled up the distance to the actors' encampment. Breaking the horse down to a trot, Bran scanned the gathering who were apparently rehearsing. He looked for signs of Kate.

He spied her talking to Christopher. His nephew stood on the stage, his hand resting on one cocked hip as if in deep consideration over whatever they were discussing.

Bran prayed she was telling his titled nephew that she didn't want to see him any longer. That would make Bran happy.

Then, at that moment, the couple laughed as if highly amused over something that had been said. The jealousy that shot through Bran was an evil thing.

He dismounted and tied Orion next to Winderton's horse. They nickered at each other and pressed noses.

Bran made his way to the stage. Kate must not have seen him approach because she gave no sign in his direction.

"The next playlet," she announced, "will be the fox and the lion. Nestor, you play the fox this time since you are already in the costume."

Christopher noticed Bran first. "It's Balfour," he called in greeting. He was in boyishly good humor. No wonder Lucy was suspicious. Bran would be himself if he hadn't known where Kate had been.

Kate glanced over her shoulder. "Ah, hello, Mr. Balfour." Her attention returned immediately to her actors. "John, Robbie, stand here. Yes, right there. Otherwise no one will see you."

And that was it. *Hello, Mr. Balfour.* No other greeting? No running into his arms? Not even a flirtatious wink?

Bran found himself watching the rehearsal with his nephew. Winderton was full of tidbits on acting. "We were talking about the staging of the play when they reach London," the duke said with great self-importance. "Certainly what they have now for set pieces won't make any impression."

That was true.

"I told her about the last play I saw. They actually had what looked like a full-size military frigate on the stage. Miss Addison is concerned about how she will afford set pieces that won't make them look provincial."

"For the play she is doing now?"

"Actually, the play to be performed in London will be *The Tempest*. She believes she needs the Bard to establish herself."

So, there would be a storm and a magic forest.

During the afternoon performance, Bran found ideas floating in his head for ways he could use his understanding of mechanics and architecture to create those scenes. The set pieces needed to be both economical and yet able to engage an audience on a grand scale.

At last his patience in waiting for Kate paid off when he managed a moment alone with her. He caught her as she was leaving the women's tent. She reached for his hand, clasping it tight. He leaned his head toward hers. "We should tell Winderton about us."

Her troubled gaze met his. "And then what will happen?"

"He will be upset but he is young. He will recover."

"Or we shall be run out of the country and, I have no doubt, there will be a disastrous scene between the two of you."

She was right.

Kate faced him. "I would not have you thrown out of your living quarters because of me. What is between us is too new, too fresh. Perhaps it would be wiser for us to keep ourselves secret until we understand exactly what we are about."

He knew what he was about—he wanted Kate. It was that simple . . . or was it?

At that moment, Reverend Summerall came driving up with a vicar from a neighboring church and their wives. Kate had to greet them. The reverend wished to expound upon the religious principles of *Aesop's Fables*. She smiled at the clergymen. "One moment please," she said before glancing back to Bran. "We shall discuss your offer later, Mr. Balfour." She acted as if they had the barest of acquaintances, and yet, there was a warmth in her eyes that held a promise.

"Yes, later," he agreed, blandly. She wasn't the only one of them who could pretend.

Reverend Summerall began telling all what a remarkably talented actress Kate was as if he had forgotten her performance at the Cotillion Dance. Bran bowed out, moving toward his horse. Winderton fell into step beside him.

"You and Miss Addison are acting more charitably toward each other than in the beginning," Christopher said.

Bran studied his nephew. The duke didn't seem angry or offended. If he suspected a closeness between Bran and Kate, he would not be so pleasant. "Is that not good?"

"It is excellent. I wish Mother would come around. She fears I will run away with an actress. As if I would be so foolish or treat Miss Addison so shabbily."

"That is comforting." For a second, Bran was tempted to tell Christopher that Kate was his, that he had claimed her.

Then, he realized, Kate was right. His nephew would consider it a betrayal. There would be an uproar. Some things might come out that needed to be dealt with sensitively.

Not for the first time, he questioned his sister's wisdom about keeping the news of the title's past perilous finances from Winderton. To be honest, in those early days after his return from India, Bran had been more interested in building his engineering firm than in thinking her edicts through.

His goal had been to repair the Winderton fortunes and he was doing a nice job. A tidy sum was starting to grow under Winderton's name. If the duke was prudent and wise, which actually meant if the duke continued to take Bran's advice, then he could have a substantial fortune to pass on to his heirs.

Bran had not regretted supporting the Winderton estate. He had more money than he needed.

However, now, he realized that he may have gone too long without telling his ward the truth. Especially since even Kate thought he lived on the generosity of the duke instead of vice versa.

But Kate was right when she warned against telling him about their love—this was not the right time. Young men had hot heads. Who knew how the duke would react when he learned that not only was his uncle sleeping with the woman he adored—but that he was also financially dependent on that uncle as well?

Then again, it was past time for Winderton to start to understand that his mother was wrong—the sun didn't circle around him.

Still, that was not a conversation Bran looked forward to.

He *did* look forward to seeing Kate again.

That night, he waited in the woods surrounding her tents for her. It was late when she finally came out. She was surprised to see him step in her path.

"Is something wrong? Why are you here?" she asked.

"I didn't want you to walk through the woods by yourself," he said taking her into his arms. Their kiss was full of promise . . . and their lovemaking that night in his bed was better than the evening before.

Chapter Fourteen

𝒯he nights that followed were magical to Kate.

Brandon was always thinking of ways to please her. He'd have special suppers prepared in the main house and set up in his own dining room, just for the two of them.

There were stuffed figs and perfectly cooked cold beef served with a mustard sauce and warm, fragrant bread. Nuts, cheese, and apples were the dessert and it was all washed down with a fine red wine.

"Do the servants mind working for you?" Kate asked.

"They never complain," Brandon answered. "And I always see to the gratuities."

Those words made her happy. They showed that even though Brandon lived on his nephew's estate, he seemed willing to care for himself.

One night after they'd finished their meal, he'd prepared a bath with soaps that smelled of lemon and lavender. The tub was the largest that Kate had ever seen and easily accommodated both of them—well, until they started making love in it.

They created a terrible mess of his bedroom that night. Water was sloshed everywhere. "You will have to tip the servants even more."

"Aye, I will," Brandon said, drying her off before lifting her up and carrying her to the bed where he made love to her again . . . and again.

They could not have enough of each other.

And when they weren't making love, they were talking about everything. Brandon shared his frustrations with the bridge commission and how difficult it was to start over.

"You were respected in India?" Kate's head rested on his chest.

"Well respected, yes. Of course, I had to work for it."

"You will have to work for it here."

He reacted as if her answer surprised him and then he smiled ruefully. "You are right. I just don't like the struggle. Not at this point of my life. Marsden assures me that the committee hasn't ruled me out completely."

"What does the earl have to do with the committee?"

He pressed a kiss to the top of her hair. "He took up my cause when he learned that Lord Dervil had promoted his man in my place. Dervil and Marsden are sworn enemies."

"Because?"

"Dervil shot his father—"

"What?" Kate started to sit up but Brandon held her down.

"It was a duel over a property line. The two families have been neighbors for centuries and have been at each other's throats for that length of time. Then I did something to upset him."

"What?"

"I convinced Lucy not to sell Smythson to Dervil. Mars believes Dervil campaigned against me as a way of striking back."

"Do you think that is true?"

Brandon lay there a long moment, his hand moving down to her shoulder where he drew lazy circles with his finger. "I have no idea," he said at last.

Something in his tone sparked her curiosity. She raised her head. "Do you want to build bridges?"

"I've built many of them."

"Yes, but do you want to build them?"

"Say, over roads or buildings. I designed those as well."

"And are they what you want to build?"

The movement of his hand stopped. "It is what I do."

"You also tell stories," Kate reminded him. "You collect them." Sometimes, after they had made love, he would tell some tale he'd tucked away. Her favorites were the ones he'd learned in India. They were like the mythic tales he had shared with her years ago.

"I'm not a writer," he told her. "I'd be bored. I like my stories already written."

Kate sat up. "And yet, when you tell them, there is a very visual strength to them."

"I doubt if there is money in repeating other people's stories."

There it was. The simple fact of his life—and hers. Money was important. "I hope the Earl of Marsden is correct and you still can build your bridge."

His response was to kiss her down to the mattress and for the next hour, they were very busy.

Kate discovered that in spite of her nocturnal activities, she wasn't tired during the days. Brandon would walk her back to her tent right before dawn. She would sneak into her cot and manage a few hours' sleep until she needed to be up for work.

Granted, she didn't continue her normal pattern. In the past, she was usually the first up. Now, she often slept later than Jess, the laziest person in the troupe.

Of course it was noticed. And all the actors, save Silas, teased her. Kate could sense his worry, even though they didn't speak about what she was about. He may have thought her smart, but that did not mean he thought her wise.

However, he was not living her life.

And it was so easy to believe that all would be well, especially since she was falling in love with Brandon. He dominated her thoughts. At different times during the day, she caught herself yearning for his touch or anxious to see his tall presence approaching and having him close at hand.

The dream of reclaiming her place on the London stage no longer held the same allure. Her overpowering resentment at the past was fading, as was her need to prove herself. London didn't seem all that important . . .

HER LAUGHTER rang through the room. Kate had tried to kick him out of bed because he'd complained about her stealing the covers and Bran's response had been to grab her foot by the ankle and pull her toward him.

"No," she begged, holding on to the other side of the cotton mattress. They were both naked.

"You do not throw me out of the bed. Or steal all the covers," he announced, coming up on his knees and jumping on her like a rowdy boy.

Kate warded him off with bent knees as he tried to tickle her. When he rolled onto his back, she was the one who tried to tickle him and gave a delighted shout when she realized he did have one very ticklish spot. She sat on top of him, tickling, laughing—

And that was the moment he fell in love.

Oh, he'd been in love with her, but he was quickly learning there were many types of love. There was the love of her body, of their union—and this was the love of *her*. He admired her mind, her drive, her determination, and the special sparkle that made her who she was. This was the sort of love that lasted an eternity.

He caught her wrists, his sides hurting from laughing. He held her arms out, looking up into her face. In that moment, he knew he wanted nothing more in his life than to hear her laughter every day. He would let her rob the covers from him every night, if it meant keeping her with him forever.

She had noticed how still he'd grown. Smiling down at him, her hair messy from their love play, she asked, "What? Why do you stare at me that way?"

Because I love you. "Because I've seen nothing more beautiful."

Kate sat back as if his words had touched her. "Perhaps you feel that way because I am *naked*," she suggested, wagging her eyebrows with a devilish grin as if teasing him.

"It's possible," he answered. "Or it could be because your passion matches my own."

"And by the last you mean what?" Oh, she knew, but he wasn't to let such an invitation pass with just words.

"This." He lifted her hips and slid her down over him.

Kate's eyes widened. She squeezed him and he thought he'd be undone before they'd started. Gently, he guided her on how to move, on what he liked. Her head fell back in pleasure. "I do so like this," she whispered before catching her breath in a moan.

And I love you, he wanted to say. The words never passed his lips. He was not ready to be so vulnerable.

Instead, he showed her.

"WHAT SURPRISE do you have for me?" Kate asked.

"You will find out," Brandon answered. "Just follow me."

He led her down the stairs of the Dower House. She was wearing his shirt and nothing else. Even her feet were bare. For his part, Brandon wore just his breeches. He carried a candlestick.

He led her into what should have been the front room of the house. There was no furniture in it save for a large table and a chair.

There were two more candlesticks on the table. He lit them. Golden light filled the room and fell on the large sheets of paper spread out on the table.

"This is what I want you to see," he said, gently pushing her into the chair in front of the table. "These are my thoughts on set pieces for *The Tempest.*"

"Your what?"

"You were telling me what you envisioned for the play and I thought I would make a few drawings."

Kate looked at the scenes on the paper—and was charmed.

He crossed around to the other side of the table. "I know it is set on an island, however, I picture a forest on the island. A magical forest." He tapped one of the pages.

She pulled it out and gasped in appreciation. The trees he'd designed were indeed magical. In their bark were the faces of mythical creatures. The same was true of the rocks.

"This is clever. Very clever," Kate said wonderingly. The mythic element would quickly bring the audience's imaginations into the play.

"You like?" He acted relieved.

"I like very much."

"Here is the tempest scene," he said, referring to the storm that was at the beginning of the play. The set was in the same shape as the forest except now there were waves with, again, sea sprites and sirens hidden in them. "Actually, what I've done is created four-sided pillars on wheels that turn. You can reposition them at different areas of the stage. Turn this piece around and it is the forest you just looked at. Here is another scene for another part of the island. Then, the fourth side of the two pillars will be painted stones." He drew out another paper. "This is for Prospero's prison or it can be the masque."

"Brandon, this is wonderful." She could do this. Her troupe could copy these designs. They were made only of painted wood; the brilliance came from his fanciful drawings, which could be easily copied.

"Excellent," he said and gave her a smile that said he was both pleased and modest about his work. He rolled the drawings up and tied them with ribbon. He offered them to her.

Kate was humbled. "Thank you. This is an incredible gift."

"I'm glad you like them. I had some worries."

"I more than like them. They are brilliant. I wasn't certain what I was going to do in London. I can afford the pillars you designed. Your talent is wasted drawing bridges and roadways. So is your imagination."

"Really?" He made a face as if he was a bit surprised at himself.

"Yes, really."

"And exactly, how much do you like my drawings?"

Kate laughed and walked around the table to him. She put her arms around him. He pressed against her and she felt the length of his arousal. He'd left the top button of his breeches unbuttoned. She undid the second one, feeling the smooth skin of his head. "I like them very much."

"Very?" He lifted her up to sit on the table and took a stance between her open legs.

Kate wrapped her arms around his neck and her legs around his hips. "Let me show you how much." She undid another button and he leaned her back.

There was no coyness between them, just a blazing desire—

A strong premonition that something was wrong gripped her. It was a warning, a sense that they might not be alone.

He immediately noticed her distraction. He stopped, their bodies joined. "Is something wrong?"

She glanced around the room. There were no drapes on the windows. The outside world was dark. She listened to the quiet. "Are we alone?"

"Yes."

She frowned. "Do you sense anything? Such as perhaps we are not? I feel as if someone is watching us."

His response was to blow out the candles, plunging them into darkness. He'd stepped back, their lovemaking forgotten, and pulled up his breeches. "Wait here."

He went outside. When he returned, he said, "I could find no one. Would you rather go upstairs?"

"I believe so," Kate admitted. And shortly, she put the whole thing out of her mind as Brandon and she resumed the activity that was her very favorite.

Later, as he escorted her back to the tents, she tried to look deep into the darkness of the woods. No one jumped out at them. Still, she was unsettled with a sense of foreboding that she couldn't quite shake.

They had reached the line of trees. He kissed her. She put a protective hand over the designs she held in her arms, not wanting him to crush them. Her action made him smile, and then he gave her arms a squeeze as if wanting to hold on to her before saying, "I want to be open about us. I don't want to hide you."

She frowned. "What does that mean, Brandon?"

"Mean?"

She took a step away from him. "What are you offering?"

"To tell Winderton about us."

"Oh, yes." *Of course* he was talking about letting the duke know. And what would Brandon say? That she was his mistress? Kate experienced a surprising stab of disappointment. "Don't tell Winderton anything—not unless—" She paused.

"Unless what, Kate?"

You wish to marry me.

The unconscious thought startled her. She wasn't the kind of woman a gentleman married. Men like her father were rare. Even her mother had said as much. And yet, there it was, her deepest desire. An impossible one.

"Unless the time is right," she answered. She was tired, she realized. Overwhelmed actually . . . and felt deflated. "Thank you for the drawings." She began moving toward the tents.

"I'll see you this evening?" he asked.

She nodded without turning around.

Inside her tent, Mary and Jess were sleeping. Kate quickly undressed and climbed into her cot. She glanced over at the other women. Mary appeared relaxed while Jess was sleeping on her side, something she didn't do very often—or were Kate's nerves stretched so thin she truly was looking for beasties everywhere?

She turned onto her side and ignored the tear that ran down her cheek. No good was going to come from her liaison with Brandon. At least, she was honest enough with herself to admit it. For a bit, she'd let herself believe all would be right. She knew now she wanted more than he could give. He was too proud a man to take on a wife he couldn't support . . . or one who, well, who would bring very little to a marriage.

And if he made an offer to keep her as his mistress? If he'd put such an offer into words?

She was no longer certain of her answer.

SOMETHING WAS bothering Kate. Bran blamed himself. Why had he even started that conversation?

It was because of the drawings. The set pieces were his gift to her. He'd been pleased that she'd liked them. However, it was only when she was looking at them that he realized she was going to leave Maidenshop. She was going to leave him.

Bran raked a hand through his hair. Something was not right between them, and he didn't know what it was save that he was desperate to resolve it.

Should he not have done the drawings?

She had walked off to the tents without looking back. Always before she'd at least give him a glance and would often return for one more kiss. Not this morning.

Or was she tired? They didn't sleep much. And he wouldn't apologize for his gift. She had been pleased. Kate could not have faked her reaction.

In fact, after seeing how happy she was, his mind began working on new sets. The blank stage she was working with for her *Aesop's Fables* was serviceable . . . but what if he designed some pieces that would convey a sense of Ancient Greece? Village crowds would like that, especially if it was something no other acting troupe had.

He also could do something about the costumes. In India, he'd been fascinated by some of the dances he'd seen, where the performers often wore masks to convey the characters they portrayed.

In fact, as he walked back to the Dower House, his imagination was alive with ideas. This was more fun than designing bridges and roads. He'd sketch a few of his thoughts and show them to her tonight. Masks would take up very little room in the theater wagon and could add so much more to their performances.

Then Kate would understand he was committed to her. He supported what she was doing. He wanted her to be happy—

A weight plowed into him, almost knocking him to the ground and crashing him into a tree.

Stunned, Bran was shocked to see that Winderton had attacked him. His nephew stood in front of him, his face outlined in fury. His hands went for Bran's throat.

"You bloody bastard. I saw you on the table with Kate Addison. How dare you put your hands on her."

Chapter Fifteen

Christopher was young and strong. However, Bran was heavier and more experienced. He brought his arms up, breaking his nephew's attempt to choke him. Bran then shoved the duke away from him. Winderton's heel caught on a tree root and he went sprawling onto the ground.

Doubling his fist, Bran stood over him. "Don't dare get up, not until you tell me what this is about." His head and back hurt from being slammed against the tree. He was willing to give his nephew a schooling he'd not soon forget.

"I saw you with her," Winderton shot out, half rising as if in defiance.

"Saw what?"

"You and Kate Addison, in the Dower House, on the table. I saw you. Or don't you remember?"

So, Kate's sense that they were being watched was not wrong.

"You damned weasel," Bran answered. "You were creeping around where I live."

"No, I was finding the truth about you."

"The truth about me?" Bran could have laughed, and then realized that perhaps this was good. The time had come to let Christopher know that his pursuit of Kate was over. Bran lowered his fists. "Well, now you know. And you'd best not say anything about it. After all, a lady's reputation is at stake." Kate would be deeply embarrassed if she learned they had been seen.

Winderton scrambled up to his feet. "Lady?" He spat the word out, poised to attack again.

Bran raised his fists. "Go ahead," he said to his ward. "You do remember that I'm known around boxing saloons as a good fighter. Insult Kate and I'll enjoy hitting you."

The duke seemed to weigh his odds and then pulled back, his face pinched and pale. "I want you gone from Smythson. You are no longer welcome under my roof. You will leave immediately. And you will have nothing to do with Miss Addison."

"Ah, there you are wrong." Bran lowered his fists and decided that now was as good a time as any to deliver some home truths. "If you were peeping in the window—"

"*I was not peeping.*"

"What word would you like? Does *spying* sound better?"

"I was . . ." Christopher's voice trailed off.

"What? What were you doing?"

"*I love her.* She is *mine.*" He thumped his chest on the last word and Bran had to keep himself from laughing. Apparently Christopher was as dramatic as his mother.

"Yours? You don't own her. She makes her own choices."

"I tell you, I *love her.*" He sounded ridiculously noble.

Bran made an impatient sound. "You can love her . . . but she decides who she loves in return."

"Which would be me if you hadn't interfered."

"There, see? You know she doesn't return your affections."

The duke did not like that comment. "I know *nothing* of the sort."

"You must, Christopher, or you wouldn't be so bloody angry with me. I knew Kate years ago, back when I was as young as you. We have a history between us." He didn't speak unkindly. He understood heartache.

"You are such—" The duke broke off his sneer as if he couldn't think of a suitable epithet to call Bran.

"Yes, I am," was Bran's agreeable answer. "And I actually understand quite well the pain you are in right now. You will recover and how we continue forward will depend a great deal on your maturity. After all, I am your uncle, and for a few months more, still your guardian."

"I will have nothing to do with you."

"That is not in your control, Your Grace. We are family."

"Family doesn't do what you've done to me."

That barb hit its mark. "You are right," Bran said soberly. "And yet, Kate is free to choose her lovers."

For a second, it appeared as if Winderton would charge him again, and then his manner changed. "All this time, you and she were laughing at me."

"No, not that, Christopher. We were going to tell you." Eventually, possibly.

Winderton drew himself up. He appeared almost ducal. "I meant what I said. I want you gone from Smythson. You will leave the Dower House immediately."

Bran sighed. This was the moment when things would grow truly uncomfortable. He would not keep the secret any longer. The time had arrived. "I will not leave, Your Grace."

"You don't have a choice. I ordered you."

"Actually, I do have a choice. I own Smythson. You can't throw me off the property."

"*You what?*"

"I own Smythson. I purchased the estate right after I arrived from India to assume my role as your guardian."

"You couldn't have purchased it. I would have known that."

"The house was not properly entailed and your father had accumulated crippling financial obligations. After his death, Her Grace had no choice but to sell or the estate would have gone to the debtors. The title is yours, but the property is not."

"You're lying."

"I wish I was. I bought up the notes against the house that your father had signed. If I had not, Dervil was after them."

"I didn't own my house?"

Bran nodded. "Or any of the lands around it. Your father was a terrible manager of his affairs."

The duke snarled as if to protest, and then a new insult hit him. "Why was I not told?"

"Now, *that* is a fair question. For the answer, you will need to talk to your mother. I can only explain my part."

"Which is?" The bark in the young duke's voice was quickly becoming annoying.

"Which is that your mother asked me to keep it quiet. I believe she wished to save face. She's a proud woman. Too proud," Bran had to admit. "I agreed because you were young and you had been close to your father. It was hard losing him." And Bran had remembered how he'd felt when his own father had died. He'd been about the same age as Christopher. "Also, London is full of shallow people. Knowledge of the state of your finances could have had repercussions that Lucy and I both wished to avoid."

The duke shook his head. "We didn't have money?" he repeated in disbelief.

"Not when compared to your debts."

"I remember there was some rumor going around school that my school fees weren't paid. Did you pay them?"

Bran did not like the challenge in his ward's voice but he did not back away from the truth. He was done with it. "I paid them." Bran took a step toward him. "I also believe you need to know the whole. As your guardian, I have been managing your affairs. I meant to sit down with you to explain matters before your birth date. Then again, this is a good time to share the gist of what I've done."

"Which is?"

"Smythson is a profitable estate. Mr. Hamlin has proven himself to be an excellent manager. You have money now invested in the funds and your renters are paying in a timely manner, something they weren't doing before I hired Mr. Hamlin. They also act pleased with his management. In time, with careful and frugal consideration, you will restore your family's fortunes."

The duke considered his words a moment, his brows drawn down in a frown. "As long as I do what you say, correct?"

Sensing the tension in the question, Bran answered neutrally, "You may do as you wish. Soon it will all be under your control."

"But I can't throw you off of *my* estates?"

"Well, you will be able to do so after you reimburse me for what I've spent. I would be happy to return Smythson back to you. I have no need of it." Besides, he had not saved Smythson for an investment. He'd purchased the notes because the duke was family.

"I see." Christopher stood still a moment, a young man processing his future. "And you are telling me I can't have Miss Addison?"

Steel came to Bran's voice. "I have no control over Kate. Neither do you."

His nephew's nostrils flared and Bran realized he'd made an enemy. "I have no doubt that you are angry with me," he told Winderton. "You might even hate me." The duke made no comment. "I made decisions to protect you. All were discussed with Her Grace."

"But not with me."

Bran wouldn't have liked being treated in such a manner either. Too late, he saw the error he and Lucy had made. "As I said, you may not believe this, or agree with the decisions, Your Grace, but I've had only your best interests at heart."

"Including about Kate?" This was the first time Bran had heard Winderton use Kate's given name.

"Definitely about Kate."

"I loved her." The young man's words hung in the air.

Bran met his eye. "I can understand why. And now, I'm going to leave. I'm tired—"

"I imagine so after what I saw—"

In one single beat, Bran's hand shot out and closed around the duke's shirt front. He dragged his nephew forward. "You will *not* hurt Kate and you will say *nothing* of what you saw to anyone. If you do, Winderton, then I will wash my hands of you and expose all the secrets that your mother has so carefully guarded."

To his credit, Winderton didn't back down. "I love her. Can you say the same?"

Bran released his hold. He took a step back, and then walked away without looking back.

However, at the Dower House, he found himself irritable over the confrontation. He should have gone to bed, but his mind would not turn off.

In truth, Bran had no regrets over informing Christopher of his inheritance. For too long the lad had been kept in the dark. Well, now he knew the truth of things and if he had any pride at all, he'd be rightly humbled.

And the duke wasn't wrong in asking what Bran's intentions were toward Kate.

He wondered about them himself. What did he want? What did she expect of him?

He found a bowl of apples in the kitchen next to yesterday's leftover buns. He munched on a piece of fruit as he walked toward the front room. The candlesticks were still on the table where he'd done his drawings, right where they had left them the night before.

He thought of Kate sitting on the table wearing nothing but his shirt. He could offer her everything her heart desired—and she'd throw it in his face.

Unless he offered marriage? For the first time, Bran wondered what would happen if he married an actress?

Lucy would scream. He could live with that.

He'd lose his membership in the Logical Men's Society, although he believed Mars and Thurlowe would wish him well. He could still turn up at The Garland for pints of ale when the mood struck him or for the lectures of scientific interest Ned was determined to arrange for the village. Actually, he was beginning to think the premise behind the Society was faulty.

Standing in the middle of an empty house, he realized he *wanted* Kate in his life.

If he married her, not only was he honoring her with his name, he'd have her forever.

Forever. The word pleased him. They had already wasted fifteen years—and he didn't wish to waste any more.

The sound of a horse and carriage interrupted his thoughts. He looked outside and saw the brougham pull up with Lucy inside. She was dressed in her black and purple. The liveried driver jumped down to open the door for her.

Bran crossed to the front door to open it. Before he could reach for the handle, the door flew open. Lucy stormed in, her arms pumping with her fury. *"You told him.* You should *not* have told him."

Bran had no doubt about who "him" was. "Come in, Your Grace. Would you like something to drink?"

His sister's eyes appeared ready to skewer him for his insolence. "I want *nothing* to drink. I want *answers.* Why did you tell him without consulting me?"

"Are you talking about the state of his affairs? Or my liaison with Miss Addison?"

Lucy went rigid. Her head circled in the air as if she was ready to swoon. She found her grounding. "Liaison?" She took a deep breath. "I don't want to know what you do with that harlot—"

"Careful. I will not have you speak ill of her."

"How can you defend her? She broke my son's heart."

"She didn't encourage him. I watched her. She was circumspect. He encouraged himself." Bran stopped, puzzled. "Wait, Lucy, I thought you wanted your son away from her?"

"I did not want him *rejected.*"

"You aren't making sense. Dear God, I could use a drink."

"Winderton wants you to leave. He has ordered it."

That was beyond enough. "I'm not leaving, Lucy."

"You can't stay here."

Bran stared at his sister. "I own here."

"I denied everything you said," she announced.

"Helpful of you, Your Grace."

"I wouldn't have had to do it if you hadn't talked to him without discussing the matter with me first."

"And did he believe you?"

"You know he didn't."

"I definitely need a drink for this conversation. Where is that port? Do you wish one?" he asked his sister.

"Of course not," she snapped. "And why are you walking off when I am talking to you?"

"Then follow," he threw over his shoulder.

Reaching the pantry, he uncapped the decanter. He took a cup and poured himself a generous measure.

Lucy appeared at the pantry door. "I've never seen Winderton so upset. He's young—"

"He's coddled. He needs to be out in the world." Bran downed the drink. "He also needs to understand that nothing is handed to a man just because he has a title. He must earn his rightful place, not whine about it."

Lucy frowned like a hen eyeing a distasteful worm. "What has come over you? You sound angry. And I should mention that he, too, is drinking hard spirits this early in the morning. See? He isn't that coddled."

"Drinking does not make a man."

His sister shrugged. "Says you with a drink in your hand."

Her words reminded Bran of his and Kate's game about being "naked." He wished Kate was here instead of Lucy. His sister was infuriating, and Bran was tired. Too much was happening over which he had no control. "Lucy, nothing happened to Christopher other than that his pride was bruised which isn't a bad thing for any of us from time to time. You didn't want him with Kate Addison. Well, he isn't with her. But *I* am."

"And I am supposed to be at peace with that?"

"You aren't supposed to be anything. It is my life."

She made a disgruntled sound. "Next thing I know, you will be telling me *you* want to marry her."

"I do."

He'd answered without conscious thought. The words had just flowed out. Bran frowned, examining what he'd just said and discovered it was true. He did wish to marry Kate. He certainly wasn't going to allow her to go to another man. She was *his*.

Lucy appeared horrified. "Are you mad? She's as old as you are."

He was still trying to overcome his own shock at his statement. "You are right. She is old."

"You won't have any children."

"Possibly. I haven't ever felt the need for any."

"Younger women are more biddable."

"They would bore me."

Lucy rocked back throwing her hands up in the air. "The world has gone mad," she muttered. "It is as if no one knows their place anymore. Or values their class."

"I make my own place, Lucy. I'm the son of a younger son."

"That doesn't mean you throw all opportunities away with a misalliance."

"I could see how you would declare the duke was making a misalliance, though I might not agree with you. But that's not the point here, I just want to marry the woman I love. The woman I've *always* loved."

"This is not going to sit well with His Grace. He is inconsolable. He's saying all sorts of outlandish things."

"And he will for a while. But he will recover. He will find some-one else to love. Kate is mine."

Lucy had to hyperventilate a moment. Bran ignored her, walking back to the front room. His earlier restlessness was gone, replaced by certainty. He was in love. This was what love felt like. He could even imagine their future. They'd set up house together. She'd quit the theater. Take care of him. This was not a bad plan. Being in love was convenient.

"And what of Christopher?" Lucy asked. She leaned against the hallway wall.

"He will be angry but this is a lesson Winderton needs to learn—"

"Angry? He is furious. Especially about your money. He demanded to know what we have been living on since the estate isn't in his name."

"Did you tell him?"

She looked stricken. "I had no choice. I told him about the allowance you gave us."

"And he didn't take that well."

"Did you not hear me? He is livid. He went running out of the house like a madman. I don't know where he has gone. I don't know what he is doing. Could we not have kept it our secret—at least a bit longer?"

"We kept it a secret too long. Here is the push he's needed to go out into the world—"

Lucy interrupted him with a mother's cry of alarm. "I like him *in Maidenshop.*"

"Maidenshop is too small a place for him. He should be in London."

"Where there are *more* actresses. Who knows what trouble he will find for himself? Just like his father did. What if he has a penchant for gambling the way his father did?"

There was the root of Lucy's fears. "I will talk to him."

"Right now he despises you."

"Right now, if he is anything like he was an hour or so ago, he is drunk. Once he sobers up and accepts that Kate's not for him, then we can discuss his future. I told him I have no desire to keep Smythson. But before I let go, he has to know how to manage a property such as this and be responsible enough to do so."

Large tears welled in his sister's eyes. "Come, Lucy, stop this. All will be well."

"For you and your actress, perhaps. If you have your way, my son will be in the city, but what about me, Brandon? Everyone will be leaving me."

Here it was, the heart of the matter . . . and he'd believed her fears were for her son. "Your Grace," he kept his tone soft, compassionate, "the time has come to set aside your mourning. No woman could have been a better wife to your husband than you. However, rusticating here is not doing you good. You would also benefit from a bit of Town bronze. You can stay at my house since the place Winderton owns is not comfortable." Or truly habitable. Gone were the days when the Duke of Winderton kept two staffs, one for the country and one for the city. "You can call on old friends."

"They have all forgotten me. No one likes young widows."

"Perhaps, but they do like single duchesses."

"I'm a *dowager*." Her wail made it sound as if it was a crime.

"Lucy, let go of the black. Come back into the world. Who knows what adventure awaits you?"

A tear she had struggled to hold back slipped down her cheek. He wiped it away. "All will be well," he promised.

"Even if it is not," she admitted sadly, "the damage has been done."

"Or we have opened ourselves up to embrace the new."

"I don't want to sit at a table with an actress."

"Then we won't see each other often."

"I don't wish that."

"Don't think too far ahead," he advised. "I will go to Winderton after he has had a chance to sober up and try to make him see the bright side of all this."

"I pray you do." She walked out the door like an aristocrat facing the guillotine—resolute, tragic, forlorn.

Bran walked to the door and watched the footmen help his sister into the vehicle. He waved as they drove away before closing the door.

His first impulse was to go to Kate, to tell her he wanted to marry her. He decided against it. The hour was too early and his love was probably trying to catch some sleep, something he needed as well.

LUCY BOUNCING on the bed woke Bran.

At first, he thought he was dreaming. He felt like he'd just closed his eyes.

She proved she wasn't a dream by shaking his shoulder. "Brandon, *wake up.* Wake up!"

"What?" He was never good first thing after sleep. "Lucy, what are you doing here?"

"I've come to say that you are wrong. You said that all would be well. *It isn't.*"

"And why is it not?"

His sister held out a letter. "This is from Winderton. I found it on the desk in his room. If I hadn't just happened to go in there, I would never have seen it."

"Lucy, you go into his room several times a day."

"No matter. He writes to inform me he has eloped with his actress." She dropped the letter on his chest. "Do you wish to tell me now how everything will be fine?"

Chapter Sixteen

"*W*hat?" Bran picked up the letter. It was Winderton's hand. He was very direct:

> *My life has been a lie—*

"That is dramatic of him," Bran muttered. "I wonder whom he takes after."

Lucy snorted her opinion.

> *—I seek my own purpose in life—*

"Another piece of nonsense," Bran observed.

> *—I am eloping with the woman I love. I'll repay you for the horses once I'm established.*

There was no signature.

Bran stared at the words. "Kate wouldn't have said yes."

"Apparently she has."

"She wouldn't."

"She did."

Bran crushed the letter in his hand. "She couldn't."

But she could. She had done it before. With Hemling. Only he had forced her.

Could Winderton be that crass? If he attempted to harm Kate in any way, Bran would kill him.

Nor did it help that old doubts resurfaced. It had taken him a month to leave London and she'd stayed with Hemling the whole time and longer, by her own admission.

The woman he loved. Winderton had only loved Kate.

"His Grace took two horses from the stables," Lucy said. "He told the stable lads to saddle Lolly because the lady who would be using her was not accustomed to hard riding. And then he set off in the direction of the actors."

"When was this?"

"Four hours ago."

Four hours? "What time is it?"

"Half past two."

Bran could catch them. "It isn't Kate with him. She wants to go to London."

"As a duchess, which is what she'll be if they marry, she may go wherever she wishes."

Her statement brought him up short. Jealousy was an ugly emotion. Bran didn't want to feel it, and yet it was there.

Kate couldn't have chosen to go with Winderton. Bran refused to believe it—which meant she could be in trouble.

He sat up and reached for his breeches, the sheet across his lap. "You may wish to turn around."

Seeing he was about to stand, his sister gave a squeak and quickly stepped out into the hall. She half closed the door, her back to it, so that she could speak to him. "I warned you that my son was going to do something irrational."

"None of it makes sense," he muttered.

"It does. He's run away with that actress. She's agreed to go. Why did you tell him the truth? *Why?*"

Because Winderton was not a bloody child, he wanted to retort.

Instead, he swore under his breath and buttoned his breeches. In fact, in all of Winderton's complaints this morning, the one issue he was right about was that his uncle and mother should have been more honest with him. "When did you last see Winderton?"

"Shortly before I confronted you this morning. I went searching for him around eleven. I was worried. He was so quiet. He wouldn't talk to me when I tried to discuss the matter civilly after speaking to you. He wouldn't even open the door to his rooms."

There was probably no "civilly" about what she had to say. "Well, Miss Addison is on the stage at this moment. So, if you are right and she has run off with him, he is still at her theater."

"How can you be so certain?"

"I know Kate. She won't miss a performance."

"Men are such goats. They think they know everything." She threw this out in disgust while giving him an evil eye through the crack in the door.

Bran's response was to shut the door. "I'll be ready in a few minutes."

She stomped down the hall and Bran took a deep breath. Kate wouldn't have left with Winderton. She wouldn't, unless the duke forced her.

Or she had been playing both Bran and the duke, an evil voice inside of him whispered.

If she had been, then Lucy was right—would such a woman turn down being a duchess?

WITHIN THE half hour, the dowager and Bran were on their way to the actors' encampment. Lucy, who rarely drove herself anywhere, was so upset she drove them both in her gig.

They arrived just as the play was coming to an end. They had heard the cheer of the crowd from the distance and now people were milling around.

Sitting in the gig, Bran scanned those gathered around the stage for a sign of Kate and Winderton.

Since Lucy's first crazed charges that had inspired his doubts, he'd managed to regain his perspective. Kate would not have eloped with Christopher. It defied common sense.

Still, where was she?

He climbed out of the gig, helping Lucy down as well. Mrs. Warbler was talking to the Irish actor. She had a sketchbook in her hand. She had been at every production Bran had. She'd sit in a bench off to the side and scribble away, an ink bottle uncapped at her feet. She was "writing," she told everyone and came to the plays to "study" what the playwright had done. Bran had just assumed it was another eccentricity of the woman.

Lucy spied her friend. "Elizabeth!"

"Don't make a scene," Bran said under his breath. "The fewer who know what is going on, the better."

His sister nodded. Mrs. Warbler came trotting over. "How good to see you, Your Grace. You missed this afternoon's performance."

Bran took over. "Where is Miss Addison?"

"I don't know," Mrs. Warbler answered. "She wasn't at this afternoon's performance."

Kate *not* at a performance?

Lucy brought her hand down on his arm in a death grip of fear, and a reminder that she had warned him.

"There was a good reason," he assured her, and himself. He left the women to walk to the stage. The Irishman had a group of young belles that included Squire Nelson's daughter around him. Bran walked past him, jumped up on the stage, and saw Silas in the tent. He walked up to him. "Where is Kate?"

The old man gave him a considering look. "She is around here some place."

"*Where* some place?" Bran asked, his voice deepening with his frustration.

Silas raised his chin, his mouth curling into a frown. "She is around, sir."

That wasn't the answer Bran wanted. He reached for the

smaller man, grabbed him by his Aesop costume and practically lifted him from the ground. "When did you see her last?"

"I don't see why I have to answer you at all," Silas returned, his own fists doubling.

"Brandon, Brandon," Lucy said coming up to him. "It is *true*, Brandon. What we feared has come true."

Rage filled him. It couldn't be true. Not again. Not a *second* time. He couldn't lose her a second time. *He loved her.*

She loved *him*. He believed it to his bones . . . which meant she had been coerced in some manner—or he could be wrong.

He practically threw the old actor away from him. Silas made a loud grunt as he landed against a stack of trunks. Bran had been too rough, but before he could speak, Lucy broke down into loud wailing as if mourning the dead—

"What did you do to Silas?" Kate's sharp voice broke through the noise.

From the corner of his eye, she came running toward her actor. She reached out to help him. Silas gave another shout of pain as if Bran had done far more than he had.

Bran didn't care. Here she was. "Where is he? Where is Winderton?"

Kate rounded on him. "What is the matter with you?"

But Bran was too caught up in the moment to answer *her* questions. "Is he forcing you? Or did the two of you plan this?" He caught her by the arms, desperate for an answer.

"No one is forcing me to do anything," Kate started, however Lucy interrupted.

"Where is the duke? Where is my son?"

Bran ignored his sister. Instead he looked into Kate's eyes. "You are not being forced? You are leaving of your own choice?"

"No one forces me to do anything," Kate assured him, and it was the wrong thing to say.

The jealousy that had once propelled him halfway around the world to put distance between them reared its ugly head. "You made a mistake then, Kate. You chose the wrong man. Winderton has nothing."

Beside him his sister gasped her distress. *"No."*

"I'm the one with the money," Bran charged on. "I own Smythson. *I own it all* and it could have been yours—because *I* was going to be foolish enough to ask you to marry me. I would have given you everything including my name. And yet, once again, you made the wrong choice. So be happy with Winderton. I don't want someone so faithless. And to think I loved you—" He released his hold and turned away, but Kate grabbed his coat.

"What are you talking about?" she demanded.

"You leaving with Winderton. Go. It doesn't matter." He couldn't even look at her.

"Have you gone daft?" Kate took a step back.

"He hasn't gone daft," Lucy said, stoutly jumping in. "We know what you and the duke have planned. We are here to stop it. Release my son from your clutches, *you scheming harlot.*"

The dowager's words rang out in the air and that was when Bran started to retrieve a bit of his sanity. His sister's language snapped him to his senses. "Lucy, please."

"I will not *please* anyone," his sister countered. "I will shout what this woman has done from the rooftops until I see my son. Until I know he is *safe* from *her.*"

"I've done nothing to Winderton," Kate answered.

"You have stolen his heart," the dowager declared to one and all. "Now you wish to steal his birthright."

"Obviously I have not because he is *not* here," Kate said.

The thought that she did not have the duke had not apparently occurred to the dowager.

Or to Bran.

After a momentary confusion, Lucy asked, "Then where is he?"

"I have no idea."

"Where have you been? You were not in your play."

Their little drama had collected far too much interest from the lingering theatergoers. Lucy acted unaware of the audience they had drawn.

"She was with me," Mars said. His appearance startled Bran. He looked up to see the earl standing at the tent's back entrance.

Bran frowned. Mars had wanted her from the very beginning. He'd assumed Mars had stepped back because of their friendship. What if he hadn't? A new jealousy sprang up. "What are you doing here?"

"Miss Addison sent for me."

"Because?"

Mars's gaze narrowed. "Because I am the magistrate. Or have you forgotten, along with your manners?"

Bran was both confused and alarmed. "Why would you need the magistrate? Has something happened to Winderton?"

Lucy gave a huge gasp and swung around, her hands flying up in the air as if she would swoon.

Bran took her arm. "Not now, Lucy. We need you with us."

"But my son—?"

"There is nothing wrong with Winderton, Your Grace," Mars said. "Or at least, not as far as I know. Miss Addison came for me because one of her actresses is missing. We were out making inquiries."

"Which actress is missing?" Bran demanded.

Kate stared at him as if she was seeing him for the first time. She did not answer.

At her silence, Bran removed his hat and raked a hand through his hair—and then it hit him. Perhaps Winderton hadn't been writing about Kate in his note?

The thought shocked him.

His thinking had been going one way, and now here was this new possibility. "Was it Jess, the petite blonde?"

Kate and Mars exchanged a look. Kate spoke. "Yes, she has never missed a performance and we can find her nowhere. I'm worried. I fear something terrible may have happened to her."

"Not truly terrible," Bran said. "But I believe she's on her way to becoming a duchess."

Lucy screamed in distress and Bran had had enough. While his sister broke down into noisy tears, he walked over to the recently closed tent flap. As he suspected, Mrs. Warbler and a host of others were standing as close as they dared to the tent. He motioned for Mrs. Warbler to come to him.

"My sister is not feeling well. Will you help see her home?"

"I would be honored, Mr. Balfour," Mrs. Warbler said.

"Can you drive the gig?"

"Of course."

Bran was thankful for the woman's lack of nonsense. Lucy needed a stern hand right now. He fetched her. She actually came along willingly. Looking up to Bran, his sister muttered, "He didn't even take the *good* actress. What is the matter with my son?"

Bran had an idea, and he feared he was guilty of the same trait. History seemed to be repeating itself. He remembered his storming into the offices of the East India Company and demanding they hire him on. He wished to be sent as far away from London as possible, and he had been.

To Mrs. Warbler, he said, "See she gets home, and make sure you give her a big glass of Madeira."

"Yes, sir." Mrs. Warbler actually sounded docile. The women drove off.

He returned to the tent. Mars and Silas were giving him well-deserved scowls while Kate seemed intent on looking everywhere but at him—and he understood.

If jealousy was an uncomfortable emotion, shame was even worse. He closed the tent flap and stood away from everyone before saying, "I believe Winderton has run off with Jess."

"Why would he do that?" Kate asked.

Bran looked at the others. Would she want this information known?

Kate took a step toward him. *"Where is Winderton? Is Jess in* danger?" Her voice had grown shrill and Bran knew she was suffering from her own fears carried from the past.

"He's eloping."

"With Jess?" she said with disbelief.

"If you haven't found Jess alive and you haven't found her body, what do you think the odds are that she is with my nephew who left a note claiming he is eloping with the woman he loves?"

Silas spoke up. "It is possible. I never liked the chit, Kate. She was like moth to the flame when she was around the duke. Every time he came here, she was following him."

"And she rubs up against him every chance she can," Nestor added. The other actors nodded.

"I didn't notice," Kate said.

"You were busy avoiding him," Silas answered.

Mary said in her quiet voice, "Jess left her cot last night and I didn't see her this morning. She also spent the night before somewhere else."

Kate looked at Bran. "He won't actually marry her, will he? I'm sad to say, but Jess is the sort only a fool would take to wife."

"Or a duke who is acting out of spite," Mars answered.

"He wouldn't be so lost to good reason as to marry someone he hardly knows," Kate said, directing the comment to the earl. She had yet to look at Bran.

"I don't know, Miss Addison," Mars said. "Let's ask someone who knows him. What do you believe, Balfour? Do you think our young duke would be so reckless?"

There was an edge in his friend's voice and it dawned on Bran just how harsh he'd sounded when he'd first seen Kate . . .

"I'm certain he could," he answered, a growing sense of his own culpability making it hard for him to meet their gazes. Action would be the cure. "I'm going after him before he makes a huge mistake."

"And I'm going with you," Kate said moving forward.

"No, you are not. I can travel faster by myself," Bran said.

She planted herself in front of him. "I will have no problem keeping up."

"Kate, I will bring them back."

"I'm not worried about the duke. I'm going to protect Jess from the two of you. And perhaps protect you from her. She's a clever one and there is no telling what has happened. Give me a moment to change."

"I don't have that kind of time," Bran started again but Kate shut him up with a snap of her fingers.

"You do not have a choice. You don't come into my home, and that is what this theater is, accusing me the way you did and allowing me to be called names—" She paused to let her meaning sink in.

She knew he had thought the worst of her.

Seeing that her point had been taken, that she had his full attention, she said, "I must protect Jess as well, even though she probably doesn't need it."

"Then you will take her back into the troupe?"

"I will do whatever I please, but first, I shall hear her side of the story," was the icy reply. "Silas, saddle Melon."

"Not the nag that pulls your wagon," Bran protested. "I'll supply you with a mount. Although, I will set a fast pace."

"I will have no problem."

"Very well then. I will return shortly." Bran left.

Yes, the crowd of villagers seemed to have grown since he had entered the tent. There were raised eyebrows and a good deal of general speculation. He walked through them. His stables were almost two miles away. He could have commandeered a pony cart but his legs could move faster.

He had just reached the rim of oaks when he heard a horse come up behind him. He turned to see Mars.

His friend nudged the horse close to him. There was no smile on his face. "Do you wish a ride?"

"I acted a perfect ass back there."

"You mastered perfect," the earl agreed.

"I'm sorry. I let my temper have the better of me. My nephew—"

"It wasn't your temper that had the best of you. And your nephew had nothing to do with it other than being a catalyst. I've seen my share of jealous men. You aren't the first to warn me back. The question I have, Balfour, is what are *your* intentions?"

"What do you mean? Why are you quizzing me of such a thing? You, of all people."

"Because I can and someone should. Kate Addison is not a woman to take lightly and she was genuinely worried about that girl. She feared someone had done something evil to her."

Like Hemling's kidnapping.

Mars continued. "Women like Kate Addison don't come along often. Granted, she is too independent by half but that tantrum you just threw—"

"I did not throw a tantrum."

"No, you just made a buffoon of yourself. I don't think you wanted to do that."

He didn't. Bran looked back at the stage and tents. Kate was nowhere to be seen. He looked up at Mars. "Are you going to give me a ride to my stables?"

"Absolutely," his friend said, offering a hand so Bran could swing up on the horse behind him. Kicking the horse forward, he added, "I will also warn you that once this matter is cleared up, I'm going after Kate Addison. She's not 'yours' any longer."

"*She is.*"

"You poor sod." Mars kicked the horse into a gallop and they didn't speak even after they reached Smythson's stables.

Chapter Seventeen

$\mathcal{K}$ate was wearing a riding habit when Bran returned to the tents with a horse for her. The dress was well cut, stylish, and appeared molded to her. Her favorite velvet cap was set at a rakish angle.

She did not greet him as he rode up on Orion. He held the reins to a smooth-trotting gray mare. From the edge of the stage, she took the reins and easily mounted sidesaddle as if she'd done it hundreds of times and required no assistance from him.

"You have a good seat," Bran said approvingly as a way to fill the silence. He was aware that her actors watched him with disapproval. Silas had his arms crossed while Nestor appeared ready to leap on Bran if he did anything untoward. Even Mary and the always silent John appeared frustrated that they could not go with them to protect Kate . . . from him?

Bran wasn't certain.

With a quick command, Kate set her horse forward. Orion immediately fell in without waiting for Bran. Apparently the stubborn gelding had decided she was the better person to follow.

Kate had fine control of the mare, which didn't give her any problems.

She was also studiously ignoring him. Bran let them ride past the line of oaks and up the road a bit before he said, "Do you have a plan for where we are going?"

"To Gretna, I assume." She bit the words out as if annoyed she had to speak to him. "It seems the likeliest possibility, and we really have little more to go on."

Since she was riding toward the Northern Road, which was exactly the route he had expected to take, he let her lead. Orion seemed perfectly happy to follow the gray and Bran asked himself exactly what had he said earlier?

And he remembered.

He'd declared he owned Smythson, the secret his sister had begged him to guard. Considering Mrs. Warbler heard everything that was said, the information had probably been tacked up on St. Martyr's door by now.

He'd informed Kate she had chosen the wrong man, that if she'd been more clever, she could have had him. He'd declared himself to her. He'd even said he loved her.

Bran had never felt so exposed in his life.

He'd said it out loud, in front of everyone. Words he had never spoken to Kate in private.

He'd even admitted he had been ready to give her all that he owned. He'd actually accused her of being a common fortune hunter, something he had actually once believed of her when she'd stayed with Hemling.

And he knew her well enough to understand that his words had been insulting to her.

Almost as insulting as his unbridled jealousy.

He had no excuse.

They reached the main road. She turned the mare north and he followed. It was a good piece of road and easy to ride side by side, except the stiffness in her back and the set of her shoulders said she was not ready for conversation.

They had ridden almost an hour before he attempted to bridge the divide between them. "Winderton sent a note saying he was eloping with an actress."

His comment was met with mute stoniness. Even the set of her jaw was hard.

"Kate?" It took courage to prod her. He'd been an ass.

"He did ask me. I said no. So he must have thrown himself on Jess, or perhaps she threw herself on him. Either way, I was never going to leave with him."

Of course she wouldn't. Bran knew that. Kate had never been interested in his nephew.

In fact, a part of him—the part of his brain that still had some common sense—had rejected the claim immediately . . .

"I'm sorry. I think I went a bit mad when I read his letter and after I learned you had not performed this afternoon." There. He'd said it, and he felt naked in front of her.

She gave no reaction. Not even a sidelong glance.

He let them travel a bit more before he said, "Kate, I ask you to pardon me for my behavior and my words."

Her head snapped round. "Do you mean the part where you were going to offer for me? Is that what you wish a pardon for because you didn't mean what you said?"

Bran sat heavily on Orion, a signal for the horse to walk. Her gray trotted a few steps more and stopped. Kate looked back at him. There was no traffic on the road. They were by themselves in the late afternoon sun.

"I love you, Kate." His heart grew with the truth of those words. "I love *you*." He repeated them with conviction, with honesty.

She studied him, her expression solemn, and then she shook her head. "You speak of love, but the truth is, you'll never forgive me for what happened years ago, will you? When you launched into me, *in front of everyone*, that was jealousy speaking there. I saw it for the first time, that emotion that you attempt to control every time you ask me about Hemling."

"Kate, I have never felt jealous over the marquis—"

She cut him off. "*Yes*, you have. It has always been there between us. As far as you are concerned, I should have escaped Hemling or I should have fought within an inch of my life. I should have done anything but stay and try to survive—"

"I don't judge you."

"Brandon, you have done nothing but judge me." She kicked her horse toward his, stopping when the animals were almost nose to nose. "There has been a question in the back of your mind ever since we grew close. Hemling was fifteen years ago. I'm not even the same woman, however, you seem to be the same man. I told you the truth and you are either not pleased with the answer or you don't believe it. Even when you don't say anything, I know it is on your mind."

"So you can read my mind now?" he said, reacting to the bold directness in her tone.

"You are not that complicated."

That was a direct blow.

He met her angry gaze. "If I have been overbearing on the matter, it is because I failed to protect you. It is me I blame, not you. And I've obviously set it all aside. Why else would I declare myself right there in front of everyone?"

"Because you were angry. You were lashing out—and that is when you tell me you love me?" She shook her head. "What hurts is that after what we've meant to each other, you jumped to a horrible conclusion about me. I thought you were different than other men, Brandon. I'd hoped."

"Kate, I—" He what? He bowed his head, reaching deep within. "Kate, it *was* jealousy." There he'd admitted it, and now he needed her to forgive him.

"You think I am so lacking in moral decency that I would throw you over for money. For a title. For a position."

"I thought you once did."

"That is my point. You will never let me forget what happened between us. I was young and very confused. Everyone in London told me that I had no choice, not after what he'd done to me. I was also ashamed, Brandon. I believed even you had abandoned me. And yet I had to go on. I had to face my mother. I had to decide who I truly was."

"I know. Kate, I'm sorry. I was a bit insane. I love you."

"And I love you." She spoke as if they were the saddest words in the world. "I'd begun picturing a life with the two of us together. I was so silly—"

"It isn't silly. It is what I want."

"It isn't what I want, not any longer."

He reached out a hand to her, as if to draw her close. The gray backed up. He dropped his hand. "I don't understand. I am truly sorry. I'm not perfect, Kate."

"I don't ask for perfection, Brandon. What I want is trust. I want someone who will against all odds believe in me. Who will stand beside me and not expect me to wear a hair shirt for past mistakes. I want someone whose faith in me is unshakable. Who would ask me first if something was true instead of forming his own conclusions. You didn't even give me a chance to respond to you, Brandon."

"I was wrong."

Kate didn't even shift her seat on the saddle, and he knew he was losing her but he didn't understand why. "What do you want from me? I will give up everything for you."

"I don't want you to give up anything. Don't you understand? I'm not a cross to be borne. I've never accepted anyone's pity—"

"You are willfully misunderstanding me," he started, his temper beginning to rise.

Calmly, she responded, "I understand you very well. Perhaps better than you understand yourself. Come, let's find this nephew of yours." She set her horse off.

"Kate," he called, wanting the matter settled, wanting his resolution where she fell into his arms and forgave him for any and all past transgressions.

Instead, she kept riding.

THEY RODE for two more hours. They checked every posting house along the way for word of a young couple matching Winderton's and Jess's descriptions.

Kate didn't engage Brandon in conversation. She'd said her piece. In truth, she was heartbroken.

Years ago, he had broken her heart because of her mistaken belief that he had been in league with Hemling. Now, he'd done it all on his own.

There had been nothing kind or loving in his accusations. He'd wanted to hurt her, and he had.

Offering her everything he owned? Why, he'd kept it a secret from her. He'd probably feared that if he told her his wealth she would have schemed to take it from him.

And it was bitterly disappointing to discover that he wasn't the noble man she had imagined. He was like all the rest—only happy if he kept her in her place.

No, she reminded herself, not *all* men were that way. Her sisters' husbands weren't. Her brother acted as if his wife was the sun in his life. When he wrote about her, the words he used to describe her glowed with his love for her.

Kate wanted what they had. She wanted a man who didn't wish to possess her as if she was something to be owned. She wanted someone whom she could trust. She'd been convinced Brandon was such a man . . . until his fit of spite and jealousy.

Her sister Alice would tell her to be thankful that she learned this now about him instead of later, but Kate could not feel gratitude. Because of Brandon, she had started to believe there was someone in the world who loved her for her intelligence, her creative spirit, and her unique gifts. Someone who would encourage her in her ambitions as well, who didn't see her as "dear" Kate—too bold, too brash, too independent.

There was no sin in trusting, she told herself, only in not heeding warning signs when they raised their vicious dragon heads—and yet, she'd thought Brandon was the one person who saw her clearly and accepted her for how she was, not how he would remake her. She'd believed that the designs he'd given her of the set pieces had been his blessing on her dreams.

She was proud of herself for not breaking down in tears now. She kept her head high and focused on the business at hand, just as she always did.

Finally, when she feared she could not remain stoic in his presence a moment longer, they stopped at a wayside inn called The Traveler's Rest.

"We should eat something," he said. "And the horses could use a rest."

He was right. She answered with a tired nod. The swirl of her emotions was draining. Seeing that he had dismounted and was coming around to help her, she kicked her foot from the stirrup and slid down. She handed her reins to the stable lad who had come out to greet them.

Brandon was not pleased that she didn't wait. His jaw hardened as if he was swallowing a comment. When he spoke, it was to tell the lad to rub down the horses and give them grain. He offered him several coins for his trouble.

Kate lifted the hem of her riding habit and headed for the inn's front door. Brandon's long legs caught up with her. She braced herself, ready for his chiding about her going off without him.

He surprised her by not speaking.

And that annoyed her as well. In truth, Kate didn't know what she wanted except to find some time to think—

The inn's front door flew open, and, to both Kate and Brandon's surprise, Jess came storming out.

Chapter Eighteen

*J*ess's face could have been a picture of feminine pouting—until she realized who stood before her.

She raised her hand to the loose blonde hair around her shoulders. "Kate—I, uh . . ."

"Yes, you *what*?" Kate said, drawing out the last word. "You are surprised to see me?" She had to laugh. "Did you truly believe you could elope with a duke and everyone would say, 'please go on, good for you,' and not try to find you?"

Jess shot a look behind her before announcing, "Well, we are not going to elope, I can tell you that. He's the most boring man I have ever met. He doesn't do anything but drink."

"Where is he?" Brandon asked.

"In the taproom," Jess answered as if it should be obvious.

Bran passed her to go inside. Kate took Jess's arm and brought her outside, allowing the door to shut.

"Well." Kate let the single word linger in the air. "You appear to be fine. Not a mark on you. Did the duke do anything wicked?" Kate had to reassure herself.

"How I wish he had. I'll be honest with you, I tried to rouse something in him." Jess spoke as if they were confidantes, cohorts in seduction. "I've never had to work so hard in my life for so little. He was too busy playing the mooncalf about you. I don't know how you tolerate him."

"I don't try to use him for what he might give me."

That earned her a pouty lip and the heavy sigh of the vastly annoyed. "Well, you can't blame me for the attempt. He said he'd marry me, that he had to marry an actress one way or the other to save face. I didn't realize at the time how drunk he was. He has no intention of marriage."

"And you were certainly going to take him up on his offer? Whether you knew him or not?"

Jess shrugged. "I had to try. It's difficult for a woman to make her way in this world. You know that."

Before Kate could answer, there came a loud sound, almost like furniture being thrown. Men began shouting.

Kate and Jess both rushed inside to see what was going on. There was a short entrance and then a doorway that opened into the taproom. The other patrons, mostly men, had gathered there. Kate pushed her way to the front with Jess on her heels.

A table and a few chairs had been overturned. Brandon stood against a rough-hewn rock wall. He ducked when Winderton threw a wild fist at him that breezed the air and landed squarely into stone and mortar.

The duke's howl of pain was almost frightening.

"Do you see what I mean?" Jess said without an ounce of sympathy. "How do you put your own fist into a wall?"

Neither Bran nor the witnesses were particularly concerned. Of those in the inn, some snickered, one cringed, and the rest appeared irritated for having their evening disturbed.

Overhearing Kate and Jess, a gentleman explained, "I was sitting at my table eating a good stew when that drunkard threw table, bowl, stew, and all at that man there." He pointed to Brandon who was busy handling his nephew.

"My hand," the duke complained. He looked as foul as Kate was certain he smelled. His hair was mussed, his jaw unshaven, and the sleeves of his jacket were torn at the seams. She knew that when he had approached her earlier in the day to make his declaration, he'd already been well into his cups. Now he was even worse.

"We will have Thurlowe look at it when we return home," Brandon answered calmly.

"It hurts."

"Broken bones do," was the crisp reply.

"Broken?" Winderton's eyes widened with alarm. "Will I lose the use of it? Can I ride? What will happen?"

Brandon looked down at his nephew with long-suffering disgust. "What will happen? You will heal and hopefully not be so ridiculous again."

"I will be fine?" The duke's words were a bit slurry.

"Well, you might have a crooked finger or two," Brandon answered.

That information threw Winderton into a lather and Kate had to smile. There was so much to love about Brandon. She would have handled the duke in the same manner.

Meanwhile, Brandon singled out the inn's owner. "We need food—" He looked to Kate and then to Jess. "For the four of us. I will pay for that gentleman's meal to be replaced as well." He indicated the one who had complained of having his meal interrupted.

"And my ale?" the man demanded.

To the innkeeper, Brandon patiently said, "And his ale. In fact I will pay for ale for everyone in the room with the exception of this one." He pointed to Winderton who held his injured hand gingerly in his other, a horrified and dazed expression on his face.

"I am thirsty," the duke said.

"Bring him water," Brandon answered.

"Men don't drink water," his nephew countered.

"You do now."

The other patrons laughed their agreement.

One young man, a shy one, sidled up to Jess and asked, "Are you all right, miss?"

"She's fine," Kate answered before Jess could respond. That earned her an evil look from her actress. Kate almost chuckled.

Yes, she and Brandon were very much of a like mind when it came to this runaway couple.

Brandon was setting things to right in the room. Others helped him as they returned to their meals or their drinks. There were many curious glances as Kate took her place at one of the tables. "Jess, have you eaten?"

"I have not."

"Then let us have a bite before we do anything else."

Dutifully, Jess sat beside her. "You are angry with me."

"Disappointed." Looking to the innkeeper who had approached their table, she said, "I will take hot tea."

"I'll have a cider," Jess said pertly.

Kate looked over at the duke. "Your Grace?" His neck snapped up at the address. Everyone else in the room seemed to freeze in place. "Will you join us?" Kate asked.

She could see it was on the tip of his tongue to refuse and yet how could he when so many had witnessed his humiliation.

Reluctantly, he came over and plopped his big body on the chair the farthest from Kate and Jess. Brandon joined them, sitting next to Kate.

Winderton scowled. "Isn't this cozy? The *two of you* together?"

"Sod off, Christopher," Brandon said evenly.

A surprised look crossed the duke's face and then his mouth closed. He fell into a glum silence.

The innkeeper brought over their drinks. He returned with a platter of cheese, meats, and bread. Kate didn't think she could eat, but the tea restored her spirits.

Jess munched away as if nothing was wrong. Brandon was thoughtful.

It was Kate who spoke first. "You will have to decide what you are going to do, Jess."

"Of course, I will return with you," the milkmaid-turned-actress said as if her opinion was important.

"You will not," Kate answered.

Jess's brows rose. "You've changed your mind about London—?"

"I haven't, save that you will not be going."

"But I am a member of the company."

"Not any longer." Kate was proud that she kept her voice calm and steady. "I will take you back to Maidenshop but not to London." From the pocket of her habit, she pulled out a heavy leather purse. "Here are your wages I owed you and funds for the next two weeks. This should tide you over until you decide what you wish to do."

Immediately, Jess fell into wheedling. "Kate, you need me. I have a role. We've rehearsed. I'm one of the goddesses. You can't perform *The Tempest* with just two actresses."

"You have destroyed the reputation of my company in Maidenshop. You took advantage of His Grace."

"I did not. He asked."

"You offered," the belligerent duke shot back. "You came to me."

"Because you wanted someone," Jess informed him. "I'm as good as she is."

"No, you're not," Winderton said decisively, weaving slightly in his chair. "You are a far cry from her." His slurry speech robbed his words of any compliment.

Jess leaned across the table as if to meet him. "You are the one who declared one actress was as good as another."

"Charming," Kate said.

The duke stared at Jess as if she was Medusa and then his head slowly turned to his uncle. "I believe I shall be quite ill."

Brandon almost bodily lifted his nephew up and hop-stepped him to the inn's front door. After pushing him out, Brandon returned to the table.

"Aren't you worried about him?" Jess asked.

"No," was the reply. "For what he is doing, the fewer witnesses, the better."

Jess grunted her agreement and tried another tack—contrition. She had huge blue eyes that could project innocence. "I was wrong. Terribly wrong. I betrayed your trust. But can't you see your way clear to giving me a second chance? I promise I will mind all the rules and I will not cause an ounce of trouble."

"Because you want to go to London?" Kate said, before cautioning, "Be careful, Jess. My question is a test of your honesty."

The milkmaid sat back in her chair. She eyed Kate for a second and then admitted, "London is the only reason I joined your troupe. I dream of going there."

"You are not alone. Half my actors are with me because they wish to appear on the London stage. Unfortunately, you have not worked hard at all. And let us continue to be honest—you have no intention of staying with my troupe once we reach London, do you?"

The claim that Kate was wrong about her was on the tip of Jess's tongue. Her protest was clear in her eyes, and then she slowly reconsidered, tilting her head and weighing the purse in her hand. "I'm bound for better things than your troupe." She stood. "Good luck, Kate." As simple as that, the girl walked away, sitting herself down at another table of rowdy men drinking.

"I believe it is time to return to Maidenshop," Kate said.

An hour later, Bran was driving a hired wagon back to Maidenshop, Kate beside him on the front seat. They had decided this was the only way to take Winderton home. His nephew was in no shape to ride and the horses were spent.

The duke now snored away in the wagon bed. He smelled worse than a pig. Even Orion and the gray tied to the back seemed to avoid catching a whiff of him.

The quiet wagon ride through the night gave Bran a chance to think.

They were almost back to Maidenshop when he decided he must try again. "I don't want to lose the one person who means the most to me. Kate, I want you for *my wife*. I love you—"

"No, you don't, Brandon."

He started to contradict her but she quieted him with a shake of her head. "It isn't time for us. Perhaps it never will be. We both have big dreams. You dream of building bridges—"

"Not any longer. I was just going through the steps, pretending that I had some meaning to my life, except I don't have any passion for it. In this week, I've felt more alive than I have over the past fifteen years."

She looked into his eyes. Hers were silver in the moonlight. Huge tears welled in them, and then she whispered, "I can't."

"You can't love me?"

"Oh, you are very easy to love."

"Then why?" he demanded.

"Because I'm not ready to give up my dreams yet. I've traveled a long way to reach this point and I must try."

"Did you feel that way yesterday?"

"Before all of this? Yes, and I believed that you understood what returning to London's stage meant to me when you gave me the set drawings."

"I do understand. I have a house in London. You can be in the theater. We can have a good life. Kate, what happened today will not repeat itself."

She faced him. "This isn't about today. Or my love for you, and I do love you, Brandon. However, I am on a journey that I started years ago, even before I met you. I must continue."

"And there isn't room for me?"

"This isn't *about* you," she said quietly. "I've given up so much to reach this moment. It's almost a calling. And if I don't try this, *my way*, then I'll always regret it. Even if I fail."

He studied her a moment and realized he had never loved her more. And, at last, he grasped what she meant about trust. About not being just attracted to the person but knowing her. Accepting her.

"You won't fail, Kate," he assured her before lifting the reins. He urged the horse forward.

They reached the tents. She didn't wait for him to help her down. Instead, she swung from the seat and practically ran from him.

And he let her go.

Bran drove the wagon to the stables. He and a lad put up the horses and they left the duke sleeping in the wagon bed.

The next morning, Bran shaved, dressed, and set off to see Kate. He had not slept well. He'd begun to doubt himself. There were things he should have said the night before. He believed he must try again. Years before, he hadn't and she had needed him.

Dreams change, he planned to say to her. *That was what life was about—starting in one direction and then realizing something better, finer lay in another.*

Would he convince her? He didn't know.

In the end, it didn't matter because when he reached the clearing, he discovered the actors were gone—wagon, tents, and stage.

Standing in the empty field, he accepted this wasn't the past repeating itself.

And he let her go.

Chapter Nineteen

$\mathcal{I}$n a week's time, Kate was in London and she discovered that many things were different about the workings of the theater world since she was last there.

She barely knew any of the theater managers and even fewer of the actors. No one seemed to have memory of her. She was starting from the very bottom of the heap as far as recognition. She had done so time and time again. After all, every new village during her years traveling with a troupe demanded she introduce herself. That didn't make it easier.

Because she had set her heart on performing *The Tempest*, she'd had to rent a theater with a royal patent. Months earlier, she had negotiated leasing the Drury Lane on Catherine Street for one week between the shows they were mounting. The pressure to make her mark in that short period of time was significant. She prayed she didn't buckle from the weight of it.

Of course they could not use the theater to rehearse so she rented a hall. She marked off Drury Lane's stage just as she had the ground in Maidenshop. She also paid for a room for the men and one for Mary and herself. Tiny rooms without air and beds that were less comfortable than the cot she slept on when traveling. Three weeks to rehearse and build Brandon's sets, one week to perform.

In *The Tempest*, Kate had chosen the part of the fairy Ariel. Silas would be the magician Prospero and Nestor, the evil Caliban.

Mary was given the role of Miranda, daughter to Prospero and Robbie would be the handsome Ferdinand.

One of the first actions to upset her plans was John's leaving the company. He didn't like London. It wasn't for him and he headed off to Manchester where he said he had family.

They were two actors down what with Kate having dismissed Jess.

She hurried to find replacements and several more to fill out the parts in *The Tempest*. Silas, Robbie, and Nestor set to work on Brandon's designs for the stage pieces while she and Mary sewed costumes. Besides the Shakespeare, they would perform several of her *Aesop's Fables*. London audiences expected a full evening.

Her dream was an expensive endeavor. By the end of the second week of rehearsals, Kate was squeezing every penny.

She was going over her expense books when Silas charged into the room she and Mary shared. Kate sat at a table, squinting at numbers by candlelight.

He slammed his hands down on the desk to gain her attention. "I've found Jess."

Kate looked up. "And this interests me because . . . ?"

"She is at Covent. She's playing Ophelia across from Kemble." John Kemble was one of the finest actors in England.

That commanded her attention. "Jess?"

"Aye." Silas reached for a stool and dragged it over to sit. "Kate, her first performance was Monday. Here it is Wednesday and they are singing her praises. They call her the 'Golden Goddess.'"

"Oh, please." Kate put down her pen. "The names they come up with. They lauded me as the 'Aphrodite of London.'"

"I can understand that, but Jess—?"

"It just means she has captured male attention." She picked up her pen. "This has nothing to do with us."

"I thought you'd wish to know."

"I do. I had no doubt she would land on her feet. May she carry on happily and stay away from our door." Silas nodded, rose, and started to leave, but Kate stopped him. "How were the reviews?"

He sighed heavily. "Fair. Of course, everything she knows, you taught her. And her winning the part has little to do with talent. The rumor is she has an important benefactor. They met at a posting house. The original actress came down sick and, well, there was Jess."

"I don't wish her ill." Kate turned her attention back to her ledger and Silas made his exit. However, after the door closed, Kate almost collapsed.

Doubt seemed to be her constant companion lately.

Too often, she thought of Brandon.

She missed him. Her life had lost its luster and he'd been more of a steadying influence than she'd realized. Now, here was Jess of all people receiving acclaim.

Kate wondered what Brandon would have to say about this turn of events. She knew he would reassure her and tell her to keep going—which was hard to do when one discovered her heart was somewhere else.

Not for the first time did she think she might have made the wrong choice that last night in Maidenshop. London was hard. The challenges were larger than she had anticipated. She wasn't afraid of them . . . she just questioned how important they were. What had once seemed vitally important now paled to the memory of having *him* close to her.

And, when there were a thousand details in her mind and everything seemed too confused and difficult, she relieved the pressure by dreaming about what was going on in Maidenshop. Probably the same thing that happened every Wednesday in the village, or every Thursday, every Friday. Such was the simple life, and she missed it. The village was surprisingly close to her heart. "But you wouldn't have known what it had meant, if you hadn't tried this," she reminded herself, speaking aloud.

And there was no turning back now. She'd put everything she owned into this one endeavor and her pride would never let her back away.

BRANDON'S SET pieces garnered a good deal of interest around the theater. Mr. Arnold, Drury Lane's manager, studied the drawings and took a personal interest in the way they were being built. "Ingenious," he kept saying. "Did you do these?" he asked Silas.

"No, sir. A Mr. Brandon Balfour created them."

"Ingenious."

Mr. Arnold rarely spoke to Kate. She sensed his tacit disapproval of her was for no other reason than she was the one making decisions—and she was a woman. She seemed to make him uncomfortable. Every time there was something to discuss, he always went to Silas first.

That changed the Friday before the performance.

They were in the rehearsal hall. Kate had just finished putting her actors through their paces when she discovered Mr. Arnold watching her from the doorway.

She walked to him. "Yes, sir?"

"I didn't know if you have seen this." He offered her a page of *The Morning Chronicle*. She didn't understand why anything in today's paper should interest her when she was so busy, until she noticed an article titled, *The Cruel Miss Addison Feared My Talent: An Interview with the Golden Goddess*. A subtitle claimed, *Actress attempts to destroy younger version of self.*

"*What?*" Kate skimmed the article. She had spoken loud enough she'd alerted Silas and the others that something was wrong. They came to read over her shoulder.

"This is ridiculous," Kate murmured.

"Unfortunately, it makes for rather salacious reading," Mr. Arnold said. "People enjoy rivalries. You know, good versus evil. I hope that you are the evil one doesn't put the audience off."

"What is this about, Kate?" Silas demanded.

Kate faced her actors. "It is Jess. She has a story here about how I conspired for the affections of the 'Duke of W' and she had to perform miracles to save him from a misalliance. All the while, she makes herself out to be a defenseless waif."

"Jess?" Nestor laughed his retort. "Wolves couldn't pull her down."

"Well, according to this article, *I'm* the wolf." Kate waved the paper at them. "She claims that I was threatened by her youth and beauty and will do anything to destroy her. I sound like an ogre. And the reason I went after the Duke of W? I hate the nobility. She even says she is motherless and saw me as the mother figure she'd always wanted. I'm not *that* old."

"And don't breathe a word of this to her mother in Crewe," Silas said.

"Perhaps that her mother lives in Crewe isn't true," Kate suggested. "Maybe she made up a mother for us? Or made up being from Crewe?" She looked down at the paper in her hands. "This is all lies and yet there is just a hint of truth. Anyone reading it would think I am some she-devil. She says I purposely followed her to London to open a play to compete with hers, that I wish to destroy her. She even claims I encouraged Arlo to elope with the vicar's daughter because I hate the church. This is outrageous, overly dramatic nonsense."

"I suspected it wasn't true," Mr. Arnold said.

"I don't know what to do about this," Kate admitted. "She is blackening my name with half-truths."

"While she is the innocent little bird. Do you want me to talk to her?" Silas asked.

"Or me?" Nestor chimed in.

"I want to ignore the whole thing," Kate replied.

"That is actually the best," Mr. Arnold agreed. "These theater matters, it is all tit for tat. No one cares . . . usually. Let it rest. It will likely spark curiosity and bring an audience our way. Why, if Lord Dervil wasn't her protector, she wouldn't have received the part of Ophelia. The actress who was playing it took ill and I understand money changed hands. She must be keeping Lord Dervil happy."

"The public doesn't know that," Kate said. "And how did she meet Lord Dervil?" She'd heard the name before, and then remembered Brandon talking about how Lord Dervil had ruined his opportunity with the bridge commission. "He's an enemy of Lord Marsden."

"The earl?" Silas said. "I can't see him with any enemies. He is too good a fellow."

"Dervil is one of those you don't cross," Mr. Arnold said. "He shows up in places most of us would rather he not be."

"Well, I've done nothing to him," Kate said.

Mary spoke. "Perhaps if we went to the papers and you told your side of the story, Kate?"

"They would be overjoyed," Mr. Arnold predicted. "And they'd make up more lies. The public would feed off of it. That is how these things work. My advice is that you ignore it. You're only here for a week as it is." He waved his hand as if everything would disappear.

"You are right," Kate said, and prayed that was the end of the matter. She even ignored Silas's muttered dark warning that all Arnold wanted was her money.

In spite of the old soldier's theory, as the day wore on, Kate was troubled to notice small gatherings of people outside on the streets in front of the rehearsal hall. They appeared to watch the door, their faces suspicious and distrusting. She chose not to go out.

One of the new actors, Harry, confirmed her suspicions when he reported he'd overheard the onlookers talking about Jess. "They are loyal to her. They carry on as if you have harmed her and they protect her."

"I didn't do anything to Jess," Kate answered. "I wouldn't."

"I believe you," Harry said, hands in the air as if to ward her off. "Except they act as if they know her personally."

"Some people are a bit proprietorial about their favorite actress," Kate said. "It's nothing to cause concern."

And she wanted to believe that, except the next day for rehearsal, Harry didn't show. One other actor went missing as well. They played minor characters and could easily be replaced. Still their leaving without a word was disturbing.

Later that afternoon, another new member of the company came in with a pamphlet that was being distributed outside with the title, *The Evil of One Miss Kate Addison*. It was full of the same rubbish that the article had been, only this one suggested that Kate practiced the dark arts.

"The dark arts?" Kate threw the pamphlet down. "Who believes in the dark arts?"

No one answered.

Placing her hands on her hips, Kate demanded, "And they can print lies about me every day?"

Again, there was silence.

"I am not going to give in to this," Kate vowed. "Come, we need to transport the props we've been using to the theater. Who will come with me?"

Robbie, Nestor, Mary, and Silas stepped forward. Reluctantly, most of the new actors joined them. They picked up tables and chairs designed specifically by Brandon for *The Tempest* and set out, Kate at their head.

Those lingering on the streets didn't approach her. There was grumbling in her direction. She chose not to hear it. Still, she could feel their eyes following her with ill intent as if she truly was some witch needing staking.

"Their minds are smaller than the Matrons of Maidenshop," Kate muttered.

Nestor responded, "Actually, I would be happy to be back there. It was a good village."

Kate agreed.

She was also not pleased to hear reports that *Hamlet* at Covent Garden was playing to huge crowds. Everyone apparently wished to see the Golden Goddess. One paper reported that, although the acting was indifferent, not a bad comment should be made about the sensitive young actress "who has suffered greatly at the hand of those older and past their own prime."

Meaning Kate.

"I haven't even stepped on the stage and I'm being dismissed," she complained to her actors.

No one disagreed with her. Silas spoke up then, "You will have to show your mettle, Kate. We all will."

It was a grim pronouncement, and a true one.

WEDNESDAY DAWNED with a clear day. A promising omen and Kate needed it.

Today, she would either be a success or ruined. She'd know by nine that evening which one it was.

She and friends arrived at Drury Lane by ten. The performance would be at six and the doors opened at five. She was surprised that there was already a crowd gathered in front of the theater.

"Do you suppose this many people are anxious to see *The Tempest*?" she asked Silas.

"I'm looking for turnips," he answered.

Kate was herself.

Nor was Mr. Arnold particularly relaxed. "It is the publicity," he said as if trying to convince himself. "All the talk has people interested."

"Of course that is true." Kate tried to sound confident.

Another actor did not show without word. It was late afternoon before they realized he wasn't coming.

Robbie claimed he could don a wig and play the very small part before returning to Ferdinand. Kate agreed, thankful for the courage of those who did show up for her. No actor liked being attacked while on stage. London's audiences could be the most hostile in the world. They considered themselves part of the entertainment if they weren't happy. It took courage to play before angry people.

Certainly it was going to take all the courage Kate had.

As the hour approached five, she put on her costume. She always felt there was a bit of ritual to taking on a character and the costume was the most important part.

She and Mary had refashioned one of her Juno gowns into a fairy dress by sewing layers of gold, blue, and green ribbons. Mary had created a crown of greenery and Kate wore her hair curling down around her.

When they had both finished dressing, Mary as Miranda left to go over one of her scenes with Robbie. "He's nervous. I am as well," she confessed before slipping out the door.

Kate relished this moment alone. Ariel was one of her favorite characters. Shakespeare referred to her as an "airy spirit." He also referred to Ariel as a male, but Kate was ignoring that direction. She also chose to play Ariel as a reluctant, almost rebellious collaborator with Prospero. She believed her changes gave the character more depth, which could be troubling if the audience expected a more traditional playing of the role. What had seemed bold two weeks ago now appeared foolhardy.

"One week," she said to herself. That was all the time she was committed to this role. She needed good houses for one week. Then she could pay off the theater and have enough to decide what she wanted to do in the future . . . because she discovered she was losing her taste for the stage.

For years, she'd battled petty rivalries, small jealousies, and disappearing actors. She'd slept on a cot and gone without eating. She'd endured insults—and for what? Because she liked to playact?

She looked at her fairy reflection in the glass and wondered if perhaps there wasn't something else out there for her? She'd never asked that question before—

A knock sounded on the door. Assuming it was Mr. Arnold to tell her how full the house was, she said, "Come in."

The handle turned. The door slowly opened and in the glass she saw Brandon Balfour standing behind her.

Kate stood paralyzed. He looked good. Too good.

He was dressed in black evening attire. He held a bouquet of roses. Lush, vibrant roses. The scent swirled through the air.

She turned. Her first impulse was to run into his arms, and

then she remembered how cruel she had been at their last meeting. He'd offered his heart and she'd refused him.

"Hello," she managed. It was hard to speak past the shame in her throat.

He appeared to feel as awkward as she did. They both acted rooted to the floor. "I wanted to let you know I was here," he said. There was a beat and then he added, "I bought these for you."

She nodded without looking at them. "They are beautiful."

They both stared at the flowers. She found it was easier than meeting his eyes that always seemed to look right into her soul.

Silence fell heavy upon them, and when she could stand it no more, she started, "Brandon—" just as he said, "Kate—" as if he, too, had felt an urge to reach out to her.

They stopped, went still. At last, she met his gaze. "Brandon, I'm sorry. I'm sorry that I was rigid the last time we were together. I'm sorry that I cut you off."

He walked to her then, intent upon her. "I'm not sorry." He stopped a foot away from her. She wanted him closer and yet something prevented her from taking the action herself.

"You made me take a hard look at how I behaved. I want to think I'm better for it for the lesson." He gave a self-deprecating smile. "I might not be. I'm stubborn when it comes to change."

"I don't wish you to change. I like you the way you are. I've missed you."

The tension left him. He leaned back as if he could not believe his luck. "My life has seemed empty since you left. I had a second chance and I learned—"

Before she could hear what he'd learned, Mr. Arnold appeared at the door, his hand up ready to knock until he saw that it was open, and that she had a guest, a male one. "I'm sorry, Miss Addison. Wanted to tell you the house is full. We are turning them away."

Brandon looked at her. "This is what you wanted. You've done it, Kate. You have made it happen."

"Yes," she said uncertainly, not sharing her fear that it was a hostile house. She didn't want Brandon to know that. He was here. That was what was important.

"It is almost time for curtain," Mr. Arnold reminded her.

"I'll be ready. Will you take Mr. Balfour to his seat? I need a moment more to myself."

"I'll be happy to. This way, sir."

"I will see you after the performance?" Brandon asked.

"Yes. Come here."

He nodded and then left with Mr. Arnold.

Kate took a last look in the mirror. She closed her eyes. *Brandon was here.* He'd come to her. And now, she needed to focus on her upcoming performance.

Releasing her breath, she straightened her shoulders and left the room.

Silas, Mary, and the actors who played the sailors were already waiting upstairs. Kate gave them all an encouraging smile.

She could hear the restless audience. It had been fifteen years since she'd listened to one this large. In a few moments, there would be a clap of thunder to signal the storm and she planned for it to be loud enough to bring them all into the story.

The sailors took their places.

Silas leaned toward Kate. "Jess is in the audience. I thought you should know."

Before she could respond, the thunder sounded, the lightning rumbled, and the curtain came up.

Chapter Twenty

$\mathcal{F}$rom where she stood in the wings, Kate could see Jess. She understood why Silas had warned her. Jess sat right in the middle of the audience, surrounded by men. Her admirers. And they were talking in carrying voices as if eager to destroy the dramatic opening of the play.

There was no way Kate would have missed her from the stage.

Kate wondered if the infamous Lord Dervil was there. She'd never met him so she wouldn't know.

Unfortunately, Jess's presence had scrambled Kate's concentration. She forced herself to breathe, to take in what was happening on the stage.

The sailors spoke about the storm. The ship rocked and then the sailors turned the pillars and the stage became that magical island.

Kate heard the audience voice its approval over Brandon's fanciful design, as she knew they would.

Prospero and Miranda began telling their story. In a few moments, Ariel would make her entrance. This was not the time for fear.

Kate placed herself in the story. She took on the bearing of the fairy spirit—and then it was time for her entrance.

She opened her arms and danced upon the stage, coming to a halt before her master, Prospero—that was when the hissing began. The audience suddenly sounded like a thousand angry geese.

Kate endeavored to ignore them. "All hail, great master! Grave sir, hail—!"

"*Go* to hell," shouted a man in the audience. The suggestion was met with catcalls and encouragement.

Kate endeavored to carry on, except her concentration had been broken. The hissing was disconcerting. She forgot her lines. Her mind was blank.

Silas picked up on her distress. He delivered his next line. "Hast thou, spirit, perform'd to point the tempest that I bade thee?"

She knew where she was. She answered, "To every article—" The shouting and hollering had ceased when Silas spoke but now they called out even louder. She could barely hear herself as she said, "I boarded the king's ship; now on the beak—"

"You can feel my *beak*," a man yelled. He stood and grabbed his crotch to let her know what he meant. The mass of people in front of him jeered their responses. The audience echoed the word *beak*. Kate was stunned by this behavior.

She'd been before difficult audiences. Having the Matrons of Maidenshop shout names at her had not been easy. Of course, they had not been the only ones who had attempted to degrade her with words. Over the years she'd been called all sorts of things.

But this was different. This was London. She'd once ruled here. *Or had she?*

She looked to Jess sitting smugly in the audience. She appeared young, clueless, and vindictive and Kate realized Silas had been right, talent had nothing to do with the milkmaid's success.

It also might not have had anything to do with Kate's success years ago either. She'd just been the next new ingenue and so many of those around her gave her credit for being nothing more than the pleasure of the moment. It was a startling and humbling realization.

And then, through the din of the crowd, she heard her name being called. Brandon was standing and shouting for her attention.

She almost cringed. She didn't want him here to see her humiliation . . . until she heard what he was saying. "Go on, Kate. It is your stage. *Make them listen.*" He clasped his hands together, the sign of a champion. He believed she could turn this around. He was here for her.

In the middle of the chaos, Kate found her strength. It came from his faith in her.

She remembered Brandon asking if she ever felt her mother's spirit and she'd claimed she did before a performance. She reached for that spirit now. She was Kate Addison, an actress, a woman with a will of her own.

Whether this audience listened or not made no difference. In fact, considering what was happening, Mr. Arnold would probably shut down her play. Audiences could riot if they were not controlled. More than once, they had been known to tear up a theater, causing great damage.

However, before she was shut down, Kate was going to give a performance that few would forget, and she'd do it for Brandon— because he believed in her.

She drew a breath, returning to her character. Silas had dropped character and looked as if he'd like to head into the crowd and knock heads together. She blocked his path. When she spoke, her voice was louder and stronger than it had ever been. She had *never* been like Jess, and this was her chance to prove it.

"To every article, I boarded the king's ship, now on the beak, now in the waist, the deck, in every cabin, I *flamed* amazement—" She threw her arms out, indicating the spell she had delivered in destroying a ship because she was *that* powerful a fairy.

"Sometime I'll divide," Ariel said, indicating where she'd created havoc with fire. "And burn in many places; on the topmast, the yards, and the bowsprit, would I flame distinctly, then meet and join."

The shouting was quieting.

She didn't care. On the surface, she was a fairy meeting the will of her master.

Inside, she could feel the blood of her mother, another woman who dared to be up on the stage, and the heartbeats and souls of every actress who had come before her. She was the emissary. They would not bow to such a crowd, and neither would she.

But best of all, Brandon was here for her. No matter what happened this night, he would be here.

Lost in the words and the magic of the theater, Kate gave a performance like no other.

The catcalls stopped. She could feel the audience move to the edge of their seats as if they dared not miss one word of the play. They believed there was a magic island where love battled the forces of vengeance and won.

And when it was done, when Prospero said his final lines, the audience rose to their feet in applause.

The actors came out for their bows. Kate always had them bow as an ensemble because she believed it took the full cast to make a play succeed. However, it was obvious the audience cheered for her.

Since she would not step forward, Silas and the others stepped back. The crowd clapped and stomped their feet all the harder, but theirs wasn't the adulation she wanted.

Her gaze searched the crowd until she found Brandon. He was applauding harder than anyone else, his eyes shining with pride.

And suddenly, overwhelmed, she fell to her knees, tears of relief and gratitude running down her cheeks.

A sound of alarm went up as everyone feared something was wrong—until they saw Brandon leap up on the stage. Actors started to stop him, thinking he might mean harm to Kate but Nestor put out an arm to ward them off.

Reverently, Brandon knelt in front of her so they were at eye level. The people grew silent.

"I could not have done it without you," she confessed.

"I was here for you. I'll always be here for you."

The truth of his words filled her with joy, and she said what was in her heart. "Mr. Balfour, would you marry me?"

A gasp went up, probably because of her audacity. Did women ask men for such a thing? Kate didn't care.

Neither did Brandon. His hand went to the back of her neck drawing her to him. "I can think of nothing I want more," he declared, right before kissing her in front of one and all.

THE REVIEWS for *The Tempest* were excellent. The house for the short run of the play was packed. Kate made her money and then some.

Most of all, she'd proven her worth on the stage, except that no longer mattered to her.

Oh, she would act. It was a connection to her mother and it was her gift in life. However, the drive to be seen, to be recognized, was not as strong because the one person whose acceptance she sought was Brandon's.

And he loved her whether she was perfect or not.

They spoke their wedding vows at the first church they came to once Brandon purchased the special license. Kate's brother, the Duke of Camberly, and his duchess were the only ones in attendance.

Afterward, instead of the traditional breakfast immediately following the sacrament, Kate and Brandon chose Maidenshop for the celebration. Kate wrote letters to her sisters and their families inviting them to join.

Two weeks later, Kate and Brandon arrived in Maidenshop to host the largest wedding breakfast ever devised by man. The village—servants, lads, and all—was invited. It would be held at St. Martyr's barn. Old Andy started brewing ale and the Smythson staff began planning for a feast.

Winderton turned down the invitation to attend. He'd told Brandon he couldn't. He was too busy going out of his way to avoid Kate.

"I wish he could be happy for us," she said.

Brandon shrugged. "It is time he learned that things don't always go the way one wants, even when one is a duke." He paused and then said, "I suggested that since Napoleon has abdicated and it is safe to travel on the Continent, he should take a tour. He agreed."

"I don't like feeling as if I have run him off."

Brandon drew her to him. "You haven't, Kate. He has his own lessons to learn. You were just part of teaching it to him."

"Is there a story about that?"

Brandon laughed. "Just a few."

As for everyone else in the village, they were happy for Kate and Brandon. Even the dowager, although she also liked the idea of her son touring the Continent. "It is what a nobleman does," she said to Kate and Mrs. Warbler.

In truth, the duchess was looking happier. She'd finally given up her black. She'd gone to purple. Brandon said everyone should be thankful for any steps forward, including small ones.

Not even Mr. Thurlowe and the earl seemed disappointed in their marriage. They discussed the Logical Society when they came to call. "We hate losing Balfour," the doctor admitted candidly to Kate and Brandon. "However, our seminar brought in two new members."

"Good, because you are going to be marrying soon," the earl reminded him.

"Not real soon."

The earl's response was a roll of his eyes that made Kate laugh. And then he clapped Brandon's hand in congratulations and kissed Kate on the cheek. "I can do that since we shall be good friends."

"I was afraid you liked her too much," Brandon confessed.

"You are a jealous oaf. Although, I was tempted," Mars said with his easy drawl, "but reason prevailed."

"And you are welcome at The Garland anytime you wish," Mr. Thurlowe told Brandon. "And for the seminars."

"I will look forward to them," was the answer.

Thinking about Miss Taylor's complaint about being left out of lectures concerning natural philosophy, Kate had to ask, "But what if I wished to attend?"

Under his breath, the earl said, "Here we go again," while Mr. Thurlowe launched into an apologetic and sorry list of reasons women couldn't possibly be invited to a seminar.

Kate had an idea that she and Mr. Thurlowe would be revisiting those silly excuses in the future. However, for now, she just smiled.

"Oh," the earl said as if just remembering, "did you hear anything from the bridge council?"

"They canceled the project," Brandon answered. "All that fuss for nothing."

"You don't seem upset," Mr. Thurlowe noted.

"I'm not. Actually, the Surveyor-General and one of the council members asked me to design a house for them."

"That is capital," Mr. Thurlowe said.

"It is certainly more interesting than a bridge. Of course, I told him I could not see to plans for their houses right away because I'm doing the drawings for a home for Kate and me."

"I wondered if you would stay in the Dower House," the earl said.

"You could move into Smythson. It is large enough," the doctor observed.

"No, that belongs to my nephew and always will," Brandon said. "Besides, Kate has rather modern ideas. I'm anxious to see this house built."

"And," Kate said proudly, "Covent Gardens Theater has asked my husband to design the set pieces of their next opera."

The earl looked at Brandon with new eyes. "Well, this is all far better than bridges." And everyone had to agree.

THEIR WEDDING feast was held on the most perfect September day ever.

The Matrons decorated the old barn as if they were planning for the Cotillion. A banquet of food was spread out for guests.

Everyone came. The dancing started at two and was still going strong at ten that night when Bran grabbed Kate's hand and led her outside.

They walked around to the back of the barn. "Do you remember our confrontation here?" he asked.

"Roughly. I can't imagine being as angry as I was with you now."

"I'm relieved, because you were furious." He took her hand, pulled her closer so that he could wrap his arms around her. "So, what is it you wanted to talk to me about that you don't wish the rest of the world to hear?"

She fit her body against his. "I think," she started, and then corrected herself. "I *know* I'm with child."

"You what?"

"I'm surprised, too. I thought I was too old, especially since years ago, nothing happened. I assumed I needn't worry."

"Are you certain?" he asked.

"All the signs are there and I talked to my sisters this afternoon. I'm pregnant."

Bran spun her around in a lively little dance. "*We* are pregnant." He had to repeat it again. "We are *pregnant*."

"And you are as happy as I am," she said as if confirming to herself.

"*We* are happy." He sealed that statement by kissing his wife. More than once, in fact. Right there under the stars of a September night with the whole village dancing away.

Love brought them back together. Love would carry forward.

And it was nothing less than a miracle.

Author's Note

Dear Readers,

I hope you enjoyed Brandon and Kate's story. Many of you first met Kate in *The Duke That I Marry*. She really captured my imagination. I adored her outspokenness and knew she must have her own tale.

However, I grappled with the idea of second chances. Especially after fifteen years? I worried if it was plausible. Doubt is my major pitfall. I worried, I fumbled, I talked to myself.

Then, as it so often does, the Universe offered a gift. I received an email from someone I'd known thirty years ago. Someone who had once been important to me and thirty years was *twice* the time Kate and Brandon had been apart.

Once again, I am reminded of how generous love is. Not just that intense let's-do-it kind of love, but also the love of kindness, of friendship, of connection. Recognition is a gift. And I firmly believe those whom we've met along the way never actually leave us, do they?

The book began to flow.

As for dukes marrying actresses, I covered that topic in my Author's Note for *A Date at the Altar*. If that isn't enough for you, please look at Prince Harry, Duke of Sussex, and his lovely wife Meghan, Duchess of Sussex. Are explanations truly needed?

Here is wishing you love in all its forms.

Many hugs,
Cathy Maxwell
Buda, Texas
June 29, 2019

Don't miss the next installment in the
Logical Man's Guide to Dangerous Women
series, coming soon from Avon Books!